Scarlet
in the
Snow

Also by Sophie Masson

(Random House Australia)

Moonlight & Ashes

Written as Isabelle Merlin

Three Wishes
Pop Princess
Cupid's Arrow
Bright Angel

The Chronicles of El Jisal series

Snow, Fire, Sword
The Curse of Zohreh
The Tyrant's Nephew
The Maharajah's Ghost

Edited by Sophie Masson

The Road to Camelot

Scarlet in the Snow

SOPHIE MASSON

RANDOM HOUSE AUSTRALIA

A Random House book
Published by Random House Australia Pty Ltd
Level 3, 100 Pacific Highway, North Sydney NSW 2060
www.randomhouse.com.au

First published by Random House Australia in 2013

Addresses for companies within the Random House Group can be found at
www.randomhouse.com.au/offices

National Library of Australia
Cataloguing-in-Publication Entry

Author: Masson, Sophie, 1959–
Title: Scarlet in the snow / Sophie Masson.
ISBN: 978 1 74275 815 2 (pbk.)
Target Audience: For secondary school age.
Subjects: Fairy tales.
Dewey Number: A823.3

Cover photographs: girl © iStockphoto.com / Stefano Lunardi;
rose © pio3 / Shutterstock.com
Cover design by Christabella Designs
Typeset by Midland Typesetters, Australia
Printed in Australia by Griffin Press, an accredited ISO AS/NZS 14001:2004
Environmental Management System printer

Random House Australia uses papers that are natural, renewable and recyclable
products and made from wood grown in sustainable forests. The logging and
manufacturing processes are expected to conform to the environmental regulations
of the country of origin.

For Sasha

спасибо Большое

One

Three sisters sat spinning at the old tower window, watching for their mother to come home. After a time the first sister said, 'I see our mother's sleigh flying through the forest, laden with fine things, with silks and satins, velvets and furs.' Then the second sister said, 'I see our mother's sleigh speeding over snowy fields, laden with valuable things, with caskets of jewels, pearls and amber and gold.' And then the third sister spoke, and she said, 'I see our mother's sleigh hurrying towards home, light as a feather with fragrant flowers, roses and lilac and jasmine and lilies. And behind the sleigh, spring is coming, the snow is melting, winter is being chased away . . .'

'Ah, there you are! I might have known I'd find you up here, scribbling like some old clerk. Look at you – you've got ink all over your fingers! No, stop, don't do that, Natasha, you'll get it on your nose too!'

Too late. The tip of my nose was already graced with a blotch. I hurriedly closed my notebook and pushed it under the pile of old blankets. Scrubbing half-heartedly at the nose-blotch with a crumpled handkerchief, I said, 'What's the matter, Liza? Is the house on fire? Have the horses run away? Are the hens off their lay? No, wait; it must be something much more important. I know. Anya's run out of hair-curling papers!'

'Ha ha, very funny,' she said sourly. 'Don't you remember? Your godfather's coming to tea. And he's due in less than an hour.'

'And you came bursting in here to tell me *that*?' I hadn't forgotten. I just hadn't wanted to think about it. I don't like my godfather, Captain Peskov. With his cold beady eyes and his spindly legs in their dusty black trousers, he reminds me of a bedraggled elderly crow. And as for his title, I cannot believe he's ever been captain of anything other than the good ship *Misery*, for he is for ever croaking about this or that unpleasant and miserable thing, usually how someone had cheated him of what was rightfully his. He's some kind of distant cousin of my father's, but aside from that I don't know why he was chosen as my godfather. He's a real *skupoy*, a real stingy person, and he's certainly never taken an interest in me. Now, though, I can't help thinking that my poor papa must have owed him money and by asking him to be my godfather, was trying to get on his good side. But I don't think that side exists.

'Why on earth is he bothering to visit us now, when he didn't even come to Papa's funeral and hasn't sent so much as a note since?' I said scornfully.

Shrugging, Liza pushed back a stray strand of her fair hair. 'Maybe he's had a change of heart and he's decided to help us.'

I laughed. 'A change of heart? He doesn't *have* a heart to change, Liza. That old *skupoy* might be rich but he's also a real miser and you know it. His purse strings are so tight you'd need a crowbar to open them and even then they'd probably stay shut.'

'You have to be nice to him,' she said, ignoring my comment. 'Mama says you must. She says it's our only chance.'

I stared at her. 'Mama said that?'

She had the grace to flush. 'All right, not the last bit she didn't. But she did say you should be nice, so it must mean she thinks that.'

'No, it doesn't,' I began hotly, and then I cut myself short. Because I know how hard it's been for Mama these last eighteen months. It's not just the grief at losing Papa, not just the loss of our old life, not just the constant money worries that have put grey streaks in her black hair and dark shadows under her green eyes. It's also knowing what it all means for us, for her daughters. Balls, parties, fine dresses, costly jewels, city living, high society, romance, hopes for a glittering marriage to an important nobleman: all that belongs to dreams of the past now. To be honest, that side of it didn't worry me, like it worried my older sisters. Anya had been the belle of the Summer Palace Ball and Liza had just made her own entry into society only a few weeks before Papa died and the true state of our finances was revealed. But back then, at fifteen I'd still been too young for all that. You can't miss what you've never known. And probably now would never know.

But I lost no sleep over that, or even over the loss of our beautiful city mansion, and everything in it, to pay the enormous debts Papa had left behind. Our country house, which had once belonged to Mama's father, was much smaller than the Byeloka mansion, but it was cosy and homely, with ample space for us all. We had plenty to eat too, for we had cows, chickens, a vegetable garden, an orchard, a fish-filled stream, and mushrooms and berries in the woods. It was true we only had one house-servant now instead of the flock we'd had before, and we'd all had to learn to do our own hair and look after our own clothes and sometimes lend a hand to Sveta in the house or with the chickens, and help Oleg and Vanya, who look after the garden and the cows. My sisters minded terribly, but I didn't. It was a small enough thing to do for Mama, who works so hard, sometimes long hours into the night, even in winter when her studio in the garden is so cheerless.

Truth is, I miss my father, but I don't miss society. I find the whole notion of it suffocating, with its gossip and matchmaking and rules for young ladies. Occasionally, we're invited to village dances, and though my sisters moan about what country-bumpkin affairs they are, with farmers and local gentry noisily mixing, I enjoy them much more than I'd have enjoyed Byeloka balls. But even more than that, I love the freedom I have here, where you can run barefoot in long summer grass or whoop as you race a sleigh across snowy fields, or get ink on your fingers and nose, and nobody cares. Nobody, that is, apart from my sisters. I don't share their feelings, but I understand them and love them. And especially I love my mother dearly and would do anything to put the sparkle back in her eye. So if Liza's right and by some miracle the stingy old Captain might be persuaded to help us and lighten Mama's burden, then for her sake I should pretend I'm glad to see him.

I sighed. 'I suppose this means we'd better look our best. Do you think my brown velvet would do?'

Liza's blue eyes widened in surprise. She's not used to me being biddable, still less asking her advice. But she soon recovered. 'What, that old thing? Certainly not. The sleeves will be too short; you'll look like a clown in it.'

'Then it will go nicely with my ink-blot nose,' I said flippantly, but Liza wasn't amused.

'Stop being silly, Natasha, and come with me. We have to ask Anya what she thinks.'

I groaned inwardly. I could see that I was in for a long and tedious session of parading in front of the mirror, but I could also see that I'd have to put up with it.

It took even longer than I thought, because Anya wasn't in a good mood. She'd found a tiny pimple on her normally flawless creamy skin, and her sea-green eyes were stormy with irritation as she dabbed at it with powder. Liza usually humours her, but today she was impatient. 'For heaven's sake, we don't have time for this! Anya, you look beautiful, you always do!' She stroked Anya's black ringlets. 'But if the Captain claps eyes on Natasha in that shabby old velvet, he'll change his mind about making her his heiress and then we'll be stuck here for ever.'

I couldn't understand how she'd gone from the faint hope that he might help us to the ridiculous fantasy that the old miser would make me his heiress, and I nearly laughed aloud, but stopped myself in time. Turning to my eldest sister, I said solemnly, 'That's right. And you're so good at understanding these things, Anya. You have such a fine eye for clothes and what they say about people.'

She gave me a hard look. No wonder. It's not exactly the sort of thing I'm in the habit of saying. But like Liza she recovered quickly enough, saying, rather ungraciously, 'Oh, very well.' She looked at me critically. 'Hmm. Now let me see . . .'

Although it was autumn and there was a definite bite in the air, in the house, with the blue and white stove burning cheerfully, it was very warm. So between them Anya and Liza decided that given the regrettable fact my face and neck still bore traces of a summer tan like a peasant girl's, and the less regrettable fact that my brown hair was still sheened with summer gold, I could play the part of the fresh-faced country maiden in a light flowery dress that would make the old miser think of spring. 'And as everyone knows,' said Anya, 'the thought of spring makes you happy, and happiness makes you generous.'

It was my turn to be surprised. Practical Anya had said something not only acute, but beautiful. I wished I'd thought of it. I made a note of it in my head, to add to my story, the story I'd started when Liza burst in. Happiness makes you generous. That would be the theme of my story. It would be like a magic charm, to work on my own family. And on myself.

Alas! All our efforts – the pretty rose-patterned muslin dress, the coral necklace Anya said would set off my brown eyes, my tidy plaited hairdo, clean face and stiff smile – were for naught, as were my sisters' rustling, perfumed presences and my mama's gentle conversation. Not to speak of the honey cake and tiny gingerbread stars and horses painstakingly iced in pink and white by Sveta, and the hot fragrant tea, poured from the best samovar into the best tea-glasses. All of it was for nothing. That greedy old Captain devoured everything without pleasure or thanks, and did not even look us in the face when he finally came to the reason for his visit: how it had 'lately come to my attention, Madame Kupeda, that your esteemed late husband, my dear Cousin Alexander, neglected to return some items he had borrowed from me'.

This was so unexpected that we all stared at him as though he was speaking in a foreign language. I saw the colour rush out of Mama's cheeks as she murmured, 'I'm sorry, Captain Peskov. I don't think I quite understand.'

He drew a list out of his pocket, adjusted his spectacles, and said, 'It's all itemised here, Madame Kupeda, but just so you know: Item 1, an umbrella, black. Item 2, a pair of socks, plain grey. Item 3, a pair of wet-weather galoshes.' He saw our baffled expressions. 'It was some years ago. Cousin Alexander called in to see me. It had been raining and his feet had got wet, so I let him borrow these items.' He sounded like he thought he'd done something very noble. And indeed it must have wrenched what passed for his heart to part with any of his things, I thought, even if no doubt they were old and shabby and fit to be thrown out. I certainly didn't remember seeing them in the house.

I saw Mama's hands clench in her lap and her features harden. I knew that set expression on her face and so did my sisters. We looked at each other, holding our breaths. But all she said was, very softly, 'And of course you wish your property to be returned, Captain Peskov. As it will be, as soon as I find it. Why, the thought that we might have retained any of your property makes me feel quite . . . quite ill.'

His face twisted in what was clearly meant to be a smile. 'Oh, but you must not upset yourself, dear Madame Kupeda. I am sure we can come to some suitable arrangement,' and he licked his lips. We all stared at him. But before any of us could say anything, he added hastily, 'I understand you're painting portraits for a living these days. And I fancy having my portrait painted. We can negotiate a suitable fee, from which the value of the items your husband borrowed can simply be deducted, so there would be no need to return them.' He beamed, well-pleased with himself. 'Now, what do you say?'

'What do I say?' she whispered. 'I say that if you don't get out of this house this very minute, this very second, I will not answer for my actions.' Her eyes flicked to the cake knife. Noting the direction of her look, the Captain scrambled to his feet in panic, spluttering, 'You're mad, woman, quite mad! Here I am giving you a favour out of the goodness of my heart and you –'

'Get out,' she said, 'just get out.' Her voice was still soft but there was such a chilling undertone in it that it was

8

much more frightening than if she'd shouted, and her eyes were like stones. I got up then, and Anya and Liza too, and together we went to stand by our mother, to protect her . . . to stop her from doing something terrible.

Under our combined gaze, my godfather mutely fumbled for his hat and coat. Just before scuttling out, he hissed over his shoulder, 'You'll regret this! Mark my words, you'll regret this. Your name will be mud. No-one will commission you, I'll make sure of it. No-one, do you hear!' The last word ended on a squeak of pain as Mama, after calmly removing one pretty shoe, threw it at his retreating backside, the sharp heel connecting perfectly with its target. And then he was gone, rushing out of the house as if Old Bony herself was after him, howling for his blood.

Two

The old miser was as good as his word, spreading poisonous rumours about us to all and sundry in Byeloka. We heard about it in letters from friends: apparently, from his reports, we lived in a squalid hermitage at the back of beyond, Mama's loss had quite turned her brain, and as for us girls, we were running wild as wolves and no-one who was anyone respectable should have anything whatsoever to do with us.

Well, as for the last part, that was already true. Since our financial ruin, the large social circle Mama and Papa used to move in had melted away like snow in the spring. Our few remaining city friends were not rich or powerful or influential, so their opinion did not matter to the bigwigs of Byeloka. Mind you, neither did Peskov's; his reputation was not exactly a shining one, for no-one much likes a miser. Still, enough mud stuck for the Byeloka merchants and their wives, who had been Mama's main clients, to think that perhaps their fat red faces and self-satisfied jowls might be better painted by someone else – anyone else. So as the weeks went by the commissions began to dry up, and a couple of clients who'd already had their portraits painted quibbled about the price, demanding a discount. Poor Mama had no option but to agree, for otherwise they would simply not have paid at all and she'd have been left not only with no money but with two canvases ruined by the ugly mugs of their owners.

By the time winter had really set in, our situation was becoming desperate. Oh, we still had more than enough to eat, thanks to our home resources: the barrels of salted meat and cabbage, the wheels of cheese, the rows of jars of preserved fruit and vegetables in the pantry. But the small reserve of money Mama had put aside from the sale of her paintings was dwindling by the day, and soon there would not be enough to afford other things, things she'd tried so hard to keep giving us: magazines, books, new shoes, a new dress, the occasional lace handkerchief or shawl.

Mama looked more and more haunted while Liza and Anya's faces grew longer by the day. As for me, I embarked on a secret money-making project. The most famous literary magazine in Ruvenya, *The Golden Pen*, ran a big writing competition every year, with large cash prizes, and you could enter up to three stories. Why shouldn't I enter? I had been writing since I was little, and because I also read a lot, I knew my stories were not bad at all. I told no-one about my project; it would stay a secret unless and until it worked out. So, in my best hand, I made a good copy of what I considered to be my three best stories, including *The Three Sisters*, the tale I'd started the fateful day Captain Peskov came to visit. (I was very proud of that one.) I gave myself the pen-name A.A. Fenicks, which I thought sounded intriguing, maybe even a little foreign, and certainly not like that of a girl of nearly seventeen living in some benighted hermitage in the provinces. I took my stories in their envelope, carefully stamped, to the post office next time we were in Kolorgrod, our small local town, giving as return address the post office itself, for I did not want anything to come to our house. The competition results would not be announced till well into the new year, and I had already devised a little plan about how I was going to tell the post office we were expecting a letter to arrive for a cousin called Messir Fenicks.

Days passed. A week. Two. Three. Christmas came – not very merry, this year. Well, in truth it hadn't been since Papa died. Oh, we tried; we made pretty paper decorations for the tree, Sveta baked a beautiful cake, and Mama had made us each a present: lovely wooden brooches, painted with our own exquisite miniature portrait. Anya's wore an emerald tiara on her ebony-black hair and emerald earrings in her ears; Liza's had a sapphire circlet on her brow, with a filmy veil over her hair like new-minted gold; and mine had hair the colour of fresh autumn leaves touched with the last of the summer sun, and a single magnificent ruby like a flame on a fine chain around her neck. I thought it was as if each of us had looked in a magic mirror and seen someone like us but touched with unearthly glamour, like a princess in a fairy tale.

'You *are* my princesses,' replied Mama when I said this. She kissed us all in turn. 'You are my princesses, more precious than any jewel, and dearer to me than anything in the world.' Then she sighed, and I knew what she was thinking.

'Oh, Mama,' I cried, 'I wish I *could* make magic – real magic – not like that of Grandmother Dove!' She was the village enchantress and a good old soul, but her spells were small, her magic little. She could make warts go away, improve a squint and weave a simple love-spell, but that was as far as it went. The kinds of things you heard the great enchanters and enchantresses could do – bend time and shapeshift and change destinies – well, they were as far beyond Grandmother Dove as the moon.

'You do have real magic, my darling, each of us does; we only need to find it,' said my mother gently. But that did not satisfy me, for it sounded to me like the kind of thing a parent says to stop you from dreaming of impossible things. 'Mama, if I could find magic to change things for us, I'd do anything to get it, even hire myself as a servant to Old Bony if I had to!'

'Don't say things like that, little one,' cried Sveta, overhearing me. 'Old Bony has long ears, and if she should chance to hear you ...' Crossing herself, she glanced fearfully at the darkened window, as if expecting at any moment to see the grey-skinned skull-face of the fearsome forest witch grinning at us with all her sharp teeth.

'Yes, if she hears you, Natasha,' said Liza, grinning, 'that old witch will have your heartstrings for her hair-ribbons, so watch out!'

The thing is, Liza does not believe in Old Bony or great enchanters or even the poor little spells of Grandmother Dove. The only kind of magic she believes in is the spell of riches – the magic dust of money, the glamour of wealth – and truth to say sometimes I think she is right. If we had money, poof! All our troubles would disappear, swept away in the whirlwind of good fortune. As for Anya, she does believe in magic, but only in the sort that will somehow bring a prince to her door and take her off into a world of cloth, gold and purple velvet – a world where there'd be a beautiful new gown for every day of the year. If Grandmother Dove could work that spell, Anya would long since have beaten a path to her door, and I'll wager she too would go into service with Old Bony for it. Not that there's any danger of that for either of us. For who has seen Old Bony these days? Not a single soul. Not once in a hundred years has she shown her long thin nose and sharp teeth to people anywhere. Who knows, maybe her brand of magic, the magic you hear of from the old stories, cannot survive in our modern world of telegraphs and trains and typewriters.

It's said that Christmas has its own magic and perhaps that's true, for only a week later came some good news, in the shape of a messenger from Count Igor Bolotovsky, a wealthy landowner who lived two or three hours' drive from us. In a note, the Count said that he had just remarried for the second time, to a woman much younger than himself. It was her birthday very soon and he had decided that he wished to give his new bride a portrait of herself as a present, and he wanted Mama to paint it. Clearly, he had not heard Captain Peskov's rumours, or if he had he didn't care. He would pay well for it, he said. But there were two conditions: first, it was to be a surprise, so Mama could not go to his house to paint a likeness from life, but must take it from the photograph he had enclosed. And second, as the Countess's birthday was in a week's time, the painting must be ready and delivered to his mansion within the week.

Normally, it takes Mama anything from two weeks to two months to complete a portrait. To do one in just a few days, without even the subject there for sittings, would be a hard undertaking, especially as she had come down with a bad cold. But equally there was no way Mama could refuse the Count's imperious request, not with things being the way they were. Besides, this was the first time he'd ever commissioned her, and it might be the start of something good. So she began work immediately, shutting herself up in her studio all day and much of the night, with Sveta and I running in and out keeping the little stove in the studio well fed with wood so she could stay as warm as possible.

Mama would occasionally let me stay a while and I'd watch her painting, marvelling at the transformation from blank canvas to living scene. She painted the young Countess in a beribboned hat and pale blue dress, holding a basket of peaches against a background of summer flowers, the kind of flowers Mama herself loves so much.

Every time I looked at the painting, I felt as though winter was no longer with us. I could smell the flowers, taste the juicy peaches on my tongue. Mama made the Countess look beautiful, much more beautiful than the pretty but bland little face in the photograph, and I knew that the Count would love it.

She painted and painted and in just three days, it was finished. But the effort had been too great for her, and the cold that she'd managed to hold at bay during the painting frenzy came back with a vengeance. Weak, coughing, eyes streaming, limbs aching, Mama was so sick that there was no way in the world she could possibly keep her promise and deliver the painting in time. And if she didn't, there'd be no fee, for the Count had made it quite clear he would not pay if his conditions weren't met to the letter. Somebody else would have to go, and not Oleg or Vanya either, for Mama was sure the Count would not be happy if the painting was delivered by a servant. One of us would have to go, she said.

'Oh, but, Mama, you know I'm a nervous driver,' said Anya fretfully.

'And I've got a sore throat,' said Liza, coughing for good effect.

Now, I knew very well that those were just excuses, and that actually neither of my sisters felt like leaving the nice warm house for a tedious errand through the snowy fields. But who cared? It gave me a chance to help. 'I'll go, Mama,' I offered. 'I'm perfectly well, and I love to drive.'

'Oh, but you are so young, and you've never driven so far . . .'

'Well, it's time I started then,' I said cheerfully. 'Besides, it's a bright morning and the snow's tight-packed; I'll go swiftly and will be back long before nightfall, before you even know it!'

Mama protested a little more, but I could see she was relieved, and very soon she gave in. She made me promise I'd wear my very warmest fur coat and take with me several blankets and two flasks of hot tea, which I'd refill at the Count's. The horses were hitched to the sleigh, the painting, carefully packed in blankets, was wedged in beside me and, bundled into my furs, I cracked the whip and we set off.

It was indeed a lovely morning; the air was clear as a crystal bell, the snow sparkling, and the winter sun shone out of a pale blue sky. I stopped once briefly for a good long swallow of hot tea, but otherwise kept going. It was very cold but in my fur coat and hat and gloves I was beautifully warm. The horses went like the wind and I was so enjoying the long drive on my own over the whispery snow that it came as something of a surprise when I saw the tall gilt gates of Count Bolotovsky's estate loom into view.

I was there less than an hour. I did not see the Countess at all, but on stating my errand was whisked straight into the Count's presence. A big bear of a man with huge shoulders and a kind, craggy face, Count Bolotovsky was delighted with the prompt delivery of his painting, and even more delighted with the look of it. So delighted was he in fact that he gave a large bonus over and above the agreed fee, slipping it into an envelope, along with an invitation to all our family to attend a dinner-party he

17

was giving in a few weeks' time, in honour of the visit to our region of his new wife's second cousin, Duke Nikolai Koronov, who was a relative of the King himself. I thanked the Count profusely, thinking of how excited Anya and Liza would be when they heard about the dinner-party. I couldn't wait to see their faces when I told them, and I couldn't wait to see Mama's when she opened that envelope and saw how much money was there!

He would have asked me to lunch but I said I must get back, so I was given a quick snack of a large delicious chicken pie in the kitchens, and my tea-flasks were refilled. As I was finishing the last crumbs of the pie, one of the servants leaned over to me and asked, 'Where does your way lie, child?'

I described it as best I could. She nodded gravely. 'Mind you go well,' she said, 'for strange things have been glimpsed thereabouts at night. Some say Old Bony herself keeps house in the forest there and lures folk in to destroy them.' I smiled and thanked her and said she must not worry, I would be sure to be home before dark, and I set off again, my heart light and my belly warm with the good food I'd just eaten. I was singing to myself as we started our journey home, somewhat slower than on the way there, for the horses were a little tired. But it didn't matter; we had several hours of daylight ahead of us, and we'd easily reach the village long before nightfall. And the servant's warning I did not worry about at all.

But we were only about halfway home when a wind sprang up and the sky began to fill with a mass of bruise-coloured clouds. Anxiously, I cracked the whip, urging the horses to go faster, faster, faster, trying to outrun the storm that I knew must be coming. And coming so fast that there was no hope of arriving at the village before it hit. I had to reach the shelter of the woods, for to be caught out in open ground when a blizzard hit was a sure recipe for disaster. Shouting desperately at the horses over the mounting shriek of the wind, I turned them in the direction of the line of woods I could see in the near distance. The poor beasts strained and strained, running as fast as they could, for they, too, instinctively knew the danger we faced.

Then the blizzard was upon us in a blinding, stinging whirl of ice and snow and howling wind. Within seconds everything had disappeared into a terrible white blankness and I could literally see no further than the rumps of the horses. In an instant, I had completely lost my bearings; I had no idea what direction the woods were in, but kept frantically urging the horses onwards, hoping against hope it was still the right way and that soon we'd be under the shelter of the trees. But as the snow fell faster and faster, the going became heavier for the horses, and I could feel them struggling. They slowed, stuck in the drifts that were piling up quicker than they could pull themselves and the sleigh out of them, and soon we were almost at a standstill.

What was that, in the distance? A sound – a sound that made my heart clench. A long howl, and then another, and another, and another. *Wolves!*

The horses heard it too and, whinnying in terror, they redoubled their efforts, pulling so hard that they broke their hitches, jerking the sleigh so that it tumbled over and

I with it. Almost out of their minds with fear, the horses scattered in all directions, leaving me alone in the snow amongst the remains of the broken sleigh. I was done for now; I knew that I would die. Oh God, I prayed wildly, please be merciful. If I am to die, please let it be of cold. Let me fall asleep in the snow; don't let me be torn apart by ravening beasts . . .

And then quite suddenly, through the snow-mist, there it was – a light, not far ahead. Not just one light, but several. It was a miracle – for there was a house, a big house, only a short distance away. I could just make out its shape through the white. Scrambling to my feet and clasping my coat around me, I set off at a stumbling run towards the light.

Three

I had no idea whose house it was, for I had gone so far out of my way in the blizzard that my small knowledge of the great houses on the way to the Count's estate would not serve me at all. As I got closer, I saw that the house was surrounded not by a solid wall of stone or brick, as would have been usual in these parts, but by a massive hedge, skeletal at this time of the year. It looked both flimsy yet formidable, like a cross between a tangled ball of hairy string and a bunch of bristling spears, and I couldn't see any opening in it and no way of getting through without serious scratches. But one look over my shoulder showed me the black shapes of the wolf pack racing towards me through the storm. Scratches be blowed. There was no time to waste. Throwing myself bodily at the hedge, I cried out in surprise as it parted suddenly, like a stage curtain, and I was through.

Behind me, the hedge closed again with a rustling, shivering sound. I didn't stop to wonder what it might mean, but ran like the wind down the long tree-lined path that led to the front steps of the house, expecting at any moment to hear the wolf pack in full cry behind me. Closer and closer the house loomed, several storeys high, painted sky-blue, edged and decorated with fine white marble. A grand and beautiful house, but I had little time then to admire it. Reaching the flight of marble steps without mishap, I hurried up. At the top I came to a massive oak door. It was ajar, and through the gap I glimpsed light and warmth. Yet there was no-one around, and for a moment I hesitated.

But not for long, as a blood-freezing howl ripped at the air. The wolves had got through the hedge! With a squeak of fear, I pushed open the door and plunged into the house. As I did so, the door swung shut with a crash that made my ears ring. Then all went quiet again, the howl of the wolves and the fury of the storm cut off as suddenly as if I'd been pulled into another world.

It took me a moment to catch my breath. My heart was racing, my hands shook, my throat was dry. But in a little while I recovered and looked around me. I was in an elegant hall, with grey and white marble floors, pale blue walls touched with gilt, and a couple of tall-backed chairs upholstered in dark blue velvet. A sweeping marble staircase led up to the next floor, and the whole area was lit by an immense, magnificent crystal chandelier which threw out a steady golden light of a far richer colour than the gas lamps of Byeloka streets yet that had neither the flicker nor the smell of candle-flame. It was as warm as a balmy spring day, too, though I could see no stove which might explain the heat. But it wasn't either of those things, strange as they were, that made the hair on the back of my neck prickle. It was the sight of the pictures that hung on those walls. Or rather, the large picture-frames, elegant in carved gilt – *but containing only blank space.*

There were six or seven of them, each picture-frame slightly different in style yet each exactly the same, for they were quite empty, enclosing not even a slice of pale blue wall but a white nothingness. As the daughter of an artist, I was used to all kinds of pictures. But I'd never seen anything like this. What kind of person hangs *non-pictures* on the walls, empty frames with nothing in them but a white blank, repeated over and over?

But it was too late to be asking questions. Outside were the blizzard and the wolves. Inside, it was warm, beautiful, well-lit, and appetising smells from somewhere were wafting to my nose. I was hungry and cold. For nothing in the world, not even fear of what might lie here, would I have poked my nose out of that door again. Yes, I did not know what dangers might lie in here. But I knew *for certain* the dangers that were out there.

'Hello? Is anyone home?' I called out nervously, not sure whether I hoped someone would answer or not. Silence. I called again, 'Thank you for the shelter, I am very grateful.' As I finished speaking, I caught my breath. Was I imagining it, or had I heard a rustling sound, like someone moving somewhere above me, someone who'd been watching me? With a little shiver, I looked up the great staircase, but could see only a shadowy darkness. I most certainly didn't want to go up there to investigate.

I wanted to stay in the light and warmth. And the good smells were getting stronger, making me feel faint with hunger. So, casting a nervous look around, and repeating, 'Thank you, I am so very grateful,' I edged out of the hall and down a corridor that soon led me to a cosy wood-panelled dining-room.

There too were empty picture-frames hanging on the walls, only I gave them a mere glance this time, for there was something much better to look at: a long table, set with three places in crystal and silver and fine porcelain, groaning under the weight of dishes that would have made even a saint's mouth water. There was red and black caviar in little glass dishes, fresh bread, golden-crusted roast chicken, mushrooms in butter sauce, jewel-bright tomatoes, plump berries, a tall meringue cake layered with cream, fragrant tea steaming in a samovar, and I don't know what else. As I hungrily gazed at it my stomach felt emptier and emptier and my throat more and more parched. I kept looking at the three place-settings, wishing that my hosts, whoever they were, would manifest themselves so we could start on the food – for somehow I knew that one of those place-settings was for me.

I sat down on one of the velvet-upholstered chairs and waited. Long minutes ticked by and still no-one came. The sight of the food tormented me. My stomach growled that everything would be getting cold, that it would be spoiled, that I must not wait. A longing grew in me to reach out a hand and just try a little of that caviar, just a tiny slice of the chicken, just one tomato. But instinct kept me back. I'd never been in an enchanted place before. I'd never known anyone, personally, who had. But I knew they existed. Occasionally you saw reports in the newspapers of somebody who had stumbled across some such place, and lived to tell the tale. But sometimes they disappeared without trace, never to be seen again. Although such reports weren't common these days, I knew from my reading that these experiences were always connected to crossing *feya* lines, the invisible web of magic that is woven through the everyday world and which is particularly strong at certain spots where a *feya* or some other magic-maker, human or non-human, might reside. The servant at the Count's had warned me about Old Bony and her enchanted realm in the forest. But this place clearly wasn't Old Bony's doing. She most certainly didn't go in for mansions or fashionable furniture or blank pictures. She was of much rougher tastes, and her enchanted cottage, it was said, was protected by fences made of skulls and bones rather than a magical hedge. Yet I must have somehow crossed a *feya* line and found myself in an enchanted place. I knew such places had rules. And one of them was to not eat the food. At least, not when uninvited.

So I tried to be strong. But still those divine smells wafted under my nose and I felt weak with longing until at last I decided that if I stayed there one second longer, I'd throw myself at the food and become trapped. I had to get out of that room before my weakness got too strong! I had to find my hosts, whoever they might be, and find out more about where I was, why I had been allowed in. And I must keep my wits about me at all times.

So I made myself get up and leave that room. I wandered down the corridor, trying very hard to stop my feet from staging a rebellion and racing me back to the laden table. As I went, I kept passing empty picture-frames hanging on the walls, framing nothing but that white blankness. And after a while, they started getting under my skin. It didn't seem just odd now, but more and more sinister, less of an absence and more of a presence: as if behind that white space there were alien eyes watching me, observing my every move.

A tingle ran up my spine. Quickening my steps, I passed a splendid sitting-room, all white and gold, but it also contained those picture-frames glaring at me, so I didn't enter. I passed another room which I didn't even look into, I was so spooked by now. Finally I came to a set of glass doors which opened out onto a large, formal court-yard garden. The storm seemed to have ended and there was a peaceful wintry loveliness about the garden, with its stone fountain, little paths, and bare bushes and small trees waiting for spring. Even the snow blanketing the garden in graceful drifts and the icicles hanging from the trees seemed like another touch of beauty, and my heart began to lift.

Then, as I gazed out at the garden through the glass, the sun came out from behind a cloud, making the snow gleam as softly and richly as a mink coat and the ice glitter like diamonds. And there too, picked out by the sun, was something else: something that burned like a bright flame at the edge of my vision. I peered through the glass, trying to see. Was that – no, it couldn't be! Not in this season, not in the dead of winter, surely.

As if in a dream, I opened the glass doors and stepped out into the garden. My boots crunched over the snow, marking the pristine white with the weight of my passing, though when I glanced back, the snow was re-forming as though I'd never touched it. I should have been fearful, but I was past feeling scared. My hunger forgotten, all I wanted now was to see the thing I had glimpsed from the house, the beautiful thing that shouldn't be there but, miraculously, was. I went down one little path and then onto another. And, at the end of the third path, there it was. I stopped, transfixed with wonder.

It was the most beautiful flower I'd ever seen, anywhere – a red rose of an amazingly deep scarlet shade, with a fragrance whose heady sweetness filled me with delight. It bloomed all on its own on a spindly bare bush, the splendour of its scarlet petals richer than the imperial ruby of the crown of Ruvenya, and by far more lovely, for this was a living thing. Yet this was not summer; this was the dead of winter, snow lay everywhere. The sight of a rose growing outdoors in this season, when a blizzard had just stopped blowing and the rosebushes did not have a single leaf, was not only astounding, it was thrilling. And it made me feel suddenly that whatever this place was, it did not mean me any harm. A place where such a rose could grow in winter could not be bad. There must be a good light within it, a spirit that loved beauty and sweetness for its own sake.

I came closer to the rose, thinking with delight that those empty frames on the walls didn't matter to me any more, because here was a picture more beautiful than any they might have contained. The snowy garden, the scarlet flower, the bright air: it was a painting that no mortal hand could have made.

As I drew nearer, the fragrance enveloped me in a warm glow, and the satiny sheen of the scarlet was even more beautiful than I'd thought. I was close enough to touch now – and so I reached out a hand towards it. But the instant my fingertip touched the rose, its petals began to fall, fast, faster, while I stared in horror and dismay, until in less time than it takes to say it, there was nothing left of that beautiful bloom, only the scarlet in the snow like splashes of blood on a white carpet.

And then came a sound that turned my limbs to ice: a roar so loud that it shook the whole garden and made the glass doors rattle. A moment later, a terrifying creature burst upon the path before me.

Four

It was a beast, and yet not a beast. A man, yet not a man.
It stood tall on two legs and was clothed in a long coat
and boots. Its intelligent eyes were of a tigerish, glowing
amber, set in a hairy face like a bear's; it had a tawny
mane like a lion's, while its open mouth displayed teeth
as white and sharp as a wolf's. I knew at once what it
was though I'd never before heard of one that could take
such a mingled form. *Abartyen.* Shapeshifter. Man-beast.
The most common were werewolves, though even they
weren't common. And not all *abartyen* were dangerous
to humans; some were even friendly. But this one most
certainly wasn't. The light in its eyes was of a murderous
rage; its cruelly clawed hands were like sharp knives ready
to rip my throat open. Falling to my knees in the snow,
amongst the fallen scarlet petals, I closed my eyes and
prayed that death would be swift.

I could smell it now as it loomed over me. It stank not of a wild beast, as I'd been expecting, but of something else, something sharp and metallic. The smell of blood, I thought dazedly. It is a creature of blood, and it will gorge itself on mine.

I winced as something heavy tapped my shoulder. The creature's paw. Its claws were grabbing at the stuff of my dress, forcing me up till I stood trembling in front of it, its hot breath on my face. And then it spoke. Its voice was that of a man, though there was a strange intonation to it.

'You have killed the only thing that brought me joy,' the *abartyen* growled. As it lifted its terrible claws to strike me down, I knew my last hour had come.

I don't know where I found the desperate strength to cry out, 'Oh, sir, I did not mean to. I only wanted to touch it because it was so beautiful, the most beautiful thing I'd ever seen. I did not know what would happen. I swear I did not know. And I am so very sorry. Please, if there is anything – anything I can do to repay you. If I can perhaps bring you another rose –'

'There is no other,' said the *abartyen*, and there was bleak desolation in its voice. 'It was the only one of its kind, and for that you must pay. With your life.'

'Wait!' It was someone else's voice, a sharp female voice, and at that moment a little old lady, dressed all in black, appeared on the path. With her brisk trot, frail shape, widow's weeds, grey chignon and silver-rimmed glasses, she was a most incongruous sight in that place. Yet she also seemed completely at home there. A small slender hope raised its tendril within me and I whispered, 'Please, Grandmother, help me.'

She didn't reply but cast me a cool glance. Instead, she looked up at the *abartyen*, who towered above her, and said, 'Yes, my lord, you are right, and she must pay, with her life. But not,' she added, as the last hope left me and my shoulders slumped, 'with her death.'

At first I didn't take it in. Then it struck me: I was not to be killed, but I must still pay with my life. So I was to be, what – enslaved? Kept prisoner? I burst out, 'If you have any mercy in you, you will let me go. I may have done wrong but I did not intend to. It is unjust to –'

'Be silent,' said the *abartyen*, and his voice this time was very quiet, but with such an undertone of menace that it chilled me to the bone. 'Be silent and let Luel speak.'

Luel. Not a Ruvenyan name, I thought. And the intonation in the *abartyen's* voice – it's simply a foreign accent. They both spoke good Ruvenyan, but their accents betrayed them. They were strangers to my country, and oddly, that made me feel a little stronger.

The old woman – Luel – looked at me and, in a voice that betrayed no emotion at all, she said, 'You have no idea what justice or injustice is, child. You came here of your own will and you destroyed my lord's rose of your own will, and so payment must be made.' She picked up one of the scarlet petals from the snow. 'You killed his only joy. So joy for joy must you repay.'

'I – I don't understand,' I stammered.

'You will.'

31

'Am I to be a slave? A prisoner?'

'You are a debtor,' she said. 'No more, no less. You will stay here until you pay that debt. But you will be comfortable and safe. That I promise you.'

'But he . . .' I murmured, casting a fearful glance at the *abartyen*, who stood silent and glowering, not looking at me but into the distance.

'My lord will not harm you,' she said, and her voice was scornful, as though it was quite incredible that I would even imagine it could be otherwise. 'He will not touch you. You do not need to trouble yourself on that account.'

My heart sank. I had hoped that she would be my ally but it did not seem that was to be. She was connected to the *abartyen* in a way I could not understand. She called him 'my lord' yet she acted nothing like a servant. 'Is there nothing I can do to change your minds?' I asked.

'No,' Luel replied, while the *abartyen* said not a word. 'Unless, of course, one of your sisters will agree to take your place.'

There was a humming in my ears and my throat felt thick. 'Never! I would not allow them to. I am responsible, not them.' How did she know I had sisters? Who was she? Questions I dared not ask.

'Very well,' said Luel. 'Then the matter is resolved.'

Panic fluttered in my belly. 'No, wait. Please, let me at least go home and inform my family that I am to stay here till –'

'No. You can write a letter,' snapped Luel. 'We will make sure it gets to them.'

Tears sprang into my eyes. 'Please. A letter – it is not the same. My mother will be worried. She will not understand. I was expected back. If I do not return, if there is only – only a letter, she will think I am in terrible danger.' I gulped. 'But if I can stand before her and tell her it is of my own free will that I stay here, it will be easier for her. And for my sisters.'

There was a little silence. 'You will not go,' Luel finally said. 'But if you must see them, then see them you will. Come with me.'

Five

She led me out of the fateful garden and back into the house. The *abartyen* did not follow us. I was glad of that, though my mind seethed with questions and fears and desperate attempts to make sense of this nightmare I found myself in. Perhaps it *was* a nightmare, I thought, and I'd wake to find myself safely back – but wait, safely back where? In the blizzard, with the wolves circling me, or dying of cold in the shattered remains of my sleigh? It was hardly desirable. Besides, this was no dream but my reality now and somehow, somehow I had to find my way home. I wasn't completely helpless: I had read, and written too, many stories in which someone was trapped in seemingly impossible dilemmas and yet, by keeping their wits about them, managed to escape. I must do that. I must not show fear. I must not be truculent either. I must listen and watch and learn – and wait for the right moment when I might make my escape.

We came to a door that Luel unlocked with a little brass key she took from her skirt pocket, revealing stairs that led down to some sort of basement or cellar. She waved at me to go down. My heart hammered. After all her promises, was I still going to be locked up? But what could I do other than meekly do as she asked? I had no power; she had it all. So I started down the stairs; and she followed after me, closing the door behind us so we were in almost complete darkness and I could only find my way by keeping close to the wall and groping my way down the stairs.

Down they went, down, down, and even further down, till I thought we must be in the very bowels of the earth. Then suddenly the stairs ended, at another door, and beyond it there was a small, gently lit room. When we entered the room I saw there was no window; the light came from a tall lamp that stood by a chair against a dark-curtained wall. Facing this wall was an alcove, also curtained; there was no other furniture in the room.

'Sit there.' Luel pointed to the chair. I did as I was told, and she walked over to the alcove and pulled back the curtain to reveal an oval mirror. There seemed nothing out of the ordinary about it until Luel stepped up to it and I saw that she had no reflection. I watched on as she passed her hand three times over the glass and murmured something I couldn't catch. Instantly, the mirror fogged over, a fog which grew thicker, thicker, and then suddenly reversed, growing thinner and thinner till the mist cleared.

'Oh,' I whispered, overcome, for I was looking into our cosy sitting-room at home. The perspective I was looking from seemed to be just above the mantelpiece, where our own mirror hung. Mama was in the room, alone, in her favourite armchair with a rug over her knees, still looking a bit weak from her illness but better than when I'd left. She was holding an open book but clearly wasn't doing much reading, for she kept glancing at the grandfather clock, an anxious expression in her eyes. I felt such a pang of homesickness at the sight that my whole body yearned towards it and I got up, reaching out for my mother as though to . . .

'Sit!' said Luel sharply. 'Or you will not be allowed to speak to her.'

I looked at Luel's face, her nice, grandmotherly face, with its crumpled-petal skin and the clear dark eyes behind the silver-rimmed glasses, and could see no human feeling there. 'Very well. I will do as you say,' I said heavily, and sat down.

'Good. Now, close your eyes.'

I did as I was told.

'Open them again. Look at your mother and call her name. Tell her what you have to say. But beware! You have a few seconds in which to speak, no more. And if you say the wrong thing, you will be cut off immediately. Do you understand?'

'Yes,' I said, knowing instinctively what she meant. I wasn't to complain. I wasn't to tell Mama I was in danger. I had to pretend everything was all right. But I could not resist saying, 'You did not need to tell me that. I do not want to frighten my mother or worry her in any way.'

Luel shot me a look. I had the impression my answer surprised her, but she did not comment on it, merely saying, 'I will count to five, and your time will start as soon as I finish counting. Are you ready?'

'Yes,' I said shakily.

She began to count and as she did, I saw my mother's head lift. There was a puzzled expression in her eyes, as if she'd heard something she couldn't place. Then Luel reached five and, looking directly at my mother, I instantly started to speak, my words tumbling over each other. 'Mama, it's me. I'm fine, I'm safe; I got lost in a bad storm and the horses ran away but luckily I was given shelter in the household of a local gentleman.'

'Natasha?' came my mother's astonished voice, so clearly it was as if I were in the same room as her. Her eyes, wide with shock, fastened on the mirror above our mantelpiece. 'Oh, my little Natashka, what is this? Where are you? How is it that I can see and hear you in our mirror?'

'The gentleman is something of a *kaldir*, like our neighbour Dr ter Zhaber in Byeloka,' I improvised desperately, reminding her of the old Faustinian refugee, part magician, part inventor, who'd lived a couple of doors away from us in the city, 'and this – er – this vision-machine, which links between mirrors, is his new invention. It's amazing magic.' I saw Luel look at me with a strange expression on her face and thought she was going to interrupt me, so I hurried on. 'He is so very clever, Mama, but very busy, and he needs someone to write up notes for him. He has offered me a job as his secretary. It is just temporary, but it will pay well, and it will help us, so I've accepted. His household will look after me, and I'll be home as soon as I can. I just didn't want you to worry.'

'But, Natasha,' said my mother in a bewildered tone, 'I'm very grateful he gave you shelter, and I'm sure he's very clever – he must be to make this machine. But what is this gentleman's name? And why this sudden decision?'

Luel shook her head, and I knew my time was almost up, so I called out desperately, 'Mama, I will write to you and tell you all you want to know but I must go now because the machine will cut out soon; it doesn't yet work quite as well as it should. Goodbye, dear Mama, goodbye.' The last goodbye was cut off abruptly and I was left staring at my mother on the other side of the mirror. But only for an instant, for that image, too, flickered out and disappeared, and I was left with my own reflection.

My stomach churned. There were tears pricking at the corners of my eyelids. This was so cruel. Did I really deserve this, just for destroying that rose? And destroying it accidentally, too. I hadn't intended any harm. I'd been drawn by its beauty, that was all. Then I remembered the delight it had given me, just to look at it, and remembered, too, the bleak desolation in the *abartyen's* voice as he spoke of it being the only one of its kind, and the strangest feeling came over me, of pity and understanding mixed. I said impulsively, 'I am truly sorry about the scarlet flower. Truly sorry.'

'I know,' said Luel quietly. 'But it is done, and that is that.' She looked at me. 'Why did you say my lord was a *kaldir*?' She gave a foreign intonation to the word.

'What was I supposed to say?' I cried. 'That he's a . . .' I cut the words off abruptly. 'I mean, I said it because, well, because of the magic mirror. It was all I could think of on the spur of the moment to explain it without saying too much. I'm sorry if I said the wrong thing.'

'On the contrary,' she said. 'You've done well. I am glad for all our sakes.'

I took advantage of her apparent softening. 'Please, will you let me send a letter to Mama then, answering her questions? I know that if I do not, her worries will only grow.'

'Yes. You may do so, but I must read it before you send it. It seems harsh, I know,' she went on gently, 'but it cannot be any other way. And I promise that no harm shall befall you while you are here. In fact, you will be treated like an honoured guest.'

I swallowed. 'How – how long must I be here?'

'That, I cannot tell you. Yet.'

I wanted to yell and scream at her that she had no right – they had no right – to keep me here, but I knew it would do no good. So instead I said, 'At least . . . What I told Mama about – about being paid; my family . . . things have been tough, and –'

'Of course. It shall be arranged,' said Luel calmly. 'Your family will be well provided for, I promise that. And in return, I ask only this: that you promise not to try to escape.'

I looked at her. 'I promise,' I lied. It was the duty of a prisoner to escape, I thought; and a gilded cage was still a cage, no matter how anyone might dress it up.

Luel shrouded the mirror again, and we went out of the room and back up the stairs. She locked the door firmly behind us, pocketed the key, then led me into the hall and up the great staircase to a room on the first floor that she said was to be mine. Looking out over a long sweep of snow-covered lawn that stretched right to the other side of the hedge at the back of the house, it was light and airy but just as warm as the other rooms in the house. Pale gold velvet curtains framed the windows, and the floor was of gleaming parquet, covered with a large, soft rug. There was a four-poster bed made up with fine linen, big pillows and a satin-edged coverlet of cream brocade, a wardrobe and chest of drawers, a dressing table, desk and chair, a small bookshelf lined with fat volumes bound in plain dark leather, and a comfortable armchair upholstered in the same gold velvet as the curtains. Best of all, though, there were no empty picture-frames.

Luel said, 'Well?'

She was actually asking my opinion! Well, I must be making progress. I said, 'It's a nice room.'

The old woman nodded. 'You will be happy here.'

I did not know what to say to this patent absurdity, for how could she possibly imagine such a thing? Instead, I said, 'I have no change of clothes with me.'

'That is no problem.' She opened the wardrobe door. Despite myself, I could not help but gasp in wonder at the sight of the rows of dresses upon their hangers, a flurry of lace and tulle and velvet and silk and fine wool, in a variety of colours which would flatter my colouring exactly. We were a long way here from my old velvet, or even the pretty sprigged print frock I'd worn for Captain Peskov's visit. These were dresses fit for a fine lady. 'And you will find they fit perfectly,' Luel said quietly.

Now why wasn't I surprised about that?

There were shoes, too, of all sorts; evening shoes in satin and silver, day shoes in fine kid, slippers in leather so soft they felt like gloves, and sturdy walking boots. Then Luel opened the drawers to reveal fine underwear and stockings and handkerchiefs and nightgowns and shawls and more – the kinds of things Anya and Liza would have given their little fingers to own again. Meanwhile, in the desk were writing paper and envelopes and elegant pens, as well as stamps and a small pot of glue. Best of all, there was a beautiful notebook bound in pale leather, with heavy cream paper of a quality that made me long to write on it.

All these things must have been tailor-made for me. Or someone very like me. Someone knew I would come stumbling out of that storm. Not the *abartyen*, I thought, but Luel. Though the *abartyen* was frightening – a brute force – it was clearly Luel who held power in this place, despite her calling him 'my lord'. But what did she want from me? I couldn't help a little shiver at the thought.

'You will no doubt want to refresh yourself,' she said, as if she were an ordinary host addressing an ordinary guest. 'There is a bathroom just for you behind that door,' and she pointed to a door in the corner of the room, 'with everything you may need. Then you will please come down to join us for dinner. I believe you already know where.'

She had been the one watching me, I thought, when I'd been sitting in the dining-room earlier. I wanted to say I wasn't hungry and would skip dinner, but I knew the 'please' hadn't made a request out of what she'd said. And besides, I was hungry. Perhaps it was a reaction to fear, but my stomach felt hollow and empty. I could have devoured a horse right then and there. Trouble was, I had a queasy feeling I'd have to sit there and watch the *abartyen* do just that.

Six

But I was wrong. Not only did he not eat a horse, the *abartyen* did not eat anything at all. In fact, he did not make an appearance at the dinner table and so it was just Luel and I, sitting across from each other. Despite my relief at the *abartyen's* absence and the excellent meal, it was not a cheery occasion. Luel seemed deep in her own thoughts, and I was hardly in a state to make light conversation. The small pleasure I'd felt upon looking at myself in the mirror – an ordinary mirror, I'd checked! – after bathing and dressing in a simple, perfectly fitting dark red cashmere dress with a snow-white lace collar, had quite evaporated, and the delicious food might as well have been bread and water for all the delight I took in it.

It was towards the very end of the meal that Luel broke her silence. 'You are afraid, I know, but there is nothing for you to be afraid of, Natasha.'

It was the first time she'd used my name, and it made me start. 'Oh,' I replied weakly. What else could I say?

'My lord is not what he seems,' she said. 'You spoke of injustice, earlier. A great injustice was done to him – a great evil – and he, well, he found himself as he is now.'

I stared at her. 'Do you mean . . .?'

'He is not what and how he is by nature,' Luel said quietly. 'Please try to remember that.'

'But what – what happened? Why? Who? How? –'

'Too many questions for tonight,' she said, waving her hand. 'There will be time for you to learn, to try to understand. To repay him.'

I forgot about my resolve not to be combative and burst out, 'Whatever happened to the *abart*– to your lord, however bad and tragic it was, it wasn't my fault. So why should I suffer for it?'

'You won't,' she said calmly. 'I told you already: joy for joy is your payment.'

'But I don't understand how I can possibly –'

'Look in your heart. You have known sorrow, but you have never known real loneliness. Real despair. Think of that. Think of why. And then you will see your way clear to an understanding what it is you must do.'

'But why can't you tell me? Why can't you at least give me a clue?' I pleaded, beside myself.

'Because it must come from you,' Luel said, without turning a hair. 'Or it will be worth nothing. It will not help my lord. It will not repay your debt.' She got up from the table. 'And now, child, it is time to retire. You must be exhausted.'

'Just a little,' I muttered ironically, half to myself.

'Tomorrow my lord will meet you after lunch, in the sitting-room. You will speak with him.'

My heart started pounding, all irony forgotten. 'Will you be there?' I whispered.

'Perhaps,' she said. 'Perhaps not.'

I don't know if it was her careless tone that goaded me. 'Why do you have these things on your walls?' I said harshly, waving a hand at the blank picture-frames.

To my surprise her expression changed, so that for the first time I saw something like real emotion in her face. 'It is part of the injustice,' she said.

The sadness in her eyes and voice touched me, despite myself. 'They are terrible things to look at,' I said gently.

'Yes,' she said, and she looked at me. 'They are.'

'Will you not tell me . . .' I began, but she had already left the room, leaving me there at the table, gazing at the blank spaces where pictures ought to be, trying to make sense of all I'd heard that night. The *abartyen* wasn't what he was by nature, she'd said: therefore, it meant he was not a shapeshifter by nature, not a born and bred one. I had read that people could be forced by evil sorcery into an *abartyen* shape. But it was very, very rare and extremely difficult to perform. Luel clearly could not break the spell or surely she would have done so. And I had the impression those empty picture-frames were also something over which she had no control.

That was a scary thought. For given the fact she had no reflection, Luel was not human, but a *feya*, like Old Bony. And her magic was powerful, for a place like this is not maintained by minor enchantment. But whoever it was who had cursed her lord in this terrible way must be even more powerful, if Luel could not break the spell herself. I didn't want to think of what that might mean, but the feeling that the danger I was in was even greater than I'd imagined hung heavy in my belly, as if I'd swallowed a stone.

❧

I thought I'd never get to sleep that night but the bed was so warm and comfortable, and the room so quiet and peaceful, that I drifted off to sleep without even being aware of it. And sometime during the night I fell into a strange dream – strange due to the fact of it being so uneventful. In the dream, I was looking into a sunny walled garden where climbing white and pink roses rambled on the walls. The air was full of their scent and that of the more exotic blooms of mimosa and jasmine. Not a Ruvenyan garden, then, but rather from some southern country where such flowers grew. I could smell the flowers, which is unusual in a dream, and I could see the bees buzzing around them, and I could hear birds singing. There was a little white wrought-iron table and chair in the garden, and a young woman sat there with her back to me. She wore a pretty, lacy summer hat, her black hair in long, loose ringlets down her back, and her dress was a flurry of pale pink ribbons and snow-white tulle of the same delicate shades as the roses. She was waving at someone I couldn't see, and it was such a vivid picture

I felt as though I could hear the tinkle of her laughter, though I could not hear anything she said. For a while, I was there, just suspended in the little scene; then it flickered out and I opened my eyes to the darkness of my room. In the dream, I had quite forgotten about what had happened to me, but now everything came flooding back and my mind kept going round and round like a mouse in a maze, trying to find a way out.

The mirror, I thought wildly, I must learn how it works; it's the key to my escape. But to do that I had to get Luel to take me down to the cellar again; I had to listen carefully to what she said and watch what she did and then later I would find a way to get the key from her. Later – later – that meant staying here for who knew how long, and meanwhile, tomorrow, I had to meet the *abartyen*. Cursed or not, natural shapeshifter or not, he wasn't fully human any more. And no matter what Luel said, I was afraid of him.

The words she'd spoken to me at dinner, about what I must do, made even less sense now and I was trembling, shaking with the thought that if I didn't get it right, I would suffer for it. She'd said I'd not be harmed, but could I trust anything she said? Clearly, all that mattered to her was the *abartyen*. She was bound to him by some tie I hadn't yet fathomed, and I was merely a pawn in a plan whose outline I couldn't yet glimpse. I had no magical powers, no special distinction, no great beauty or extreme cleverness. I was an ordinary girl with a small talent in storytelling, that was all. And how could that help me now?

And then I remembered something my mother had told me. As a very small child, when I was scared or tired or out of sorts, I could only be calmed by having a story told to me, over and over again. Now I reached back into my memory and told myself my own story, the story of the three sisters. *Three sisters sat spinning at the old tower window, watching for their mother to come home.* And as I told myself the story, I could feel my pulse slowing, my limbs stop shaking and the panic leaving me until gradually I became calmer. I must have fallen asleep, for when I woke next bright sunlight was flooding the room.

I got up and padded to the window in my bare feet. The curtains had been drawn and there was a tray of hot tea and appetising little pastries on the dressing table. Outside, the sun was shining brightly though snow still lay on the ground. It was very quiet; there were no bird calls, which wasn't surprising, as they hardly stir in the wintertime. In the distance, beyond the lawns, I could see the hedge towering high into the sky, and a figure patrolling its edge, up and down, up and down, like a tiger in a cage. The *abartyen.*

I quickly drew away from the window, in case he should look up and see me. In an ordinary place, at that distance, of course he could never have seen me. But this place was far from ordinary and I felt as if anything could happen here – anything at all.

Seven

I had some tea and pastries, and after washing and dressing in a plain green dress, I prowled around my room, trying to work out something – anything – from my surroundings. Nothing told me much though, apart from the books on the shelf. By now I was used to the idea that things had been arranged in this room specially for me, so it was with some surprise that I discovered the books were not the kind I liked to read. There was no fiction, no poetry, no plays, only a six-volume encyclopedia and a battered Ruvenyan–Faustinian dictionary. If I was desperately bored, I thought, I could read the encyclopedia, but when I flipped through it, I discovered it was full of endless reams of dull information on obscure subjects. Even the biographical entries were boring; I didn't recognise a single name and the style was so long-winded that my heart sank and my eyes glazed over just looking at it. Only the dictionary held a marginal interest for me, because at least it was about words. I wondered whether the accent of my unlikely hosts was Faustinian. They didn't sound like my old tutor but they could have come from a different part of that powerful empire to our west, with its many different principalities and dukedoms.

And then, with a prickle of excitement, I remembered that magic was banned in the Faustine Empire, except for that under the control of an official order called the Mancers. That was why our old neighbour Dr ter Zhaber had fled to Ruvenya when he was young. Could the *abartyen* and Luel be Faustinian refugees too? Was that the 'terrible injustice' Luel had mentioned?

Driven by a sense that I might at last be on the verge of shedding some light on the mystery – a mystery I knew I had to solve if I was ever to get out of here – I leafed feverishly through all the books again, in the hopes of finding a clue.

My efforts were in vain. I put the books back on the shelf and sat at the desk to compose a letter to Mama. But the lying words I needed to soothe her wouldn't come, and my spirit of invention seemed to have failed me. Then I had an idea. I decided to write down the facts first – the truth of what had happened to me – and not what I had to tell Mama. So I took out the notebook, opened it to the first page and began to write. But though I tried to start recounting my experiences, I couldn't find the right words. I started something, crossed it out, started again, to no avail.

This was a new experience for me. I'd always been able to write fluently, easily, 'too easily' as another of our tutors said to me once, but then, she also thought that imagination was a character flaw that must be eradicated. Thank goodness she didn't last long. My father heard her say that if we were her daughters, she'd make sure all frivolous pastimes were banned. 'You are not their mother, thank God,' he'd told her tartly, 'and if you don't approve of our family, there's always the door.' Which she took, in high dudgeon, while my sisters and I happily watched from the stairs.

And that's how I found myself writing, my pen loosened at last. About those funny old childhood memories, Liza and Anya and I united in our glee and Papa, standing there with his colour high and his moustache bristling as he told that killjoy exactly what needed to be said. When Mama came back from her outing, we told her what had happened, and she had looked at him with such love and gladness!

Tears sprang to my eyes. How she must miss him, even more than my sisters and I did, though to be sure that was hard enough. But to lose the man you love when you are still deeply in love must be so much worse. And for some reason, as I wrote those words down, the dream I'd had the night before came back to my mind, the sunlit garden, and the girl in her summer clothes, laughing merrily with someone who was just outside my line of sight, but who I was sure now must be her beloved. And a strange feeling crept over me, a feeling that something bad had happened to that girl and her lover.

I put my pen down and stared at what I had just written. It was almost, I thought uneasily, as though they were somebody else's words. As though some spirit had been whispering them into my ear . . . No, stop that, Natasha,

I scolded myself. *You have enough to worry about without being spooked by your own runaway imagination!*

I didn't feel like writing any more. Shoving the notebook back into the desk drawer and out of my sight, I got up and went to the window again. The *abartyen* was no longer to be seen, and the lawns were deserted. The sky, bright blue now with a hard frosty gleam, was empty of cloud. I watched as a tiny speck of black on the far horizon drew closer to resolve itself into a single circling crow, its melancholy cawing audible even from where I stood. It was the first outside sound I'd heard since I came here, I realised suddenly. Normally, a crow's call would not figure high on my list of favourite sounds, but today, cut off from everyone I loved and everything I under-stood, it rang in my ears like the most silvery of bells, and I reached for the handle of the window to open it, wanting to hear the sound more clearly.

'Step away from there at once.' Luel's voice made me jump. She must have a footfall as silent as a cat's, I thought, as I spun around and glared at her defiantly.

'Why should I?' I muttered.

'Just do as you're told and don't argue.' She tugged the curtains across, but not before I'd seen her swift glance out of the window, and the anxiety that leaped into her eyes.

'What's the matter?' I asked, not expecting an answer.

'I don't think he can see you,' Luel said quietly, looking at me. 'I hope not.'

Instantly, my heart started banging against my ribs. 'What do you mean?'

'I took a risk with you. I hope I'm not wrong.'

Exasperated, I burst out, 'Why do you always talk in riddles? For once, give me a straight answer! Who is *he*?'

'Better you don't know,' Luel said after a silence. 'You are safe as long as you don't.'

I glared at her. 'I'd hardly call my present circumstances safe, locked up in a magic cage and threatened with death or enslavement!'

'Nobody is threatening you with either,' she said with breathtaking cheek. 'You have been given everything you might wish for – beautiful clothes and a comfortable bed, delicious food and an end to your family's financial worries – and still you complain!'

I clenched my fists, trying to stop myself from yelling. 'You have taken my freedom and my family from me, and you think I should be grateful? Are you mad, or just plain evil?'

I realised too late what I'd said, and stood there aghast, certain I would pay bitterly for it, but all Luel did was shrug her shoulders. 'Think of me what you will, it matters little to me. Whatever I do, it is for my lord, who awaits you in his sitting-room.'

I stared at her. 'But he ... but I thought it was after lunch that he ...' My anger was quite forgotten now in the new rush of anxiety that flooded over me. I did not want to face the *abartyen* just yet. Not just now.

'He has changed his mind. He wants to see you now,' she said calmly.

'But I'm not ready ...'

'Ready or not, you will go,' she said firmly, and with a wave of her arm, ushered me out of the room, following close behind.

Eight

As I went down the great marble stairs and into the hall, it seemed as though all those blank picture-frames were glaring at me, like white alien eyes ready to devour me if I put a foot wrong. I cast my eyes down, not wanting to look, and almost tripped and fell, catching myself just in time. Behind me, Luel made a tutting sound, and I felt the anger rise within me again, chasing away the fear for an instant. Concentrate on your anger, I told myself, then you won't be afraid. You won't be afraid . . .

A most unexpected sound floated down the corridor towards us and I stopped. 'What was that?'

Luel gave a thin smile. 'Have you never heard music before?'

'But it's . . .' I hesitated. 'It's lovely.'

'Yes, it is.'

I wanted to find out more, but one glance at her face told me not to bother. Instead, I followed her through the hall and down the long corridor, not to the gold and white sitting-room I'd glimpsed the day before, but to a cosy wood-panelled room with a real fire burning cheerfully in a plain fireplace and, heavens be praised, no empty picture-frames. Two armchairs sat facing the fire, with a little table between them. There was a music box on the table, of the kind you might find in a Christmas market, with brightly painted skating figures whirling endlessly round and round, to a sweet and melancholy tune. It was that tune, now fading away gently as the spring ran down, that I'd heard.

The *abartyen* sat unmoving in one of the chairs, with his back to me. All I could see was his shaggy mane of hair and the sides of his black velvet robe. And one heavy clawed hand on the armrest. I halted, my heart pounding.

'She is here, my lord,' said Luel, jabbing me in the back.

Silence.

She jabbed me in the back again, propelling me forward. Now I could see the *abartyen's* profile – his crooked nose, the thick bristles on his cheeks, the sweep of thick dark eyelashes hiding that feral yellow glare. Under his robe he wore an elegant grey suit that looked quite out of place on his thick-set, bestial body, and his clawed feet were hidden in black felt indoor boots, twisted out of shape by what they had to conceal.

'Luel, you may leave us.' His voice was softer than yesterday, but still with that growling undertone of menace. I shot a panicky glance at Luel, my eyes pleading with her not to do as he said.

She stared right back at me and said quietly, 'Very well, my lord.' A swish of skirts and she was gone, the door closing gently behind her.

I was alone with the *abartyen*. For a fearful moment in which I could clearly hear my own heart beating, there was silence.

'Sit,' the *abartyen* said, without looking at me.

My skin prickling, I did as I was told. I was so close to him now that I could smell him, like I had yesterday. Only this time it wasn't the sharp metallic tang of blood that caught in my nostrils. Nor was it any kind of wild animal stench or indeed any normal human smell, like sweat or even the faint scent of skin warmed by the fire. No, I can only describe it as something bleak and cold, like the smell of gloom. There was another silence, which seemed to go on for ever while I sat there in agony, wanting to say something but unable to. Every word dried up in my throat, every thought dissolved, except the terror a living creature feels when it is close to a predator. I tried to cope with my rising panic by staring into the bright cheer of the fire. But it didn't help much.

'Luel tells me I frightened you yesterday.'

I started, my head jerking up. What kind of cruel game was this? He *knew* I had been terrified – and for good reason. My ears burned. My stomach roiled with nausea. But I still could not speak.

'You see, I do not remember,' he said, as if he could read my thoughts.

I looked at him now, properly. His face was still turned away from mine, but I could see the clenched hand gripping the armrest. 'I don't understand,' I stammered.

'The darkness – it takes so much,' he said very quietly. 'I remember some things: the rose opening, the scarlet joy of it. I had forgotten what that felt like.' He broke off and was silent so long I thought he wouldn't speak again. Then he said, 'Do you know how long the rose lasted?'

'Er, no,' I said tremulously.

'It had only just opened when you came into the garden.'

I winced.

'And then,' he went on, 'it was gone, and there was the scarlet in the snow, at your feet. And that is all I remember. But Luel tells me . . . there was more.' He lifted his head and those tigerish eyes stared straight into mine, pinning me to the spot, breathless and confused. 'Is that so?'

Was this a trick? I'd never imagined anything like this. What did he want? What would he do to me if I said the wrong thing? Should I lie? Should I pretend I hadn't been scared or that nothing had happened? But I found my lips opening and my mouth forming the single word, 'Yes.'

'Ah,' he said, on a long sigh. 'I will not ask for your forgiveness, for why should you give it? But if it were possible for me to change what happened, then I . . . then I would do it.'

At his words, spoken with such a quiet desolation, an unexpected feeling arose in me. It was a feeling of immense pity, so intense that tears sprang to my eyes. I looked away, not wanting him to see them, not wanting to feel such a thing. I could not allow soft feelings to lull me into a sense of false security around this creature. Whether or not he was telling the truth about not remembering what he'd done, he was dangerous. Either he was a deliberate liar and manipulator, or he was insane. Either way, I knew not to trust him or his words. But I must not make a show of defiance either. So I simply said, 'I see.'

'I do not think you do. If I could undo what has been done, you could go home and forget all about us.'

'Oh, sir, please,' I cried, unable to stop myself as hope rose wildly in me. 'Please, could a way not be found to do it?'

'No, there is no way,' he said heavily. 'I cannot take back what I did and –'

'You cannot change that but you can change what happens after,' I dared to say. 'You can free me from my debt.'

'No, that is not the way things work here,' he said sadly, then paused. 'And besides, it is too dangerous now for you to leave. It will be known that . . .' He trailed off.

'Please, sir,' I gasped, 'please, I must know. What is this danger? Why can't I leave? Why can't you change whatever you want to –'

'That's enough, young woman.' It was Luel, re-entering the room so promptly I was sure she must have been listening at the door. 'My lord cannot answer these questions, and even if he could, the answers would not help you.'

'How do you know that?' I was beside myself with fury, my fear almost forgotten. I turned to the *abartyen*. 'Sir, if I – if I understood, maybe . . .' I gulped. 'Maybe I could – could also help *you*.'

I broke off in confusion. The words had come unbidden to my lips and now I couldn't believe I'd said them. What on earth had possessed me to say I'd help such a creature? I knew only that the words had come from deep inside me and could not be unsaid.

But if I was surprised at myself, it was nothing to the reaction I saw in the others. For the first time, I saw real disbelief flicker into the *abartyen's* eyes, and Luel seemed genuinely taken aback, momentarily speechless.

But it was she who recovered first. 'Do you know what you are saying? You are bound to repay your debt. That is an obligation. But this help you speak of you do not owe.'

'I know that,' I said, shuddering inwardly, because in truth I did not know at all what I was letting myself in for. Yet somehow I was instinctively more certain with every instant that passed that I must go through with my rash pledge. 'Nevertheless, I am prepared to help.'

Luel raised her eyebrows. 'Understand we cannot free you until –'

'No,' said the *abartyen*, speaking at last. 'No, I won't have it.' There was that undertone of growling menace in his voice again, and for a moment the golden eyes burned into my face with a disturbing intensity.

'My lord –' began Luel.

'We cannot ask for this,' said the *abartyen* tightly. 'It is too much. You know what it would expose her to.'

'My lord, it is a risk, yes, but one that I believe we could manage.' She glanced at me. 'And Natasha has freely and willingly offered –'

'No, Luel. I cannot allow any more harm to be done. Not to her, not to anyone.' He got to his feet, breathing raggedly as he drew the folds of his robe around him, and I sensed a titanic struggle within him. I shrank back as, looming over me for an instant, he said, 'The darkness may take me, but at least I shall have done no more to deserve it.' And then he strode out of the room, slamming the door behind him so hard that everything rattled. The music box fell off the table. Its winding mechanism jolted briefly to life and it began to play a sweet tune – its lilting sound incongruous in the heavy atmosphere.

Nine

'Well,' said Luel, 'what are we to do then, child?' Bending down, she picked up the music box and set it on the table, and slowly the tune wound down.

Staring at the skating figures as though somehow they might give me a clue, I stammered, 'I – I don't know.'

'Hmm.' She threw me a little smile, the first she'd given me. 'It has been a long time since I have experienced anything like this.'

'Anything like what?' I asked.

'I have lived a long time – much more than any human span – as I'm sure you have guessed already,' she said, her eyes twinkling. 'And I thought nothing about the world could ever surprise me. Yet a little bit of a girl with ink-blots on her fingers has done more to astonish me than any of the magic-wielders I have ever known, human or otherwise. How did you know what to do?'

I could feel the fiery blush spreading up my neck and into my cheeks. 'I didn't,' I said lamely. 'The words just came. I – I've done nothing, really.'

'Oh yes, you have. You have done an extraordinary thing. Hope came into this room with your words, and hope has never been a visitor here before.'

'Please, stop,' I cried. 'I am so confused. I understand nothing. I do not even know what possessed me to say that I –'

'It does not matter,' she said. 'It came from inside you. Nobody made you say it. You were not bound in any way. It was freely given.'

'But your lord . . . he did not seem pleased at all and –'

'He cannot recognise hope. Not yet. But that will change, believe me.'

'I am glad if that is so,' I said simply and, to my own surprise, discovered I really did feel glad.

'I am sorry if I was a little hard and hasty with you before,' Luel said, a slightly sheepish expression coming over her face. 'But I did not quite know what to make of you.'

'That wasn't the impression I got,' I said wryly. 'You seemed to know everything about me, and I knew nothing other than that somehow you had engineered my coming to your door. The storm – was it your doing?'

Luel chuckled. 'Of course not. I may have some . . . powers . . . but storm-calling is not one of them. Besides, even if I did have that power, I am not from here and the local winds would not obey me.'

'Have other lost travellers come to your door before?' I asked.

'No. Only two have reached the hedge. I didn't like the look of them. I have to be very careful, you see. I made sure to conjure up a picture of an impenetrable wilderness beyond the hedge, and they turned back. Nobody has ever come as far as you.'

'Why me?'

'I saw you in the mirror. I consulted it to see who you were. I thought maybe you were different,' Luel said carefully. 'And I watched how you behaved when you first entered here.'

I'd been right about the watching eyes yesterday, I thought.

'My lord did not know of your presence,' she went on. 'He did not know till you were in the garden. That bush, you see, has never given a flower before. I couldn't make it, for though all the others bloomed, it stayed dry and bare. Then, two weeks ago, he noticed a tiny bud on it. He's been watching that bud ever since – watering the plant, caring for it. When it finally opened, it gave him real joy for the first time in so long.'

I swallowed. 'I am truly sorry. I only wish that I could –'

'Listen,' Luel said impatiently, brushing aside my apology, 'the very day – no – the very moment such a beautiful flower blooms on a bush that has always been barren, *you come*.' Her eyes grew bright. 'I knew you were here for a reason. Now I know why. There is something powerful in you, something very special. I can feel it.'

'No, you don't understand. I have no magic powers, nothing special.' I took a deep breath. 'Though my words were rash and unthinking, I haven't changed my mind. I really do want to help. And if I am to do so, then you must allow me to ask questions.'

The old woman looked at me. 'Very well, as you wish. I can tell you about the past and about this place.'

'But?' I prompted.

'Let us come to that when we do,' she said, evasively. 'Now, you must be hungry. Shall we have some lunch? While we eat, you may question me and I will answer as best I can. Agreed?'

'Fine,' I said, trying to speak lightly.

I wasn't surprised to see the table in the dining-room already set for two, and laden with all kinds of good things selected from the delicious bounty of the waters, from succulent prawns to crayfish served in their shells with golden mayonnaise, pike-perch whose whiteness of flesh contrasted with the coral blush of river trout, and a sturgeon soup so fragrant that it made my knees knock together from pure pleasure. Add to that fried potatoes and onions, sour-sweet red cabbage, and a large salad stuffed with olives and tomatoes and different kinds of greens, and you had a feast which made my mouth water immediately.

'How do you do it?' I asked, as we sat down. 'There are no servants here to do the work.'

Luel smiled. 'That's so. There is no-one here but us. But, really, this is the easiest magic of all.'

I waved a hand at the food. 'You conjure all this up from nothing?'

'Of course not. Does it taste like food made of air?'

I shook my head.

'It's not enchanted,' she went on, 'except in the manner of its arrival. It's come from the very best tables, you see.'

I stared at her. 'What do you mean?'

'I go to the mirror and I ask it to show me who's having a feast that day – not just in this region but all over the country – and I devise the day's menus from it, choosing only the best. Naturally.'

'Naturally,' I echoed, helping myself to some lobster. 'But how do you get it here?'

'I call it to this table,' she said, as though it were the simplest thing in the world. 'And it answers the call.'

'Oh,' I said, dazed by the strange picture this conjured up of Luel snapping her fingers and dishes flying through the air like obedient dogs to their master, 'but they – the people whose tables you've lightened – do they not notice?'

'I daresay they do,' she said with a shrug. 'But I never take more than one dish from any one table. They probably put it down to a mistake of some sort. Or possibly a light-fingered servant, naughty child or cheeky dog.'

'Whose tables have you … sampled in this way?' I asked, tackling some prawns.

'Many different ones. And only those who can afford it.'

'And the clothes in my room – did they come here in a similar way?'

Luel shot me a wry look. 'Yes. I must say, you must be feeling better, asking me questions like these.'

I coloured a little. 'I suppose I am.' And I did feel lighter, as if the hope Luel had said I'd given had entered my own heart and mind. I took a first sip of sturgeon soup. 'Why do you never call your lord by his name?'

There was surprise in Luel's face again as she gave me a long, searching look. 'To protect him. He is still being sought. If I should ever say my lord's name out loud, then . . .'

'Then what?'

'It might reach the wrong ears.'

The way she spoke these words made me shiver. 'But he calls you by your name. Wouldn't that also –'

'No, I am using my inner name here, not the name I was known by in the world. This one carries no echoes. And neither, at the moment, does yours, for different reasons.'

'What are those reasons?'

'They don't know of your existence,' she said simply. 'And they won't, unless . . .'

'Unless what? Please, tell me. I have a right to know.'

'Unless you make it so,' she said quietly. 'And I think you know what that means.'

I swallowed. She meant if I tried to run away. But even though only a few hours ago that would have been uppermost in my mind, I was now more curious than frightened. 'How long have you been here?'

'Three years in clock-reckoning. Much longer if you count it in the relentless hours of my lord's agony.'

'And where are you from?'

'I cannot tell you that for the same reason I cannot speak my lord's name. If I were to speak the name of our home . . .' Luel paused and I saw a flicker of sadness cross her face, 'the feeling in it would alert them. We are not from this country. That is all I can say.'

I was silent a moment, then I said, carefully, 'What happened to your lord? Was it a curse?'

'Yes. He crossed a powerful and very dangerous man.' Her lips peeled back into a snarl. 'Quite how dangerous, we did not know until it was too late and the spell was cast. I managed to halt the full workings of it and to whisk my lord away. But that is all I could do.'

Suddenly, I didn't feel hungry at all and pushed my plate away. 'You said that your lord is still being – sought. Does that mean –'

'Our enemy does not consider his revenge complete yet. It will not be complete until my lord is utterly destroyed.' She spoke calmly, but her words chilled me to the bone.

I whispered, 'The crow this morning . . .'

'It may be from him. It may not. I checked our defences again, and they have not been breached. But I still cannot take the chance.'

I shivered. 'Forgive me, Luel, for asking this, but you are a *feya*, are you not?' She nodded in reply. 'And you are connected to your lord by no ordinary bond.'

'That is so. I've served the family for a long, long time. And I have known my lord for all of his twenty-one years, since the very day he was born.'

Twenty-one, I thought, shocked. Why, the *abartyen* was only a few years older than me. To think that that terrible thing had happened to him when he was eighteen. A sharp pang went through me, a mixture of pity and horror. 'One of your kind is surely stronger than a mere human sorcerer,' I said. 'So why –'

'There is no *mere* about it,' Luel snapped. 'Our enemy is most certainly no ordinary sorcerer. And yes, I'm what you people call a *feya*, but there are many grades and ranks of powers amongst us. Mine is only a small one.'

My eyes widened. I waved a hand around. 'But this place . . . it is your doing.'

'Yes. So what? I have tried to keep my lord safe and make him comfortable. I have even tried to give him moments of respite, of beauty, like the rose. But every day it grows harder.'

'The . . . the empty frames – are they part of it?'

Luel nodded.

'Why don't you wish them away, or whatever it is you do?'

'It is not so simple,' she said sadly.

I was tempted to say that someone who could control a magic mirror and make dishes and dresses fly from places all over the land should have no difficulty with getting rid of empty spaces.

'Child, you must understand. There are so many things I cannot do, much as I long to. I cannot reverse the spell. I cannot restore what was taken from my lord – everything he once loved, the life he once lived. I cannot protect him from the darkness that eats away at him. I cannot save him from a cruel injustice that day by merciless day devours more and more of his memory and with it his humanity.'

'Oh, Luel,' I cried, shaken to the core by the horror of it, 'the man who did this must surely be no man but a demon from the deepest pit of hell. For how could a human being do such a terrible thing to another and still not consider that his revenge was complete?'

There was a great sadness in the old woman's eyes as she looked at me. 'My dear sweet Natasha,' she said, 'he is no demon but indeed a man.'

'Well, if he is no demon, it is simple.'

Luel's eyebrows shot up, questioning me.

'What one human can do, another can undo,' I went on. 'There *must* be a way to break this spell. And I want to do it. Come what may. With your help, of course,' I added.

Luel's face filled with light. She grasped my hand, and I felt the strange coolness of her *feya* skin. 'Oh, Natasha, my dear child, you have made me so happy,' she whispered. 'You cannot know how happy. Before, you gave me hope. Now, you have given so much more. For yes, there may be a way to break the spell, but I could not say so before this very moment.'

'Why not?' I asked, puzzled.

'Listen to me,' Luel said. 'I took a risk letting you in, for I knew it might weaken the spell that has protected this place from unfriendly eyes. But I took that risk because I knew you were different, and I hoped so much that maybe you were the right one. Yet I had to be sure. Because it is only to the right one that I may say it.' She smiled radiantly. 'And you have just proven you are the one.'

Ten

What Luel told me then stilled my tongue and made my heart hang heavy as lead. I listened to her speak of the one way that would break the spell, and tried to school my own expression to conceal the horror I felt at what was being asked of me. She looked at me when she'd finished. 'Well?'

'I . . .' The simple word snagged in my throat. 'I . . .'

'It is a shock, I know. But in time . . .'

I held up a trembling hand. 'Is there . . .' I swallowed. 'Is there no possibility of . . . Are you sure this is the only way?'

'It is the only way I know.' She laid a hand on mine. 'Natasha, don't look so terrified. My lord – what you see now is not what he really is. If you knew him as I do . . .'

'But I don't,' I said shakily. 'That is just it.'

'If you turn your back on my lord now, his fate is sealed. There is nothing surer.'

'I will not turn my back, but I . . . I will do anything to save him but that,' I said, rising and pushing back my chair so hurriedly that it fell with a crash. 'You cannot demand such a thing of me! I cannot be forced to think of him as my . . .' The words caught in my throat.

'You are right. You cannot be forced to love him. You cannot be forced to marry him. And nobody can demand it of you,' Luel said sadly. 'My dear child, I'd hoped you understood that. All I can do is suggest it. It must be done of your own free will or it is worthless.'

With a cry, I fled the room and ran down the corridor, expecting at any moment to hear her coming in pursuit of me. But I reached the glass doors that led to the garden without her voice hailing me. Blindly, feeling as though I were about to suffocate, I pulled open the doors and stumbled out into the empty garden, the crisp cold air making me gasp, half in relief, half in pain.

I reached a stone bench and sat down. Doubling over, I rocked from side to side, murmuring desperate prayers. I tried to still the panic that burned within me, the fear that Luel was lying and that I was already trapped by my own thoughtless words into a terrifying marriage with a beast.

My eye was caught at that moment by a splash of scarlet on white – the withered petals of the fateful flower, lying in the snow. Hardly knowing what I was doing, I got up groggily and staggered to where a single petal lay. All the others had vanished as though they'd never existed and the bush was completely bare.

I picked up the petal. Withered as it was, it still exuded a faint fragrance, and its ragged shape and deep colour reminded me eerily of a heart. A bloody, dying heart, broken beyond repair. And that image undid the last of my precarious self-control, so that I put my face in my hands and wept, the petal slipping unregarded through my fingers.

'She has told you.' The voice was quiet, but it made me start violently. I turned to see the *abartyen* standing on the path. He stood absolutely still and his yellow eyes held no expression at all but glowed like lanterns in his monstrous face. He made a terrifying sight.

'Yes,' I whispered, quailing before him.

'She has no right,' he said, so quietly that I strained to hear him. 'No right. I did not ask it. I *will* not ask it.' His voice rose a little with each word, so that by the time he got to the end, it was a deep, menacing growl.

I took a step back. 'It is all right, sir, I am not –'

'Don't lie to me,' he said harshly. 'I know every fibre in you rebels at the thought, every sense shrinks. Is that not so? Answer me.'

I did not dare to look at him. 'Yes,' I whispered. 'Forgive me.'

'There is nothing to forgive. Whose flesh would not crawl at the sight of me? I am a monster, hollowed out by darkness. But not yet fallen so low as to allow this – this sacrifice of an innocent. I would rather live and die the hideous monster that I am.' His voice broke a little. For the first time I looked at the *abartyen* and saw not a grotesquely nightmarish alien thing to be feared or pitied, but a ruined human being valiantly trying to cling to the last shreds of honour.

Impulsively, I said, 'Oh, sir, you are no monster but a fellow mortal unjustly condemned to a cruel fate, and it is my dearest wish to help you. I cannot in truth do as Luel asks. I cannot be your lover, your wife but . . .' Trembling, I took a step towards him, then another. He did not move a muscle and stood there staring at me with his tiger eyes. They didn't seem quite as glowingly yellow any more but shadowed deep down with a darker, softer shade. I held out my hand. 'But that does not mean I cannot be your friend.'

He gave a low groan. 'No, it is too late.'

'I will not believe that,' I said, trying to speak lightly. 'Sir, is it the custom in your country for a gentleman to leave a lady's hand dangling as if she were a cheeky beggar asking for alms?'

I saw him blink – the first time I had seen such a homely human tic disturb those alien eyes. 'Why, I . . .' He broke off and then resumed a little more strongly, 'You must excuse me, my lady, but my manners are . . . somewhat rusty.' Taking my hand shyly and delicately in his, so that I felt neither coarse hair nor ragged claw, but only a very gentle touch, like the soft pad of a cat, he held it for just an instant before dropping it again.

'We are agreed, then,' I said, my heart thumping so hard against my ribs that I was sure he must hear it. 'We are to be friends.'

'Yes,' he whispered. 'But if ever . . . if ever you cannot bear the sight of me, you must say so. Send me away. I will understand.'

A lump formed in my throat. 'Now why would I do that? Unless, of course, you start taking after Captain Peskov.'

The anguish on his face was replaced by bewilderment, exactly as I had hoped. 'Who is Captain Peskov?' he asked faintly.

'I will tell you all about him, if you want,' I said briskly. 'Now, if you do not mind, my feet are rather cold from standing about in this snow. Shall we go inside?'

'Oh. Yes,' he said, sounding rather dazed. But just before he turned to follow me, I saw him bend down furtively, pick up the petal that I had dropped, and put it away in an inner pocket of his coat. I acted as if I had not seen, though an odd little tremor rippled through me as I led the way towards the glass doors, gossiping about Captain Peskov as though I had not a care in the world.

Luel met us in the corridor. She looked at us both with shining eyes. 'It's cold out there. Perhaps you would like some hot tea and fresh cakes sent to your sitting-room, my lord?'

'Ah, um,' he replied. His voice sounded a little choked, as if this ordinary request wasn't something he was used to dealing with. Luel shot me a questioning look.

'I think that's an excellent idea,' I said heartily. 'And you'll join us too, won't you?'

'Of course,' she said, and smiled. 'They will be my favourite cream cakes. I wouldn't miss them for the world.' Her eyes locked on mine, and I understood the meaning behind her words. This was a moment for great celebration, for everything has changed. Oh no, perhaps she assumed that it meant I'd agreed to marry him? I must disillusion her of that, and fast, because she might broach the subject in front of her lord and that would be too cruel. I was no longer afraid of the *abartyen*; my offer of friendship had been genuine, if nervous, and I felt instinctively that we could indeed become friends. But there was no chance I could ever feel *that* way about him. Not for anything in the world could I imagine myself as his lover or his bride, as Luel hoped. And yet not for anything in the world did I want to hurt him, one who had already suffered so much.

To my relief she said nothing about it. We sat around the fire and drank fragrant steaming tea from a tall china samovar and ate little cream cakes that were piled on a gilded cake stand. At least, Luel and I did, she many more than I, for the bird-like little *feya* had the prodigious appetite of a blacksmith. But her lord hardly touched a thing, leaving his first cake untouched except for one bite. Yet he seemed, if not cheerful, at least not morose and brooding as before. And he listened as Luel asked me questions about my family, then after a while he shyly asked questions of his own. I answered in the most interesting and natural way I could, trying hard to bring the ordinary human world of my home into this enchanted exile. It wasn't just for his sake but for mine too.

Under all my bright chatter and my new determination, a nagging worry kept intruding. I was no longer a prisoner here. But I might as well be. If the spell was not broken, and Luel's lord not returned to his own shape and his own life, then was I not, too, condemned to this place, unable to leave it because of what his enemy might do to me? Remembering the little Luel had told me, I knew enough to understand that the warnings I'd been given were not idle. There was a great evil prowling somewhere out there beyond the frail edifice of magical safety Luel had built, an evil thirsting still for the blood of its victim; an evil as ruthless as it was powerful, and one I had no hope of defeating or deceiving if a *feya* such as Luel could only just hold it at bay.

But I said nothing of this, of course. There was no point in souring the tentative sweetness of those hours, the beginnings of an unlikely friendship forged in such an unexpected way. For the longer we sat together, the closer I felt to them. And the more I became uncomfortable at the fact I had no name for him in my mind. 'Sir, I understand why I cannot know your true name, but is there none I might know you by? "Sir" is simply not good enough.'

He shot Luel a glance.

She shook her head. 'There is no name we can safely give that truly belongs to him.'

'Then will it be all right if I invent my own?' I asked, daringly.

They both stared at me. Then Luel said slowly, 'Do you have any objections, my lord?'

He shook his shaggy head. 'As long as you do not call me after Peskov,' he said, and his lips curled back. To my astonishment – and Luel's – I realised that he had made a joke. A small, weak joke, to be sure, but a joke nonetheless.

I smiled. 'Set your mind at ease; I would not give that name to a frog croaking in the swamp! I was thinking of Ivan, because it is a name both so common in our country that it must make it difficult to track, and yet also the name of many legendary heroes who triumph over great odds.'

'Ivan! Why not? It is a good name,' he said, with a lilt in his voice I'd never heard before. 'Do you not think so, Luel?'

'I think it is excellent,' the old woman replied, and there was genuine admiration in her eyes as she glanced at me. 'I think it is most excellent, my lord,' she added, 'and it fits you like a glove.'

'I only wish that gloves would fit me so well,' said Ivan, with a wry glance at one hairy clawed hand. That was his second joke, all the more remarkable because it addressed the very source of his pain. From that moment he became Ivan, and the invented name made his besieged humanity more real to me than anything else could have done.

Later, much later, Ivan fell gently asleep in front of the fire, and Luel motioned to me to tiptoe out. In the corridor, with the door closed behind us, she turned to me and said, with real emotion, 'My dear, dear child, ask of me whatever you will and I will give it to you if it is in my power to do so.'

'Luel,' I said uncomfortably, 'I must tell you that I did not agree to – to . . . what you'd asked of me.'

'I know,' she said. 'He told me. He was glad. He was unhappy with me, that I had even asked you.' She paused.

'Maybe I was wrong. Maybe there *is* another way. And perhaps you have found it.'

'Do you think so?' I said, with incredulous hope.

'I don't know yet. But in just a few hours you have done what I could not do in all these years. You have pushed back the darkness for more than a few minutes. His eyes – did you notice? There is more colour in them now.'

'Yes,' I said, then impulsively added, 'and that makes me happy, Luel.' It was true. In that instant, I was purely, brightly happy.

She put a hand on my arm. 'Ah, my dear, dear Natasha. I bless the storm that brought you to our door. And I want so much to give you something in return for what you have done. Is there anything – aside from what you know I cannot give you – that you might want?'

'Might I be allowed to use the mirror sometimes? I know I cannot go home, but if I could speak to my family – if I could see my home – then it would not be so hard for me.' I hadn't planned it, the words had just come out of my mouth, and as soon as they did, I knew it was truly the only thing I wanted.

She smiled. 'Of course,' she said softly. 'Tomorrow I will teach you how to use the mirror, and you will be able to consult it as often as you wish.' Her tone changed. 'But beware! On no account must you try to see anything beyond the walls of your home, or speak to anyone other than your family. And you must not tell them the truth but keep to that story you invented or we will all be in great danger. Do you promise?'

'Of course,' I cried joyfully. 'Oh, Luel, thank you! Thank you!' I reached over and planted a kiss on her cool cheek, making her grumble that I was as noisy and boisterous as an untrained puppy, but looking just a little pleased all the same.

Eleven

Dinner that night had a festive feel, and it wasn't only because of the delicious food. By unspoken agreement Luel and I kept the talk bright and light, and Ivan listened peacefully with an expression which told me that for the moment, the darkness had rolled back like a bitter sea from the shores of his troubled mind. Once again he hardly touched his meal. I had begun to suspect, with a wrench of pity, that his clawed hands were too clumsy to allow him to politely wield a knife and fork and so he did not want to eat in front of me. But I pretended not to notice and so did Luel, and the time passed pleasantly, much more pleasantly than I would have dared to imagine even a few hours ago. Not even the blank pictures disturbed me as much as they had before.

I went up to bed in a very different frame of mind from the previous night. Back in my room, I stood at the window, looking out over the quiet moonlit lawns and thinking that even if my predicament was not at an end, at least now I was no longer afraid for my life. Tomorrow I could speak to my mother with a lighter heart.

I was just about to close the curtains when I saw it. A solitary black shape in the night sky, just beyond the hedge. The crow.

No. I refused to give in to fear. This man – this evil sorcerer – had no way of getting through. Luel had said the defences had not been breached. Her magic was much too strong, I told myself stoutly as I undressed and got ready for bed. But though I got into bed and tried to sleep, I couldn't. I tossed and turned till I finally gave up. I lit the lamp and took the notebook out from the desk. Now, I thought, I'll be able to write what happened. But first I read back what I had written that morning, about the girl in my dream, and when I took up the pen and started to write, it was something quite different to what I'd originally intended that came rushing onto the page.

In a warm and pleasant country, where bright flowers bloom much of the year, and skies are blue as Our Lady's robe, lived a young girl called Rosette, I wrote. *She was a little dressmaker, from a modest family; pretty as the flower she was named after, bright as a mountain stream, and good as new-baked bread. Despite her modest birth, suitors queued for her hand, but she refused them all till she met Robert. A handsome, gentle young man, he fell as deeply in love with Rosette as she with him, and the pair were eager to get married as soon as they could.*

Robert was of rich and noble birth but had not yet reached his majority when he fell in love with Rosette, so under the law he was obliged to ask his guardian for his consent to the marriage. His guardian was his uncle, one of the King's chief councillors, and a proud and arrogant man known as the Master of Crows because he always dressed in black, as did his closest retainers. He professed to love Robert but, in truth, in the depths of his stony heart he hated his nephew and wished only for his unhappiness. What was more, he had been steadily spending Robert's fortune over the years, and if his nephew married and set up home with his bride, Robert would be independent and then the true state of affairs would be revealed. So when Robert came to him and asked for his consent, he harshly refused it, saying the girl was not fit to marry into their family and that Robert should forget all about her.

Robert refused and said he hoped his uncle would change his mind, but if that did not happen, he would petition the King and so go over his guardian's head. He had been a quiet and biddable young man till then but something had changed in him when he met Rosette, and the Master of Crows knew he would not be able to control things for long. He had to do something. So he decided to get rid of Rosette, imagining that once she was gone, his nephew would become biddable once more.

The dreadful day came when Robert received news that Rosette had died on her way to meet him. She had tripped and fallen from a platform into the path of an oncoming train and was killed at once. Robert was beside himself with grief but he did not suspect his uncle had had a hand in her death, for who would think such a monstrous thing? Who would believe that the man who had the King's ear could employ a vicious backstreet murderer to push an innocent young girl to a terrible death? Indeed, the Master of Crows wept many hypocritical tears over Rosette's death and then revealed to his nephew that that very morning, he'd changed his mind about the marriage and decided to give his consent. As an apology, he had sent a tiny posy of white roses to Rosette, to pin on her coat, and she had been wearing it when she fell.

I could see and smell those white roses, so pure and fragrant and beautiful and horrifying, as my own imagination drove me onwards through a story that was quite unlike anything I had ever written before.

Robert was very much touched by this and embraced his uncle, and the coldness between them was forgotten. The Master of Crows suggested Robert go on a long trip abroad to try to forget his sorrow. Robert's home and usual surroundings had become unbearable to him now that Rosette was gone, and so Robert agreed, though he knew he would not forget.

For weeks and months Robert wandered around the world, with no real taste for anywhere or anything. Then one day he came to a grim and grey mountain town where he put up for the night, intending to go on in the morning. He took a meal in a dingy dining-room and it was there that he met an ill-favoured beetle-browed man who was very drunk and who rambled on about his unsavoury life and the people he'd known, people who would 'make your hair curl, boy'. Robert had no appetite for such tales but he also had no energy to leave, so he sat there, only half-listening. The drunkard began speaking of a man he'd known, now dead, who had worked as a hired killer for the rich and powerful. 'There was this one job he did,' said Robert's chance acquaintance, 'which turned even his hardened stomach. He had so much remorse about it he hanged himself not long after. He said he saw the girl he'd killed every night in his dreams, a girl with the face of an angel and a posy of snow-white roses on her bloodstained breast, the roses that had marked her out as his victim, and every night he heard her cry as she fell and he –'

'What did you say?' said Robert sharply, cutting the man off.

Robert's face was so pale, his eyes so wild that the strangeness of it struck his new acquaintance even in the midst of his drunkard's fumes. 'What's wrong with you?' he muttered.

'The roses – you said they marked her out. What do you mean?'

'What do you think, friend? Whoever ordered the killing knew she would be wearing the posy and had probably sent it to her himself. He most likely thought that . . .' But the beetle-browed man was talking to empty air, for Robert had gone. He was on his way back to his own country, his heart no longer full of grief for his lost love but filled instead with burning hatred against his uncle, the Master of Crows.

In the first port in his home country, Robert bought a gun, resolving to shoot his uncle straight through his black, wicked heart. But what he did not know was that his return had been noted, for the Master of Crows had many spies. Robert had been seen buying the gun. And his uncle, guessing his nephew's intention, devised a terrible plan. When Robert appeared at his uncle's door, they were ready *for him; the King's police arrested him for the murder of his own Rosette and for conspiring to murder his uncle, who tearfully said that he had found incriminating evidence against his nephew. And he had documents to prove it. Robert angrily protested his innocence, but his story was not believed, for the Master of Crows was clever and had arranged everything to support his case.*

Robert was tried and sentenced to life in a prison camp in a remote place of dark forest and endless ice and snow, from which there could be no pardon and no reprieve. For years he endured it there, at first still full of rage and hate, but then hopelessly, mutely, numbly, his mind clouding day by day and his memories fading.

One day when Robert and his companions in misfortune were returning from a day of cutting wood in the forest, they came across a spindly rosebush. On that bush was a single delicate flower, white as snow. It released such a beautiful warm scent on the air that it was as though it were summer.

Robert picked it, put it to his nose and closed his eyes. In that moment he remembered Rosette, remembered not her cruel death but her beautiful life and the joy of their love. The tears came at last, gently watering his frozen, broken heart and coaxing forth the first tender shoots of hope.

I was weeping myself. When I'd sat down this evening, I'd intended to write an account of what had happened to me. I hadn't – and yet I had. For the story had come out of being here, out of all the things I'd seen and heard and felt, transformed into something the likes of which I'd never written before. And as I wept over it, my heart constricted with grief at the cruelties of the world. Still, in writing it down, the fear I'd previously felt had transformed into a determination as hard as it was bright. I had extended the hand of friendship to poor Ivan. And I'd given him a few hours of respite. But a friend is more than someone who helps you forget your troubles in light chatter. I had to coax him to tell me his story if I was to help in banishing the darkness that was trying to swallow him. Tomorrow, I would start doing just that.

Twelve

In the morning I woke to a lowering sky and a hint of rain. Looking out of the window, I saw no sign of the crow, which lightened my heart considerably. After washing, I dressed in the beautiful red cashmere frock I'd worn the first evening, thinking that the master of the house would be at breakfast this morning and I should dress up a little for the occasion. But when I entered the dining-room, I found Luel alone, looking a little tired and drawn. 'Ivan's not had a good night,' she said, when I inquired after him. 'He won't be down this morning, or at all today. We will see.'

'But I thought . . .' I said, dismayed. 'I thought, after yesterday . . .'

'He is ashamed,' she said simply.

'Of what?' I asked, puzzled.

'Of the way he was when you first came. He frightened you and he cannot forgive himself for that.'

'But *I've* forgiven him,' I said. 'I will not pretend he did not frighten me, but things have changed. He must know that.'

'Yes, my dear,' she said softly. 'I know. But the return of memory can be a painful thing, and hope can be a hard thing to truly believe in when you have lived without it for so long. He has come such a long way already, more than I could have dared to imagine. You must give it time.'

'Of course,' I said. Though to be truthful, patience has never been one of my strong points. And I'd been so full of hopeful determination last night that it had seemed to me that everything must shortly be ... My eye fell upon the empty frames, and I couldn't help giving a little cry.

'What's the matter?' Luel said sharply.

'That one –' I said, pointing a trembling finger at a picture-frame. I blinked. The sinister crow I'd glimpsed on the white space had vanished, leaving nothing but white blankness, just like before. I stammered, 'I saw ... I thought I saw ...'

'What did you see, child?' Luel asked, her eyes fixed on me.

'Noth ... nothing. It doesn't matter.'

'You must tell me. Was it a crow?'

I swallowed. 'Yes.' Why, after all my heartfast resolve of last night, was I still so spooked by the mere imagined sight of a crow on a blank canvas?

'Don't worry, Natasha, they cannot get in. You are safe here, body and soul, while I am here. I promise you that.'

'But what ... how ...' I murmured shakily. 'What I saw – was that real or unreal?'

'It was both. For it was part of Ivan's nightmare you saw,' she said. 'Last night it troubled him again and again, till he could no longer sleep for it.'

My breath was ragged in my throat as I said, 'But why – why would I see it?'

'You and he are bound by more than a debt now,' she said steadily, then paused. 'Tell me, did you dream of a white rose?'

I started so violently that I almost knocked over my glass. 'Why do you ask?' I whispered.

'Because he told me this morning that as he lay awake, an image came to his mind, the only thing that comforted him even slightly. And it was a white rose – pure white as snow.'

A shiver rippled over me from head to foot as the strangest feeling assailed me, a feeling I could find no name for – part awe and part fear and yet neither. 'I am glad if he was a little comforted, but I did not dream of a white rose.'

Strictly speaking, that was true. I hadn't dreamed it in my sleep, only in that strange state in which stories are born. I could see she didn't believe me. But I couldn't – *wouldn't* – explain the truth. It was too private, too disturbing, and I shrank from putting it into words.

'Very well,' she said, after a little silence. 'Now, if you like, I can take you to the mirror and you may speak to your mother.'

'Oh yes, please,' I said hastily, glad to change the subject, and I followed Luel to the cellar. As we went down into the darkness of the stairs, I said, 'Does Ivan ever come down here?'

'Of course not,' she said. 'Do you think he wants anyone he knew to see him in this state? Better they think he's dead, as they must think now. Besides, even if he wanted to, I wouldn't let him. It's not safe. It is like with his true name. Ivan is human. It is his reflection that would go out through my mirror and into one in your world, just as it did with you. And each reflection sends out its own faint pattern of echoes that is carried on the air. That is how the magic works. For me, it is safe for I do not have a reflection, as you may have noticed,' she added dryly. 'When I look through the mirror, no human can see me; it is only I who can see them. But Ivan's reflection would betray him.'

'You mean the sorcerer could home in on it?' I said uneasily.

'Exactly. It is for the same reason I keep the mirror down here, locked away deep in the earth, far away from the rest of the house, and with a neutral background that can tell no-one anything. It is better to be doubly and even triply sure.'

We reached the room where the magic mirror sat shrouded in its blue velvet. Luel did not uncover it at once, but first turned to me and said, 'Watch carefully, Natasha. You will need to know exactly what to do. First, pass your hand over the glass three times: once to the right, once to the left, once to the centre. Next, you must say the following words: *Mirror, show what I want to see. Mirror, give my wish to me.* And then you say the name of the person or place you want to see, and they shall appear. It depends then on what you intend to do. If you are just looking, you need do nothing more. If you want to speak to someone, you close your eyes and count to five. On the count of five, open your eyes and you can start speaking. But for speaking, the mirror will never give more than a few minutes, as you have seen.'

'And that's all?' I asked. 'Is that how you make the dishes come to you too?'

Luel laughed. 'There's a bit more to it than that. But you don't need to know that. What I've given you is what you need.'

'Tell me, Luel. Do you ever use the mirror to look at your own country? Just for news?'

'Occasionally,' she said quietly. 'There – and other places.'

'Is that how you know Ivan's enemy still seeks him?'

'Yes,' she said, and there was a clipped finality in her voice that made me understand she did not want to discuss the matter further. Uncovering the mirror, she went on, 'I'll do it today, but you watch and listen so next time you'll know how to do it yourself.'

She slowly passed her hand over the mirror three times, once to the right, once to the left, once to the centre. Luel then recited the verse, followed by 'Madame Kupeda, mother of Nataliya Alexandrovna Kupeda, known as Natasha'. Instantly the mirror fogged over. As before, the fog thickened, then thinned out gradually till suddenly it was clear and I was looking into my own dining-room at home. My mother was sitting at the table, reading a letter, while on either side of her my sisters, still in their dressing-gowns and slippers, yawned over their coffee.

Once I counted to five and opened my eyes, I found my tongue quickly enough. 'Oh, Liza, Anya,' I called out, 'wake up, you lazy lie-abeds; it's nearly lunchtime!'

They almost jumped out of their skins, and I couldn't help laughing at the sight of their astonished faces. 'Natasha?' Liza said weakly, staring straight at me. 'Mama told us about this.'

'But we didn't think it was possible,' added Anya. 'Hey,' she went on, staring harder at me, 'is that a new dress you're wearing?'

'Yes,' I said. 'It's my . . . uniform. Everyone on staff here has to wear one.'

'It's not bad for a uniform,' said Anya. 'Simple but elegant.'

'I'll be sure to tell them that,' I said dryly.

My mother, who had been listening to our banter with a smile, broke in at that point. 'Good morning, my little Natashka. I am so glad to hear your voice.'

'Oh, and I yours, Mama! Have you recovered from your cold?'

'Yes, I am much better, thank you. Now, more importantly, how are you?'

'I'm fine. But I'm sorry I haven't written you a letter yet. I haven't had time; I've been so busy working for the gentleman *kaldir*, that is, Professor . . . I improvised wildly, 'Professor Ivan Feyovin.'

'Feyovin,' said my mother, sounding puzzled. 'I have not heard that name before in these parts.'

'No, he is only lately come to our region. He is from the – from the east, and has come here for his health, because the climate in the east did not agree with him.'

'Tell us, Natashka, what's he like? Is he old and rich?' asked Liza.

'Or young and handsome?' added Anya.

'Girls,' said my mother sternly, 'these are not suitable questions to ask your sister about her employer. I am sure he is a good and honourable gentleman, and that is all we need to know. Isn't that right, Natasha?'

'Yes, Mama,' I said, 'he is both good and honourable, just not a man who likes society very much. And his household have been very kind to me.' I shot a glance at Luel. 'Mama, I will soon be paid the first of my wages, so you will receive some money to ease . . .'

'Well, as for money,' my mother said, gently interrupting, 'I have some news for you, my dearest girl.' She held up the letter, and I saw now it wasn't a standard letter, but one of those pale blue forms from the telegraph office. 'This is from our lawyer in Byeloka and contains some very welcoming and surprising news, which not even your sisters know yet.'

'What is it, Mama?' all three of us sisters exclaimed at once.

'It is a most wonderful coincidence, actually. You remember mentioning our Byeloka neighbour yesterday, Natasha? Dear old Dr ter Zhaber, who died a few years ago?'

'Yes, of course,' I said, perplexed. 'What of it?'

'He was from Faustina, originally, and had no family, and indeed everyone thought he had nothing to leave anyone, for he had spent everything he had on his research, even mortgaging his house. Anyway, it so

93

happens that many years ago, your father put up some money so Dr ter Zhaber could patent one of his magical inventions – do you remember the one he called the armchair traveller?'

I did remember. It was typical of Dr ter Zhaber's charming but impractical ideas: an armchair which would transport you to your favourite settings in your favourite books, at the press of a button. It had never come to anything, but as a little girl I used to dream about sitting back in the armchair and flying across the world to all those places I'd read about.

My mother went on. 'As you know, nothing came of it. Or so we thought. But this telegraph informs me otherwise. You see, what none of us knew was that kind Dr ter Zhaber made a stipulation that if the patent was bought, your father and his heirs should receive the proceeds. And now it appears that a company based in Faustina has bought the patent and is developing it. As Alexander's heirs, we are due a good-sized sum immediately, which will pay all outstanding debts with enough left over to enable us to live comfortably for a while. There'll be more to come too.'

'Oh, Mama!' shouted Liza. 'Does this mean we are rich again?'

'When do we move back to Byeloka?' cried Anya.

'Oh, Mama, I'm so glad,' I said warmly.

'So am I,' said my mother, her radiant smile making her look ten years younger. 'So glad, my darlings! No, we are not rich,' she went on, 'but we will be a good deal more comfortable, and though we cannot yet afford to maintain a house in Byeloka, we may rent one for the ball season perhaps. What do you think?'

There were shrieks of joy from my sisters and a wary smile from me. 'Now we have this windfall, Natasha,' my mother continued, 'we do not need the income from Professor Feyovin's job, and you can come home.'

I felt a pang as I said, 'Oh, Mama, I would like to come home, but I cannot let the professor down. I made a promise to stay till the job was finished. I must honour it.'

Mama sighed. 'I understand. Of course you must, but I miss you.'

My throat thickened. 'I miss you too, Mama. I miss you very much. I shall be home soon.' Luel made a sign and I knew my time was almost up. 'Mama, I have to go, but I will speak to you again tomorrow.'

'Till tomorrow then, my little one,' said my mother, her voice growing fainter with every word as the image flickered out and then disappeared altogether. As Luel covered the mirror again in its velvet, I stood there silently. 'Thank you.'

'What for?' she replied tartly. 'I promised you could use the mirror. I always keep my promises.'

'Including the one where you said my family would be well provided for. Because that was your doing, wasn't it, Luel?'

'Well,' she shrugged, looking a little sheepish. 'I had to do something.'

If I'd thought about it at all, I'd have imagined she'd have a basket of gold sent to our house, or some other splashy *feya* extravagance. But she'd listened and watched and come up with the perfect solution, so that my throw-away line about our old neighbour had become the key to the perfect way to provide for my family: a way guaranteed not to make them uneasy or cause gossip that might get to the wrong ears. It would seem lucky, but not unnaturally so.

'Thank you,' I repeated, 'from the bottom of my heart. That was very cleverly and kindly done.'

Luel's eyes twinkled. 'It was a pleasure, my dear. I haven't had so much fun in years.'

'I had heard of Dr ter Zhaber's armchair traveller,' I said. 'And I know it exists on paper at least. But then he had thought up so many things, none of which came to anything. And his legacy to my father – and the company in Faustina – that doesn't exist in reality, does it?'

'Dr ter Zhaber was a good old man from all I was able to learn of him,' said Luel calmly, as we went up the stairs, 'and I'm sure if he'd thought about it, it was exactly what he would have done. As to the Faustina Armchair Travel-ler Company, well, it exists in a manner of speaking, even if it is only as a fine letterhead on good notepaper. And it will pay out exactly what was promised to your family. Just as Dr ter Zhaber would have wished it.'

Evasive answers as always with Luel, but still with a grain of truth in them. And a further clue that my first thought had been right, and Luel and Ivan hailed origi-nally from the Faustine Empire. That must mean that the sorcerer also came from there, or at least lived there. Did that mean, then, that he was one of the dreaded Mancers? That was most likely, given that Luel had said he was a powerful and dangerous man. And the Mancers were both. But Luel was a *feya*, and *feyas* didn't live there, surely, where magic was forbidden? I didn't know enough about the Faustinians to know for sure. And I knew that if I asked Luel, she'd just evade the question.

There was the encyclopedia. I didn't expect much from it, for I'd seen nothing of any use when I'd leafed through its volumes. But it was worth taking a look, just in case. There had to be some reason that these particular books were in the room. Unless, I thought a little dispiritedly, Luel had just plucked them at random from some distant dusty library, to make the bookshelf look well stocked.

Back in my room, after telling Luel I was a little tired and in need of rest, I soon came to the conclusion that my dispirited theory was most likely correct. In one of the volumes, in the F section, there was a long entry on the Faustine Empire, true, but without the kind of information I needed.

There was also a general entry on magic, but somehow the editors of these distressingly dull volumes managed to make a fascinating subject sound about as interesting as a discussion of the weight of a Faustinian coin compared to a Ruvenyan coin, which, God help us, was a subject that covered an entire three pages. There was a brief and unilluminating entry on *feyas*, which read: *Non-human beings with certain magical powers, found all over the world. Populations are small, as* feyas *are essentially solitary. It is reported that there have been less* feya *sightings in our day than in earlier times. Examples of* feyas *range from the fearsome forest witch Old Bony, from Ruvenya, to Almeric, mountain wanderer of Almain.* Feyas *should be approached with caution as they are considered to be unpredictable.*

There was also an entry on *abartyens* and in particular a slightly fuller description of the werewolf clan, the Ironhearts, which had an honoured place in Ruvenyan history. Even a plodding publication such as this could not entirely ignore the stirring story of how once, long ago, a werewolf of the Ironheart clan had braved the greatest dangers to rescue a Ruvenyan prince from certain death at the hands of a bandit chieftain. Still, the encyclopedia managed to turn the wonderful tale, which I, like every other Ruvenyan, had heard from the youngest age, into a dull procession of tedious words, none of which was of the slightest assistance to me.

In disgust, but unwilling to give up, I cast aside the encyclopedia and picked up the dictionary. I leafed through each page carefully, just in case there was something I'd missed. And that was how I found, jammed between two pages, the small stub of a first-class train ticket on the Golden Express, a luxury train that ran between Faustina, the capital of the empire, and Palume, the capital of the Republic of Champaine, a country to the west of the Faustine Empire. Glittering, elegant, artistic Palume was the playground of aristocrats and the wealthy from all over the world, and if Ivan came from a great Faustinian family, then it was quite likely he'd been there. I couldn't prove the ticket was his; there was no passenger name, and no date of travel visible either, only the well-known symbol of the Golden Express with its decorated gilded locomotive.

But in all that weary and fruitless searching, it was the first real nugget of information I'd unearthed. Perhaps, I thought excitedly, that was how Ivan and Luel had come across the Master of Crows. Not in Faustina but in Palume. It could mean the sorcerer was either a Champainian native or else a foreign exile from the Faustine Empire!

Pulling out the notebook, I opened it to a fresh page. I took out the small pot of stamp-glue from the desk, carefully stuck the Golden Express ticket down on the page, picked up my pen and wrote:

Is Sorcerer based in Palume?

1(a) If from Champaine, could he be a kaldir *like Dr ter Zhaber, except evil of course? Kaldiring is a more common form of magic in Champaine than any other country, and as I remember it, Dr ter Zhaber himself had been partly trained in Palume. 1(b) Is that why Luel gave me that odd look yesterday when I told Mama that my supposed employer was a* kaldir? *Did she think I guessed something? 1(c) Why would Ivan be in touch with a Champainian* kaldir? *Was there something he had come to Palume for?*

2(a) If sorcerer is from Faustina, he may have come to Champaine to be safe from persecution as an illegal magician, and Ivan might have met him by chance. 2(b) He could be a Mancer in the diplomatic service, keeping an eye on the Faustinian Ambassador and others? 2(c) If the latter, did Ivan discover something that the sorcerer was up to, which caused him to be silenced in this monstrous way?

I put down my pen and looked at what I had written. Yes, I was sure there was something in it. But it was no good asking Luel; she'd only evade my questions. I had to speak to Ivan himself. But I could not wait until he was ready to see me. I had to go in search of him. Right now.

Thirteen

All the time I'd been here, I'd not explored the first floor beyond my room. I didn't even know if Luel and Ivan had their rooms on this floor. Now, clutching the notebook, I set off nervously down the long corridor that led away from my room and the stairs.

Luel had said I needed patience. Time. But not only is it not my nature to wait, I had the strong feeling that we had little time – that something was getting closer and closer all the time, and that if all we did was hide behind the wall, sooner or later it would get in . . .

I came to a door and knocked quietly. No answer. I tried the handle and found it to be unlocked. I opened the door and peered in. It was obviously Luel's room, for I could see her black coat lying on the bed. For a moment I thought about going in and poking around to see what I could find. But I thought better of it and, closing the door behind me, continued down the corridor.

At the very end was another door, and discovering it too was unlocked, I opened the door. Behind was not a room, as I'd expected, but a narrow set of wooden stairs that twisted up to the third floor. I set off up the stairs; they creaked terribly, making me halt more than once, half-expecting Luel to come storming up after me. But I reached the top without challenge and found myself at the entrance to a corridor. And halfway down that, a door.

I took a deep breath. Half of me wanted to turn back, suddenly afraid of how I might find him. Luel had said he was ashamed of how he'd behaved that first day. What if he'd locked himself away because the darkness had returned and the beast-rage was strong within him again? But the other half of me scorned such fears. Come what may, I'd pledged my word. Ivan was now my friend. If I wanted to help him, I had to show him I wasn't afraid. I had to make him understand he could trust me. So I walked to the door and rapped quietly. No answer. I tried the handle but it was locked. I could hear him behind the door. Or rather, I could hear his silence. It was as tangible as though he'd spoken.

'Ivan,' I said, in a voice that only just managed not to quaver. 'Ivan, it's me. It's Natasha. Won't you please let me in? I need to speak to you.'

I heard a quiet intake of breath.

'Please. I don't want to force you to come down or anything. I – I just need your opinion. I've written a story and I want to try it out on someone. And Luel isn't interested.' It wasn't at all what I'd planned to say, but the instant I said the words, I knew this was much better, because it would surprise him.

It did. 'You need my opinion? About a story?' he said blankly.

'Yes. I need to read it to you. To tell me if it works.'

'Now?' he said faintly.

'If I have to change it, I'd rather know now,' I said. 'Luel says I should wait, but I don't have any patience.'

'No, you don't,' he said, and I could hear a very slight smile in his voice, which made my heart lighten with relief.

'So, are you going to open up,' I said sharply, 'or do you propose to make me tell you the story through the keyhole?'

'I don't think that's necessary,' he said, the smile now stronger in his voice. 'Wait a moment.' I heard his steps move away and then return moments later. There was a rattle of bolts and keys as he unlocked the door, and in the next instant, there he was, standing in the doorway.

I only just repressed a cry, for in that first glimpse I thought his face had been blotted out in a white blankness, like the pictures. Then I realised he was wearing a mask, a white silk mask, which covered his face but for his eyes. He was again dressed in the black velvet robe, pulled tightly around him so only a little of the dark-coloured shirt and trousers he wore underneath could be seen, and there were boots on his feet and thick gloves on his hands.

'I'm sorry about this,' he said, and pointed at the mask. 'But my skin is ... peeling ... and I would spare you the sight.'

Through the slits in the mask, his eyes met mine. They were not yellow any more, or at least not fully yellow. Though there were still patches of that feral colour in his eyes, the deeper shade I'd seen in them yesterday had grown, so that now it was clearly discernible as green, a very human grey-green. It could be the real colour of Ivan's eyes, I thought, with an odd little skip of the heart. And set so strangely in the white silk of the mask, without the brutal beast-like features around them, his eyes spoke to me more directly than at any time before.

I laid a hand very briefly on his velvet-clad arm. 'If you prefer it, then of course.'

'Thank you,' he said, stepping away quickly, but not before I'd felt him tremble slightly. 'Please, come in.'

The room he ushered me into wasn't a bedroom but a kind of antechamber, bare of any furniture except for a chair. There were two doors leading off it, one ajar, the other closed. Ivan walked over to the half-open door and stood aside to let me in.

'Oh!' It was a beautiful but plain, restful sort of room, painted in shades of cream and the palest caramel, and filled with light. This came not from windows but from a large skylight in the ceiling. Almost directly under the skylight was a long wicker settee set with pale cushions, and facing it, a small low table on which reposed the music box I'd seen yesterday.

Ivan heard my exclamation and his eyes smiled. 'Please, sit down.'

'You too, then,' I said, mock-severely when he showed no sign of doing so. 'I can't read a story to someone who's looming over my shoulder like that. It puts me off.'

'Very well,' he said, and sat down at the furthest edge of the settee from me. I opened my notebook and said, 'Now you must tell me honestly what you think; it's no use telling me it's good and leaving it at that. Mama's always telling me that, and it's hard for me to know if she really means it or she's just saying it to me because I'm her daughter and in her eyes everything I do is good. And as for my sisters, they will never sit still long enough to listen properly. Not that I ask them very often.'

'I can see indeed,' said Ivan, and there was a laughing lilt to his voice that I'd never heard before. 'I give you my word, Natasha. I'll be an honest critic.'

'Good.' I cleared my throat. *'In a warm and pleasant country, where bright flowers bloom much of the year, and skies are blue as Our Lady's robe, lived a young girl called Rosette,'* I began. As I went on, I could feel his eyes fixed on me, but he made no sound nor gesture. After a moment, I stopped reading. 'You don't like it, do you? I can stop right now if –'

'No, go on,' he said in a voice that was quite without expression.

So I went on, but when I reached the part where the Master of Crows tells his nephew that he sent white roses to Rosette as an apology, I could hear my own voice quavering. I must be mad, I thought. What on earth had possessed me to read this story to him? It would have been far wiser to choose *The Three Sisters*, pretending that's what I had written last night, for that would have no echoes for him; it would merely be a pleasant distraction. I sneaked a look at him and saw that his eyes weren't fixed on me any more. He was looking away and his hands were no longer shaking; they were knotted together, so tightly that the bones stood out sharply against the cloth of the gloves. And every rigid line of his body showed that he was desperately holding himself in check against some violent emotion.

But I did not stop. To stop would make things worse. So I stumbled on with my story, inwardly berating myself, not only for my foolhardiness but also for my insensitivity. I'd called myself his friend and yet here I was telling him a story that was hardly calculated to make him happy. I'd destroyed that fragile bubble of lightness that had existed between us in the moments before. He must think I was a tower of witless self-regard, first to use his own tragedy as inspiration for a stupid made-up story, and then to inflict it upon him, apparently out of mere vanity. Miserably, I trailed off to the ending, stuttering to a stop.

'It was you,' he said softly. So unexpected were the words that I thought the voice was in my head. I looked up, into the steadily greening eyes that were regarding me through the mask, with an expression that made my blood quicken. 'You gave it to me. I should have known.'

'I don't . . . I don't understand,' I said weakly, lying.

He smiled. 'It doesn't matter,' he said, his voice gentle.

I felt a little squirm in my belly. Why was I lying to him? That, I did not understand. I'd asked him to be honest with me, and here was I, lying. And he knew it. He knew it for sure. I could tell by the tone in his voice, and that made me feel even more uncomfortable. 'I'm sorry if I –' I began confusedly.

'You asked me for my opinion of your story,' he said, his voice now light, almost bantering.

'Well, then, I'm waiting,' I said, trying to make my voice sound as light as his.

'It is made not of mere ink and paper but the blood of true feeling. And so it lives and breathes,' he said quietly.

I was stunned. No-one had ever said anything remotely like that to me before. I felt tears pricking at the edges of my eyelids and fiercely blinked them away. 'Oh, Ivan, thank you,' I choked out. 'I'm so glad you –'

'But there is just one thing,' he said, gently interrupting me. 'I imagine an editor might say it is not quite finished.'

Again, his eyes met mine, and I only dragged my gaze away with an effort, murmuring, 'You're right. I will think about how I can do it.' I hesitated. 'Ivan, you speak as though you understand literature. Were you – are you – a writer?'

'No,' he said, 'merely a reader.' A pause. 'I once told stories too, though not in words.'

My glance fell on the music box. 'You were a musician?'

'No, not a musician.' I saw that he was shaking like a leaf. And suddenly, in a blinding insight, I knew. 'Oh, you are a painter.'

'Once. Not any more. Not ever again,' he cried, and there was so much desolation in his voice that it struck me to the heart. Impulsively, I moved closer to him but he shrank away. 'What is it that separates man from the beasts?' he whispered, 'if it is not creation, inspiration, art? Once I delighted so in it and I thought there was nothing more important in the world, and that was my undoing.

For now ... These hands you see,' he went on harshly, holding them up, 'these hands are the clumsy misshapen hands of a beast who cannot paint, cannot create, can do nothing that is beautiful.'

'No, no, no,' I said, my heart aching, tears in my eyes. 'That is not so, Ivan. What of the scarlet flower? It was you who cared for the bud, watered it, made it open. When I first saw it in the garden, against the snow, it seemed to me just like a painting, the most beautiful one I'd ever seen, because it was living. And it was I who killed it.'

He groaned. 'You do not understand. This face,' he said, pointing at his own face with loathing in his voice, 'this is not even that of a beast, which can gaze in dumb love at beauty. This is the face of a monster. The rose bloomed when you came. It died when I gazed upon it. All I can do is destroy, blank out the beauty I long for.' And as he spoke these last words, I could not repress a gasp of horror as I realised the truth. In my mind's eye I saw those empty frames downstairs, and filled them with beautiful painted scenes, with colour and pattern and shape that then faded and disappeared, till nothing was left but the white emptiness. It was the worst injustice, the most cruel part of the spell.

He was an artist who couldn't paint. But even the consolation of looking at paintings had been denied him. He couldn't even gaze upon them without them disappearing. Were they his own lost pictures? Or ones Luel had acquired? I did not know and I would not ask. Truth was, I couldn't. I had already pushed him far enough. I had not meant to, I had meant only to help, but this – this did not help. To probe further would only make his pain greater.

But there was something I *could* do for him. Something I should have done before. I took a deep breath. 'Ivan. I must say this. I did not tell the truth to you before.'

He stilled but did not speak or look at me.

I swallowed. 'I knew what you meant about the white rose in my story.' A pause. 'I must also tell you I saw the shape of a crow on one of those blank canvases downstairs. And Luel said it was your nightmare.' He gave a start, but before he could speak, I rushed on. 'And I think even before that, I saw something in a dream, something that inspired me to write that story. I saw a lovely girl in a white dress, sitting in a sunny garden full of flowers. It was beautiful but also sad, because it felt like something bad had happened to her. That was *your* dream – *your* memory – wasn't it?'

He stared at me but said nothing.

'Please,' I said. 'If you care anything for me, if you are indeed my friend, you will tell me the answer.'

He put his head in his hands. 'God forgive me,' he whispered. 'Yes, you are right.'

There was a lump in my throat. My hands shook. My stomach churned. But I managed to say, 'Then, Ivan, listen. It proves that there is great hope, because you and I – we – are linked in no ordinary way.'

He looked up then, directly into my eyes, the yellow-flecked green of his eyes steady, almost cold. 'You must go. At once.' And before I could recover from my stunned surprise, he leaped to his feet and strode out of the room, calling Luel's name.

Fourteen

Snatching up the discarded notebook, I ran after him. 'What is it, Ivan?' I cried. 'What did I do wrong?'

He did not answer but went off down the stairs, without a backward glance. Baffled and distressed, I slowly followed, reaching the top of the first-floor stairs in time to see him and Luel with their heads together, talking. No, not talking – arguing.

Luel looked up and saw me, her face twisted. 'I told you he wasn't well,' she hissed. 'I told you to be patient!'

'I'm sorry,' I murmured, close to tears.

'Stop it, Luel,' said Ivan, so explosively that the white silk billowed away from his face, and from above, I caught a wincing glimpse of his skin, peeling and patched like a lizard's discarded coat. 'It is not her fault. Now, will you do what I ask you freely or will you stand against me?'

Shock flooded her face, draining it of colour. 'My lord,' she protested faintly, 'what have I done to displease you so?'

'Please don't take it out on Luel,' I said quietly, coming down the stairs towards them. 'It is I who troubled you, and if you would only tell me what I can do to . . .'

'It was wrong to keep you here,' he said levelly. 'You were given no choice.'

'No,' I whispered.

'You can go home. Isn't that so, Luel?'

'It shall be as you wish, my lord,' she said through tight-set lips. She did not look at me, only at him.

'But, Ivan – I thought I couldn't go because –'

'Because it wasn't safe,' he finished. 'That is so. Usually. But there is one way that it can be done without endangering you.'

'And you? What of the danger to *you*?' I cried.

Now Luel did look at me, sharply, but with surprise rather than hostility. 'She is right, my lord. There is a risk that . . .'

'Stop. I have lived in fear for too long,' he said tightly. 'I refuse to do it any longer. Would you make me, Luel?'

She flushed. 'Of course not, my lord.'

'Then you will do as I ask.'

I looked from one to the other. 'But things have changed since I first arrived, and I can . . . I can wait to go home,' I stammered. 'You are my friend now, Ivan. I cannot just leave you. I want to help you.'

A strange expression flickered across his eyes, then he turned away. 'And so you *will* help me if you do this. Go home. Go home to your family. And when you are there, if you should freely decide that you want to return here, then it will be done. And only then can I truly know that

111

it is of your own accord that you are here, not because you are threatened. But if you should decide to stay home and never return, you will not be troubled again.'

'But . . .' I murmured, close to tears, torn between wanting to be free – to go home – and fear for him, for what it might do to his state of mind. 'What would happen to you?'

'You have already given me so much, Natasha,' he said quietly. 'Stories. Laughter. Hope. Friendship.' He paused. 'And a white rose, blooming in my dreams. These are things that have made me stronger. You must not worry about me.' He reached inside his robe and pulled out something small and bright. The last petal of the scarlet rose. Only it wasn't withered any more. It was as fresh as the day it had been part of the flower, its fragrance so sweet my senses reeled.

'It's so beautiful,' I breathed.

His eyes smiled. 'Yes, it is. And this, too, is your doing.'

It was my turn to flush. 'I don't know how,' I said lamely.

He handed it to me. 'I give you a rose for a rose. Keep it with you. If you should decide to return, you need only place it in front of a mirror and breathe on it. I will know you want to come back. If you do not want to, then do with it what you wish.'

'I *will* come back,' I said fervently, as I carefully put the petal in my pocket. 'I promise, Ivan.'

'No promises,' he said. 'No vows. No binding. You must be free. And nothing you have been given is to be taken from you.' He turned to Luel. 'You understand, don't you, Luel?'

'I do, my lord,' she replied, no longer sounding angry or upset but resigned. 'It shall be done.'

'Then we must say our goodbyes, Natasha,' he said. 'May God bless you and give you happiness and joy for all the days of your life.' And he would have gone like that, slipping away without touching me, without coming closer, only I could not bear for that to happen. Covering the distance between us in two rapid strides, I took his hand in one of mine and, with the other, gently lifted the mask from his poor ruined face. Taken by surprise, he stood as still as a statue. Reaching up, I kissed him quickly on the cheek, feeling a burning on my lips as I did so. He looked at me then with the stricken eyes of a hunted deer and, murmuring something indistinct, he freed himself from my grasp and fled.

Left alone with Luel, I shot her a cautious glance. My heart was racing, my lips still burning, my fingertips tingling. 'I'm sorry for upsetting him,' I muttered. 'I really didn't mean for any of this to –'

'No,' she said, 'I'm sure you didn't. But it is done now.' Her words were curt, but not her voice. 'Go. You must pack. We leave in five minutes.'

'*We?*' I echoed.

'You and me,' she said. 'If you are to be truly safe, I must take you back myself. You will be shielded behind my protection.'

'But then Ivan will be left alone and unprotected,' I breathed.

She looked steadily at me. 'Not quite unprotected. I will strengthen the defences here before I go. And I will be back quickly. The risk is small. Besides, it is true what my lord said. He *is* stronger than he was. Look.' She pointed at the picture-frames behind me. I turned around to see, with a cry of gladness, they were now starting to fill at the edges with faint silvery greys and pale greens, like the first tiny stirrings of life under a shroud of snow.

'How I wish that –' I began.

'Careful,' Luel said, with a lift of the eyebrow. 'Remember where you are. And don't worry too much,' she added in a softer tone. 'If he is stronger, it is due to you. And so I owe you that at least, and hold no hard feelings.'

'Oh, Luel!' I cried. 'I don't know what to think any more. What I feel, what's right, what I should do. What I want . . .'

'Then he is right, and you must go,' she said, 'or you will never know for sure. Go upstairs and pack. You will find a holdall at the back of the wardrobe. Take whatever you want and meet me down here. The sooner we leave, the sooner I can return.'

I would have said more, but Luel had already bustled off. I hurried upstairs, found the holdall and started packing. I looked longingly at the row of dresses of lace and tulle and velvet, but in the end I decided to take only my own old one, plus the red cashmere dress I was already wearing, for I did not want too many awkward questions at home. From the drawers, I selected two fine lace petti-coats, still wrapped in their pale blue tissue paper, which would make fine gifts for Liza and Anya. For my mother I took a white woollen shawl as soft and light as cobwebs.

I would tell them that I had purchased them from a travelling hawker with my first week's wages. Lastly, taking out the scarlet petal from my pocket, I carefully placed it for safekeeping within the leaves of the notebook, in the middle of my story, and put it in my bag.

Everything now packed, I put on my old coat with its fur-lined hood and my thick gloves, and cast a last look around the room. My eyes fell on the bookshelf. On an impulse, I snatched up the dictionary and threw it in my bag too. As I did so, I glanced out of the window and saw not the crows circling but the lonely, restless figure of Ivan, pacing up and down beside the hedge as he had that first morning. This time, though, I wished with all my heart that he would look up and see me. But he didn't. I removed a sheet of paper from the sheaf in the desk and wrote: *Till we meet again.* I signed my name and rapidly sketched a rosebud underneath.

'Natasha! We must go!' Luel's anxious voice floated up to me.

'Coming,' I said. I quickly folded the paper, scribbled 'Ivan' on it and left it on the desk. Then I hurried out of the room, down the stairs to where Luel waited in the hall, rather comically wrapped in a fur coat that looked several sizes too big for her.

I had no idea how we were going and half-expected it would be through the mirror. But instead of heading to the cellar, Luel led the way to a side door, which I hadn't even noticed before, and I found myself emerging into a large barn, the kind that has a wide wooden ramp to one side so sleighs can easily be brought in and out. And there to my surprise was my sleigh, the one I had abandoned in the snow. It was no longer broken but was in fact looking as good as new. It was loaded with my old blankets, now clean and glossy, and a big cloth-covered basket filled with food. Luel saw the expression on my face and gave a little smile. 'Can't have your mother thinking Professor Feyovin is a tight-fisted sort, now can we? Or she'd never let you come back.'

'It's very kind of you,' I said, touched.

She shrugged. 'Throw your bag in. Then we can be moving.' I did so, and Luel, putting her fingers to her lips, gave a long low whistle. At once the sleigh slid down the ramp and out into the snow, while we went out by the barn door. And there, harnessed to the sleigh, were my old horses, looking a little younger, their coats shining, manes brushed and eyes bright. They snorted and puffed in the bright cold air, and when they saw me they whickered with soft pleasure. To my shame, I had not given them a moment's thought since I had arrived, for I had assumed they'd died of cold or had been eaten by wolves. 'Thank you,' I said to Luel, 'for looking after them.'

'Bah, they were safe enough,' she said. 'They were just scared, that's all. I wasn't intending to tell you about them for a good while yet.' She picked up the reins. 'Well, are you coming?'

'Can't I drive?' I said, climbing on.

'No, it'll have to be me if we are to get there quickly,' she said. 'And hang on tight. Here we go!'

She suited the action to the word, and we took off down the path like an arrow from a bow, the hedge parting before us. I whooped with delight as we went through, my uneasy feeling about leaving Ivan alone almost forgotten in the joyous gladness of going home.

Fifteen

The sleigh went like the wind on the hard-packed snow, so blindingly swift that I could hardly take anything in of our surroundings apart from a blurred, dark line of forest to our right and the cloudless sky. And though we were going very fast, I felt no sting of wind on my cheek and heard only the soft jingle of the horses' bells, like the silvery music at an other-worldly ball. It was as if we were in a kind of bubble, light and clear as air.

Neither of us spoke. There was no need to. We sped on, always skirting the forest, and flew past the turning which led to Count Bolotovsky's mansion, where I'd delivered Mama's painting. I had to remind myself that had only been the other day, not like the weeks it felt. Soon we reached a little village and raced through it. Although there were two or three people about, not one of them turned their heads or stopped to watch us go by even though we passed very close to them. It was as if they didn't see us. Only a cat, lying in the sun on a windowsill, stood up, its back arched and eyes big. Of course, as is well known, animals can sense things humans can't, and even a *feya's* spell of invisibility will not altogether close the eyes of a cat to her passing.

We went through fields sleeping under snow, through woods where people were gathering nuts, past streams shrouded in ice, and still no-one seemed to notice us. We rushed down the streets of Kolorgrod and out into the familiar countryside. Finally, there we were, gliding in through the modest gates of my family's estate and drawing up outside my house.

Luel jumped out of the sleigh after me, helping me to unload my luggage and depositing it by the front steps. 'Your family will be able to see you as soon as I am gone,' she said, 'so go in to them at once, but, mind, on no account change the story you told them or reveal anything you have seen or heard about my lord, for if you do, you will put him in terrible danger. Promise me that.'

'Of course,' I said, 'you have my most solemn word.' I hesitated, then went on. 'Luel, there is one thing I would ask of you. Will you speak to me when you get back and tell me if all is well? For otherwise I know I shall be anxious.'

She looked at me and for a moment I thought she was about to refuse. Then she nodded. 'Is there a mirror in your bedroom?'

'Yes,' I said, 'on my wardrobe door.'

'Very well,' she said. 'I will speak to you at midnight tonight. Now I must go. Farewell, Natasha, and may good luck go with you.'

'It is not "farewell" but "till we meet again",' I said, but my words were carried on the empty air, for she had already vanished.

I took a deep breath, then picked up my bag, walked up the steps and rapped on the front door. A moment later, I heard Sveta's slippered shuffling and the door opened, revealing her large, rosy-cheeked, surprised face under its untidy grey bun.

'Oh my goodness!' she cried, embracing me. 'Oh, Natashka! Oh, my little dove! You're back! Oh, what a surprise! What about your job? And oh ho, someone's been working on that sleigh, eh? And how well the horses look!' And without drawing breath or waiting for my comments, she clumped outside and shouted for Oleg to come at once and take the horses and the sleigh to the barn. 'And what, my girl, is *that*?' she said, pointing at the basket.

'That, dear Sveta,' I said affectionately, 'is to help fill the larder. Professor Feyovin's housekeeper was most insistent I should bring it.'

'The very idea,' grumbled Sveta. 'As if my housekeeping isn't good enough.' But she took the basket cheerfully enough when I handed it to her, and said, 'Well, I suppose with you back, my little dove, we'll need more food on the table. You always did have a better appetite than your sisters. Come on, come on, no good standing around in the cold as if this was some stranger's home and not your very own!'

'It's good to be home, Sveta,' I said, laughing. After greeting Oleg, who had just arrived, panting, from around the side of the house, I followed her in. 'I've missed you. I've missed everyone.'

'And so I should think,' said Sveta, puffing as she carried the laden basket. 'A young girl like you having to work for a *kaldir*, with all those bad smells and bangs and explosions and heaven knows what. It's not right. I remember Dr ter Zhaber's servant Mina saying that she always expected the house would come down on their heads one day, what with all that poking and prying into the most jumpy kind of magic there is!'

At that moment, the door to the sitting-room opened and my mother came out, frowning a little. 'Sveta, what is the meaning of this hullabaloo?' Then she caught sight of me and gave a little cry. 'Oh, Natasha! My darling! What's happened? What's wrong?'

'Nothing,' I said, 'it's just that Professor Feyovin has given me a short holiday as he has to go to Byeloka on business, so I'm home, Mama!'

She hugged me. 'Oh, that is very good! I'm so glad to see you.'

'Me too, Mama,' I said, hugging her back.

'And just you look at this,' put in Sveta, gruffly, holding out the basket. 'This professor of hers thought she might starve, I suppose.'

'Oh, my goodness,' said Mama, peering into the basket. 'Look! There's a jar of the best caviar! And quails' eggs! Oh, and the finest smoked herring and salmon from the north! And Byeloka ham! And such colourful bonbons, and oh, look, the most beautiful crystallised cumquats, and cherries and apricots! Oh my, oh my! This is so generous, so very generous, I hardly know what to say. Surely we cannot accept such bounty – it is too much!'

'Mama, you would greatly offend the professor if you refused,' I said hurriedly. 'And even more his housekeeper, Madame Luel, and believe me, that lady is a force of nature and not likely to take no for an answer!'

'Oh,' said my mother, 'then of course we must accept and we are very grateful, very grateful indeed. I will write and thank them both myself this very day. Now, let us go into the sitting-room and have a cup of tea; it's freshly made. Liza! Anya!' she called, as we passed the stairs. 'Come down, girls, and see who has come back!'

As we went into the sitting-room, I couldn't help glancing at the mirror above the mantelpiece, half-thinking that I might catch a glimpse of the enchanted mansion in it. But of course, all I saw was the reflection of our own cosy sitting-room, with its cheerfully burning fire, big old shabby comfortable chairs, silver-framed photographs on the dresser and the usual untidy clutter of half-read books and magazines and other bits and pieces on the little side table. Everything was just the same as before, and though I was very glad to be back, it also gave me a weird feeling. After all that had happened to me, it felt strange that nothing should have changed here, that life should have gone on in just the same ordinary pattern as before.

Except, of course, it hadn't, for our prospects had changed due to what Mama called 'the miraculous legacy of Dr ter Zhaber'. When Liza and Anya came sailing into the room a few minutes later, greeting me with the casual pleasure of sisters, I saw that the joy of that discovery still lingered with them, far outweighing any genuine curiosity they might have had about my enigmatic employer, who they'd already decided was some kind of crotchety old eccentric. It made things a good deal easier for me. Oh, they were delighted with the petticoats, as was Mama with her shawl, though Mama shook her head and said I should not have spent so much of my wages on gifts for others.

Over a delicious light lunch of dill soup and freshly poached eggs with smoked salmon, the talk soon turned from my adventures at Professor Feyovin's – or rather, my lack of adventures, as I was at pains to point out, describing imaginary days spent transcribing spidery scrawls into clear print – to my family's plans for renting a house in Byeloka. My sisters had already pored over the brochures and each had a firm favourite; now I was invited to look at the brochures myself and pick which house I thought best. I didn't care much one way or the other. I was glad to see my sisters happy, but the thought of going back to the city wasn't particularly attractive to me, and the thought of the ball season even less so. In the end I rather mischievously pointed to a completely different house to the ones they'd set their hearts on, and so of course that set them off on a new round of bickering till Mama declared she'd had quite enough of our nonsense and took herself off to her studio to paint.

I too left Liza and Anya to their squabbles, going off to unpack in my familiar but suddenly strange room. When I'd finished, I sat on my bed and took out the notebook. I hadn't shown it to anyone and wasn't intending to. It felt too private, something I shrank from sharing. Apart from me, it was only Ivan who knew my story existed. As I opened the book, the fragrance of the rose petal reached my nostrils and I was struck by a sudden urge to weep. I could see Ivan in my mind's eye, sitting in that light-filled room, listening to my story. I could hear his soft words, and I felt a pang as intense as it was disconcerting. Why had he sent me away so abruptly? I couldn't understand it. We were starting to become real friends, beginning to understand each other. I had told him the truth about what I had seen. Why then did he cut me off so quickly, so harshly? Yes, I knew what he had said about wanting to give me a choice, and it moved me greatly. But I could have waited. I'd been willing to wait, to discover more about him so I could work out the best way to try to break the spell. As it was, right now I had so little to go on . . .

Cupping the petal in my warm hands, I inhaled its fragrance, remembering how even that very first day, that terrifying day, I had felt instinctively that a place where such a rose could grow in winter could not be bad. There must be a good light within it, a spirit that loved beauty and sweetness for its own sake. That spirit, I knew now, was Ivan's.

My scalp prickled. It was Ivan's spirit that had brought the rosebud to life, despite the dreadful torture he'd been put through. And that gave me hope and a new idea. There *was* a way I could help him, even before I went back. Facts are a good deal easier to come by when you are not shut away from the world but can consult such things as newspapers and libraries. First thing tomorrow, I would begin my search.

Placing the petal carefully into my finest handkerchief, I folded over the corners and hid it in the depths of my drawers. Then I sat down and mentally ticked off what I already knew about Ivan: he'd been a painter, he was twenty-one years old and was a foreigner. His enemy was both powerful and dangerous. And possibly their paths had crossed during a visit Ivan had made to Palume, which he'd travelled to on the Golden Express. The last item I was less sure of, but still intended investigating.

The most significant fact I had learned, I thought, was that Ivan had been a painter. That meant there was something I could do right now, even before starting my research in town. Closing the door of my room behind me, I went to find my mother in her studio, and sat watching as she worked on a beautiful, glowing still life of fruit and eggs on a wooden plate. It was not a commission but something she was doing for herself, she'd said, for she was hoping to create enough paintings for an exhibition in Byeloka in the summer, her first for many a year. And then, quite natur-ally, she gave me the opening I'd been hoping for, as she stopped, looked at me. 'You know, Natasha, there are those who say that my way of earning a living is not suitable for a lady, but what would have become of us if I had not been granted some talent with the brush?'

'We would have been homeless and begging for alms,' I said warmly. 'And all those who say that earning your living with the brush is not suitable for a lady would be passing us by with their noses in the air, so I do not think we need to care about them. And besides, Mama, a painter must paint or wither away inside, is that not so?'

'It is, Natashka,' she said softly, 'just as a writer must write or a musician play. Without the core of our being, what are any of us fit for? Even those we love may suffer from it. I think that after I lost your father, I could not have been a true mother to you if I had not been able to paint, if my gift had deserted me at a time of such terrible pain.'

I hugged her tightly. 'You have always been a true mother to us.'

'I am glad you think so, my darling,' she smiled. 'And it was also your love, your presence, which kept my art alive.'

'Oh, Mama, I think it must be such a terrible thing, the very worst thing for an artist, to be unable to paint, through accident or sickness or ma– or anything else.' I'd been about to say 'magic' but changed my mind at the last moment, just in case.

'Oh yes,' she said, 'it would be a terrible fate indeed. When I was a child my art tutor suffered just such a tragedy when he broke his hands in a riding accident. The surgeon did not set the bones properly, and so he lost the full use of his hands, unable to hold a paintbrush or a pencil. The poor man went to pieces.'

'Oh, that's so sad.'

'And there was that case – when was it – three, four years ago? That famous painter, now what was his name? He wasn't from Ruvenya but from some foreign country.' She frowned, trying to remember. I hardly dared to breathe. 'Yes, that's right, from Almain.'

'From Almain? Oh.' It wasn't where I'd deduced Ivan came from, but after all, I didn't know that for sure, did I? 'What happened to him?' I prompted. 'Did he have an accident too?'

'No, not an accident. Something harder to fight, in a way. Especially at his age.'

'His age? Was he very young, Mama?' I said, struggling to keep the excitement from my voice.

'Young? Oh no, darling. He was about fifty. Gelden. Timon Gelden was his name, that's right. He'd had a long and distinguished career and was still most active,' she went on, not noticing my crestfallen expression. 'Until the scandal, of course.'

'What scandal, Mama?' I asked mechanically, knowing now this would not be of any use.

'Oh, he tried to punch a critic who said that Gelden was well past his best. Trouble was, it was the critic who floored him. Gelden was made to look both ridiculous and ill-mannered. And then somehow everyone decided the critic was right, that Gelden's work was bad, and he just went to ground and vanished from sight. I heard later that he'd gone into a monastery.'

It was nothing like Ivan's story, I thought, disappointed, but trying not to show it. Oh well. I hadn't really expected it to come so easily, had I?

The rest of the day passed peacefully and uneventfully, but by dinnertime I was so tired I could hardly keep my eyes open during the excellent meal, and excused myself immediately afterwards to go to bed. I set my alarm clock for half-past eleven and put it under my pillow, where only I would hear it. I fell asleep straightaway and into a dream where I was running down a long tree-lined path, one I recognised at once for it was the one that led to the enchanted house. I could see a tall figure at the end of the path, and I knew it was Ivan and that he was standing there watching me. But the faster I ran, the less ground I made, so that Ivan's figure grew further and further away. It was frustrating and upsetting, and in my dream I kept trying to call out to him to come towards me but my words were snatched away on the wind and he did not hear.

Finally, I was rudely jerked awake by the insistent peal of my alarm clock's bell. Leaping out of bed like a jack-in-the-box, I pulled on my dressing-gown and sat shivering by the last embers of the fire, waiting for midnight.

At length it came, the clock striking each chime slowly as I peered into the long wardrobe mirror, waiting for Luel to appear. Nothing happened till the final chime died away – and suddenly there she was, whispering my name.

'I'm here, I'm here,' I said, peering deeper into the mirror, for it was disconcerting to be talking to a disembodied voice in what looked like an empty room. I knew why it was like that – because Luel had no reflection – but it was still strange and a little uncomfortable. 'How is he? Is everything well?'

'All is well,' she whispered, 'but my lord is restless and I hear him pacing his room tonight.'

'Did you tell him you were speaking to me?' I asked.

'No, I did not think it a good idea.'

'Please, please tell him you did. That I am glad to be home. But I do not forget him. Tell him. Won't you, Luel?'

'I will see,' she murmured. 'If I think it right. And now it is time I went.'

'Wait, wait! Promise me you'll contact me again soon,' I said desperately. But it was too late, for the picture of the cellar room had already flickered out and all that was left was the dimly lit reflection of my own room.

Slowly, I went back to bed. It took me a long time to get warm again, and almost as long as that to finally drop off into a heavy, exhausted sleep, with a multitude of jagged dreams I could not remember in the morning.

Sixteen

I did not even have to make up an excuse to go to town, for Mama announced at breakfast that she had decided on the house we were going to rent in Byeloka and would go in to arrange things with the agent. Of course then my sisters wanted to know which house, and when it proved to be a small but charming one set on a canal not far from the central square, but also one neither of them had put high on their list, they made a bit of a fuss before admitting that it wasn't too bad. And when Mama said that she also intended to begin choosing furnishings and curtains from the agent's order books, they jumped at the chance to be part of it, laughing at me for saying I didn't mind leaving it all to their good taste, as I had some research I'd promised to do for Professor Feyovin in the library.

'You want to watch out you don't turn into some dusty bespectacled old body just like him,' said Anya.

'With holes in your stockings and blotches on your nose,' added Liza, teasingly.

Mama told them both sternly that they should be ashamed of themselves, that Professor Feyovin was obviously a good and generous man, who had done us proud in every way, and that furthermore she respected my loyalty and dedication and that if Liza and Anya didn't apologise immediately, they could stay home and help Sveta with the chickens. Of course they did exactly as she said, though Liza couldn't resist whispering to me, as we were going up the stairs, 'Scribble, scribble, scribble! When did that ever make the world go round?'

I gave her a haughty look. 'What, so you think you know more of the world than me?'

'Much more, I'd say, than someone with her nose always stuck in a book,' she retorted.

'Ha! Little do you know,' I said crossly. 'You've just been here while I –'

'While you what?' she said sharply, as I cursed myself inwardly for my imprudence.

'While I learned about really important things,' I said quickly, 'like the . . . the formula for levitation, and a gadget that may help us to understand the speech of animals, and –'

'Pooh!' scoffed Liza. 'Who cares? Magicians are always going on about their great works that will change the world for ever, but I've yet to hear of one who did anything worthwhile, like make money grow on trees, for instance, or roast ducks that fly straight onto your plate.'

I couldn't help smiling, thinking of Luel doing that very thing.

Liza gave me a sharp look. 'What are you hiding, Natasha? What's going on?'

'Nothing,' I hurried to say, 'I just think it's funny you can't see what's right in front of your nose. For wasn't Dr ter Zhaber a magician, and didn't his legacy make exactly the kind of magic for us that you speak of?'

Liza looked startled for a moment, then exclaimed crossly, 'Oh, you've always got to have the last word!'

'No, that's you,' I said teasingly, and she laughed.

'Honestly, Natasha, you can be impossible sometimes!'

I had successfully managed to evade her suspicions, but it had taught me a lesson. If I was to keep my secret, I had to guard my tongue a little more carefully.

It was market day in Kolorgrod and the town was very busy. Oleg, who had driven us in, had to drop us off in the main square and go to find somewhere else to park the sleigh, for there was no room in the usual spots. Mama arranged for him to meet us at midday, which gave me just over two hours for my search. I left Mama and my sisters in front of the agent's office and hurried to the newspaper office a few doors down. A surly young woman at the entrance desk told me reluctantly that, yes, they did have an archive, and yes, the public might consult it, but first I had to get permission from the editor, who was away on an assignment and not expected to return for a day or two.

But I wasn't going to be beaten as easily as that. 'I am secretary to a very great gentleman scholar,' I said grandly.

'His name is Professor Feyovin. You may have heard of him; he has given papers at all the learned academies, and just last month he presented a copy of his latest work to the King. And he has charged me with looking up a certain matter arising three years ago; he told me that it was surely to be found in your archives for, as he said, the *Kolorgrod Messenger* is one of the best and most thorough newspapers in the land.'

'He said that, did he?' said the surly girl, softening.

'Yes, he did, and he also said that he would be making full acknowledgements in his book, and sending the editor a copy of it as well,' I embroidered. 'You may also be interested to know that this book is to be presented to the Emperor himself, so that the name of the *Kolorgrod Messenger* will reach the highest ears in the land.'

Even I thought I might be laying the butter on a little too thick here, but she lapped it up. 'Of course we will be more than happy to help a true scholar,' she said eagerly, reaching under the desk and taking out a heavy brass key. 'Please follow me, Miss, and perhaps if you like I may be of assistance to find what you want?'

'Oh no, it is quite fine. I know you must have a good deal of work at the desk; it's so busy in a newspaper office,' I said hastily. 'But thank you very much for the offer. I will be sure to mention you to my employer, who I know will be most grateful too.'

'Oh, that is quite all right,' she simpered, the surliness quite gone as she led me a little way down a corridor to a door which she unlocked with the brass key. 'If you find you do need my help after all, please don't hesitate to ask.'

'Thank you,' I said a little faintly, for although the room was small it was a daunting sight, with dusty boxes piled upon dusty boxes, each labelled with dates, and stacks of newspapers tied with string covered just about every other spare surface. But there was no way I wanted her peering over my shoulder while I looked. 'And now I'd better start, I suppose,' I said, smiling. She took the hint and left, taking the brass key with her, to my dismay.

Still, who else was likely to come into this dusty bolthole? The *Kolorgrod Messenger*, despite my hypocritical praise, was hardly the stuff of legend, and its pages mostly sent you to sleep. But occasionally there were news items about more sensational happenings from far and wide, sometimes of a magical nature, dotted like crystallised fruit in everyday porridge, and this is what I looked for as I slowly and painstakingly picked my way through all the editions of the *Kolorgrod Messenger* from three years back to the present.

I found some extraordinary snippets, such as a lurid tale of a love potion gone wrong, a fur-trapper's report of stumbling into an enchanted village in the forest, and a macabre story of a man devoured by a spirit-wolf called up by a northern shaman. But I discovered nothing that bore any relationship to what I was looking for. Whatever spell the sorcerer had used to transform poor Ivan into an *abartyen*, it had not been noticed – at least not by our august newspaper.

So I tried another tack, and went through them all again looking for any mention of art and artists. There was very little of any consequence, though I did find a small mention of Gelden and his fisticuffs with the critic in an Almain art gallery. It was most discouraging. And the dust was tickling my nose and my throat and making me sneeze.

It was sheer luck that my eye happened to light upon something down the bottom of a page of a Christmas issue. A rather uneasy mix of news and advertisement, it bore the tagline 'Golden Express Brings Art World's Brightest Stars to Faustina Festival', and went on to say: *Artists from all over the world have converged on Faustina for the city's new Imperial Art Festival and its offers of rich prizes. The festival is in part sponsored by the luxury Golden Express, which provides discounted fares for every artist whose work has been accepted for the festival. On the train from Palume to Faustina this year were some of the finest artists from Champaine, Almain, and the Prettanic Islands, to mention only a few.* Below the article was a rather blurry tinted photograph of a large group of men and three or four women, all of them in evening dress, grinning at the camera in the luxurious surrounds of the Golden Express dining car.

My skin prickled with excitement. Real information at last! And it gave me a different theory to the one I'd had before: this train had run from Palume to Faustina, so if Ivan had been on it, Palume was where he'd come from. So he probably wasn't Faustinian, but Champainian. And maybe it was in Faustina, at the Imperial Art Festival, that the fatal event had occurred, which meant Ivan had made an enemy of a 'powerful and very dangerous man'.

My ears burned. My fingertips tingled. I felt like a hound on the scent, eager for my prey. I went to the door and cautiously looked down the corridor. No-one was around, so I hurried back to the newspaper, ripped out the page I needed, folded it very small and put it deep into the pocket of my dress. No-one would notice, I thought, as I hurriedly put all the rest of the papers from that year on top and replaced the box. Opening the first box I'd looked at, I scribbled down a few random things from those newspapers in my notebook, just in case the surly girl wanted to see the results of my research. Not that I thought she would, but it was better to be safe than sorry. Then, my cheeks burning, my throat tight, I put every-thing away and headed back to the reception desk.

A weedy young man was talking to the surly girl. He wore a dark suit and stovepipe hat, and had a bushy blond moustache that ate up nearly half his face. He broke off his conversation when I appeared and politely raised his hat to me. I nodded a little nervously and, turning to the girl, said, 'Thank you very much; the professor will be so grateful.'

'Did you find what you wanted?' the girl asked.

'I did, thank you.'

I was about to leave when the girl said, 'It's a funny thing, you know, but this gentleman also wants to consult the archives. Nobody from one year to the next, and then there's two in the one morning!'

'Er, yes, indeed,' I said, shooting a glance at the man, who smiled discreetly and, doffing his hat, went off down the corridor towards the archives room. I hoped he wouldn't notice I'd torn out that page. 'How far back was the gentleman looking, as a matter of interest?' I said, trying to sound casual.

'Oh, only about a year or two,' she said. 'He's looking for information on land sales in the district around that time.'

I was relieved. There would be no need at all for him to go looking into that older box. I was safe. No-one would know what I'd done.

It was nearly eleven-thirty now, so I had no time to waste. I dashed into the library, picked up a few books at random on various subjects 'Professor Feyovin' might be expected to be interested in, and asked the librarian if she had any information on the Imperial Art Festival in Faustina.

'I believe there may be a pamphlet somewhere,' she replied, 'but unfortunately, my dear, it's all in Faustinian, so it might be not very useful for you.'

'That's all right, I can read the language a little and I have a dictionary at home,' I said quickly.

The librarian left and returned with a four-leaf pamphlet that featured a coloured picture of the imperial family of Faustina, with the logo of the Golden Express company. Inside was a good deal of print, of which I could only understand a few words. But at the back there was also an address, and it gave me an idea.

'Are you thinking your mother might like to enter it, my dear?' said the librarian, looking at me a little curiously. She knew my family circumstances, of course.

'Yes, I thought she might,' I lied brazenly. 'Is it all right if I borrow this too?'

'I'm not sure if the prize is really what she ...' the librarian began, but I had already tucked the pamphlet with the books under my arm and, with a cheery thanks, headed out of the library to my final destination – the post and telegraph office.

That morning Mama had announced that she could give us an allowance now, so we each had a little money of our own. I did not want to spend too much of mine, so after thinking carefully, I wrote the following short telegraph: *Urgently need list participants in first competition, for book. Prof Ivan Feyovin, c/o Kupeda residence, Kolor Province, Ruvenya.* I paid for it and watched as the woman sent it down the line to the address on the back of the pamphlet. Now it was gone, and all I needed to do was wait until they answered.

Meanwhile, I had the page and the photograph on the Golden Express. With a magnifying glass, I might be able to make out those faces more clearly. And one of them was probably Ivan's. Of course I had not seen him as he was before the spell had made his face monstrous, but I had looked into his eyes and I had seen his spirit. Something told me there was a good chance I would recognise him, and it made my heart beat faster to think that soon I might know who he really was.

Seventeen

All the way home, and all through the lunch that Sveta had ready on the table for us as soon as we arrived, Mama and my sisters talked excitedly about the house they'd rented, making plans for when we would move there. I only listened with half an ear, for I longed to get back to my room and look at the newspaper photograph properly. Of course my silence could not fail to be noticed, and at length Mama broke off her conversation to say, 'Is everything all right, Natashka? You look so far away.'

'What? Oh, yes. Sorry, Mama,' I said hastily. 'All's fine. I was just thinking.'

'Not about the house, I'll be bound,' said Anya. 'Have you heard anything we've said?'

'Yes, yes. Of course. It all sounds . . . interesting.'

'Interesting?' said Liza. 'Is that all you can say?'

'What do you expect me to say? You know what I think of the city.' I sighed. 'And I have other things on my mind.'

'What, about your professor's job again? Anyone would think he'd put you under a work-spell, the way you've been going on about it,' grumbled Anya.

'You wouldn't know about that, would you?' I retorted. 'Spell or no spell, you have no idea what work means.'

'Girls, girls!' Mama said, sighing. 'That'll do. Now, please clear the table, Liza and Anya. Natasha, you stay here. There's something I want to say to you.'

'Yes, Mama,' chorused my sisters, meekly. I sat there on the edge of my seat, nervous about what was coming next, but even more desperate to get back to my search, the photograph I'd filched burning a hole in my pocket.

'Natasha,' said my mother, 'look at me.'

Reluctantly, I did so.

'I'm a little worried about you, my dearest daughter. There's something on your mind. Since you've been back, you seem different,' she said gently. 'Are you sure you're all right?'

I swallowed. 'Quite sure, Mama.'

'Is it something to do with what the professor has been asking you to transcribe?' she asked, searching my face. 'Is that what troubles you? Is he writing about dark magic, perhaps?'

'Oh, no,' I said, startled. 'Nothing like that. Iv– the professor is a good man. I am just . . . a little tired, Mama. And you know, well, frankly, I didn't miss Byeloka. So I find it hard to get as enthusiastic as my sisters. But I'm sorry if I have been rude.'

'Oh, my dear girl,' said my mother, sighing, 'you know I have come to love our place here and that I shrink a little at the thought of being back in society. But I am merely a middle-aged widow – no, don't protest, Natasha, that is what I am – whilst you girls are young and life is before you. And you need to see more of life than just our little world here. You need to know more people than we can know here, if you are to find your place in the big wide world, and the right man to share your life with – a man who will make you as happy as your dear father made me.'

'Mama,' I said, blushing, 'there is time enough for that, and besides, I have seen the men of Byeloka and none of them interests me. They are all full of their own self-importance and think that a woman should have no mind of her own.'

'It is surely rather harsh,' said my mother, laughing, 'to condemn the entire male population of Byeloka when you only know a fraction of it! I am sure there will be amongst them more than one who would be drawn to you as much for your intelligence and spirit as –'

'Please, Mama, I don't want to talk about it,' I interrupted her. My belly was churning with an undefined emotion, my throat a little dry. 'I do not think there are any such men.'

'Well, I thought exactly the same once,' she said. 'Then I met your father, and I knew I was wrong and that I would go through fire and flood and all the terrors of the world for him. One day, you will understand what I mean.' She saw my mutinous expression and sighed. 'Meanwhile, my darling daughter, think that you are only seventeen and that you should not have to spend your life worrying about the papers of a professor.'

'I'm not,' I said crossly. 'I'm not thinking about them at all.'

'Well then,' she said, 'will you come with us this afternoon to visit Madame Elena?'

Madame Elena lived in the next village. She wasn't quite Byeloka standard, but pretty good for a village dressmaker. I shook my head gently. 'I'm sorry, Mama. I am very tired and must rest.'

'Very well,' she said a little sadly, and I knew it was because she felt I was not being frank with her. But how could I help it?

❧

Back in my room, with the door locked behind me, I tried to read the pamphlet. It proved to be slow going, even with the help of the dictionary. And as it seemed to be of no immediate help to me, I soon cast the pamphlet aside and turned to the newspaper clipping, peering at the photograph through the magnifying glass I'd swiped from the study on my way upstairs. Even with the magnification, it was hard to make out their individual features, not to mention that some were standing in such a way that they were half-hidden by others.

But I refused to be defeated, and slowly I scanned each single face. Some were easy to dismiss, such as the women and the older gentlemen with greying beards and moustaches. But there were at least ten young men in that group who looked around the right age, and three of them had their features quite obscured by the glass they were lifting, or by someone's hand. So I looked very carefully first at those young men whose faces weren't obscured, and the way they carried themselves, to conclude that most likely none of them was Ivan. That left only three.

I heard the front door bang as my family left on their outing. For a moment, I felt a little guilty I hadn't joined them. Then I shrugged and returned to my task, squinting through the glass. Was it him? Or him? Or him? Again and again I looked, trying to decide till my eyes began to hurt and my head ache. I had placed so much store on this and now it didn't look as though it would help me at all. Oh, Ivan, I thought, I wish you could tell me! If only I could speak to you . . .

Wait a moment. What had he said? Leaving the newspaper on the bed, I hurried over to the chest of drawers and carefully lifted out the handkerchief that held the rose petal. I gently unfolded the cloth and at once the rose's scent filled my nostrils. I lifted the petal to my face and gently breathed in its aroma. Then I stood in front of the wardrobe mirror with it and closed my eyes. 'Oh, Ivan,' I whispered. 'Ivan, my dear friend, please show yourself to me. Please speak to me.'

I could feel his presence so close to me that when I opened my eyes and looked into the mirror I was sure I would see him there. But there was nothing except my own reflection, staring back wildly at me. Luel, I thought. Luel won't let him use the mirror. She'll think it's not safe. She won't even reply to me. I was only to do this when I was ready to return, and I hadn't said that's what I wanted. I hesitated. Should I return? No, not yet. It would do no good. I had to know his name. I had to wait for the reply from the Imperial Art Festival. I had to wait till I knew more, till I could be sure.

I sat on the bed with the photograph on my lap. And with my heart pounding and the breath catching in my throat, I laid the scarlet petal down gently on the face of the first young man whose features I couldn't make out. I left it there an instant and then lifted the petal off. When I looked at it again under the magnifying glass, the man's face suddenly leaped into focus – so clearly I could almost see the pores of his skin. But it wasn't Ivan. I tried the next man, but it wasn't him either. And then, taking a deep breath, I laid the petal gently upon the last one.

To my horror the newsprint began to curl up at the edges, as though it was being held over a flame. I quickly snatched up the petal to save it. And a split second before the photograph burst into flames and crumbled into ash, I saw the third man. He was handsome with a straight grey-green gaze, a head of thick, red-brown hair, and a proud, almost arrogant demeanour. I recognised him at once, with the thrill of absolute recognition. It was Ivan.

'Natashka! Natashka!' Sveta's voice outside my door nearly made me jump out of my skin. 'There's someone waiting in the sitting-room to see you, my dove. A friend of your professor.'

My heart thumped. Ivan had heard me! Luel had come! Pocketing the petal but leaving everything else behind, I hurried out. Sveta was hovering in the corridor. 'I've got some lemon cake just come out of the oven – that'll do nicely with tea, yes?'

'Yes,' I said vaguely, eager only to get to the sitting-room. 'That'll do just fine.'

'Luel, I'm sorry if I alarmed you,' I said as I went in, 'but I needed to speak to Ivan urgently and . . .'

The words died on my lips as I saw who was sitting in the armchair by the fire. Not Luel. Indeed, not a woman but a man. It was the weedy young man I'd seen only that morning at the newspaper office.

The shock jolted me so that I could not utter a word, only stare at him as he calmly looked back at me. I had not noticed his eyes before. They were blue – a clear, shallow blue, and unblinking. 'Mam'selle Kupeda,' he said, in a soft, sibilant whisper, with an accent I could not place. 'The post office told me Professor Feyovin might be found here.'

'What? No. They were wrong.' The eyes were having a strange effect on me. They were so clear and blue I felt almost as though I could see right to the back of them, to the back of his skull. For there was nothing in them, no emotion I could place at all.

'Oh, that is a pity,' he said tonelessly. 'Perhaps then you might tell me where he is to be found? I am most anxious to see him.'

'Why?' I said. My skin was creeping, my neck prickling.

'I am a friend of his, Mam'selle Kupeda. We were students together. I know he will be glad to see me.' He smiled, unsettling me.

'I don't believe you,' I managed to say. 'Get out. I have nothing to say to you. Nothing.'

'I doubt that,' the man said, and in two strides he was upon me. I would have run, I would have struggled, I would have screamed for help, but I could not. Every one of my muscles seemed paralysed, every movement impossible. Then he pointed his index finger at me and said something in a voice that seemed to come both from inside and outside of him. I instantly was seized with such a terrible pain in my chest that I almost blacked out.

'Do you still have nothing to say to me?' the man said, his blue eyes fixed on me. I could see something behind them now, something that lurked at the back – no, not at the back of his eyes, but further still – behind him, a sense of another presence, as if the man standing before me were a mere puppet or a ventriloquist's doll. 'Tell me where he is,' he said. 'That is all you have to do.'

I found my voice. 'Never,' I said. 'I will never tell you.' Summoning all my strength, I reared up and spat in his face.

'That was not clever,' the man hissed. 'Not clever at all.' He raised his index finger, but as he did so, a deep growl resounded in the room, and the blond man fell back, staring up at the mantelpiece mirror in shock.

'Oh, Ivan,' I gasped. 'No, no, no . . .' Hulking and terrible in his *abartyen* form, he stood there beyond the mirror, eyes burning like wildfire in the peeling ruin of his face, the skin underneath as raw as if it had been burned, lips drawn back in a wolfish snarl.

He did not look at me but straight at the blond man, and his voice rumbled with menace. 'Touch a hair on her head again and I will tear you apart.'

'Well, well, how very touching.' The blond man had recovered himself. 'After all this time, you walk right into my trap. But then you always were a reckless fool.' The cold blue eyes flicked to me, and again I found myself pinned by their gaze, unable to move a muscle or say a word. 'Threaten me again,' he went on in sinister calm, 'and she'll be dead in an instant. Though, come to think of it, she'll be of more use to my master alive. He's been needing a new subject for his work.'

Ivan's clawed hands twisted against each other and his eyes flashed with fierce hatred as he said, very softly, 'Leave her be, Felix, or you'll be sorry.'

'Don't make me laugh! You are powerless. You can do nothing to help her.'

'That's where you're wrong.' A spasm crossed Ivan's face. 'I still have this: leave her be and you can deliver me to your master.'

The blond man started. For an instant he looked baffled. Then he smiled. It wasn't a nice smile. 'You swear?'

'I swear.'

'Very well. Your bargain is accepted.' And so saying he stepped towards the mirror.

'No!' I cried desperately, regaining my voice and my power of movement now the blond man's gaze no longer rooted me to the spot. 'No, Ivan, please, listen. You can't do this. Luel won't let you – she won't –'

'She cannot stop me,' he said. 'And neither can you.' His voice and his glance were so harsh and cold with pain that it cut me to the quick.

'Oh, Ivan, my dearest Ivan, don't do this, I cannot bear it,' I wept. 'I love you.' The words were torn out of me, expressing what I had not accepted or even understood until that very moment, a realisation that shook my whole world. I saw the shudder that went through him and knew why he'd sent me away so abruptly – he had known what lay between us long before I had. He had known because he had already loved me and was afraid for me. Trembling, I whispered, 'Yes, I love you, with my whole heart and of my own will. So the spell must from this moment be broken.'

As I spoke, Ivan began to change. The *abartyen* skin lifted up as though it had been a mask, his features remoulding themselves into human form, distinctively handsome planes of bone and flesh and skin, his hair thick and shining, his body straightening into that of a tall, broad-shouldered young man, and his hands no longer clawed and scaly but strong and shapely. I saw his lips form my name, and his beautiful eyes were filled with such love and such sorrow that I cried out in fear. 'Oh, my love, what is it?'

'It is too late, for he has bound himself to my master in order to save you,' said a mocking voice beside me. 'Oh, he will not die, for that would be too easy. He will for ever be out of your reach, and nothing will change that now.' And the man my love had called Felix pointed his index finger at the mirror, which shuddered and rippled like water. At once his body shrank and changed shape, and in the blink of an eye he had turned into a crow, which flew into the watery glass and vanished. Then Ivan, the crow and even the reflection of our room were gone as the mirror went black as night.

Behind me there was a gasp and the crash of breaking crockery. Sveta had come back just in time to see what had happened.

Eighteen

'Sveta, listen to me.' I was cold all over but calm, strangely calm, as I bent down to help her pick up the broken china. Sveta was almost hysterical, crossing herself repeatedly, crying that she'd let a demon into our house, that we were all cursed now and that it was all her fault. 'He's not a demon but the tool of a wicked magician, and it's not your fault, dear Sveta,' I said gently. 'But you must listen to me, for I do not have much time, and you must remember what I'm about to tell you. Will you promise?'

She looked at me with wide, frightened eyes and nodded.

'You must tell Mama this: the man you glimpsed in the room beyond the mirror, the young man with the grey eyes, is the man I love. He was under an evil spell through no fault of his own. I have called him Professor Feyovin but that is not his true name. I do not know what it is. All I know is that he is in mortal danger from that sorcerer and that I must do everything in my power to find him. Do you see?'

'Yes,' she said softly.

'Tell Mama I understand now what she meant about going through anything for the one you love. And tell her not to worry about me. I will write as soon as I can.'

'But, Natasha, where will you go? And what will you . . .' I did not hear the rest, for I was already running up the stairs, two at a time. Back in my room, I put on my coat and walking boots, flung two changes of under-clothes, a nightgown, the cashmere dress, the dictionary, the pamphlet, and my notebook and purse into my bag. But the scarlet petal I held in my hand, close to my face. I stepped up to the wardrobe, facing the long mirror, breathed on the petal and said, 'Luel, bring me back.'

I had no idea whether it would work. No idea what had happened to her enchantment now the spell was broken. No idea what Felix might have done to her, only that he could not do much, for after all she was an immortal – a *feya*. No idea if she was even there any more. I knew none of these things save that I must speak with her and this was the only way I knew.

An instant passed in which the mirror remained stubbornly reflective of my own pale, drawn face. I was about to speak again when something made me stop. And there, in a corner of the mirror, a ripple began. It grew and grew and grew till the glass became like clear dark curtains of water, and behind it, unmistakeably reflected, was Luel, beckoning me through. I swallowed, tucked the petal into my bodice, against my breast and over my heart. Clutching my holdall firmly, I stepped right into the mirror . . .

And straight into what felt like a howling snowstorm, so intense and violent that I was blinded and deafened, ears popping, skin freezing, tongue heavy in my mouth, limbs paralysed – all my senses deserting me in an instant. The storm caught me and tossed me like a rag doll in the air, stinging shatterings of thin sharp crystals exploding all around me, and I felt my heart slow to a crawl and my mind blink and go out. Just before it did, the whiteness was ripped aside like a veil and behind it I saw a face looming over me, a malevolent face, skeletal with eyes sharp as daggers, pointed teeth bared in triumph, and I gave a great cry of despair. And died.

'No, you foolish girl, you did not. You are alive and well. But not for long, if you don't hurry.'

I opened my eyes. I was in the cellar, lying in the pulverised remains of the mirror. My coat and dress were torn, and I felt bruised all over. My bag had vanished and all my belongings with it. And *she* was sitting there, looking at me with small black eyes gleaming in the dull grey skin that was tightly stretched over the bones of her gaunt face. I'd never seen her before, not in the flesh, if you could use such a word for a being old as time, old as whispered stories around ancient firesides, warnings of not straying too far into the forest, where she held sway. I'd never seen her and yet I knew who she was. There might not have been a confirmed sighting of her for decades but she had never gone away. And she never would. Hers was a timeless world that cared nothing for the silly human notion that we had moved beyond her. But why was she here?

'The stranger followed her nursling,' Old Bony said, watching my face. She could read my thoughts – that was clear. 'You don't have much time. Get up.'

Groggily, I staggered to my feet. The walls of the cellar were webbed with cracks and the floor heaved under my feet. A rumble started from deep below, jerking me out of my numbness to the danger I was in. I sprinted for the stairs, ran up and through the open door, down one corridor and into another. All the while the mansion was shaking and rumbling and things were flying around me – broken tables and chairs, shredded carpets, shattered lights, torn books. Still I ran and ran for what seemed like an age till I finally reached the hall and saw out of the corner of my eye that the pictures had gone from the walls, as though they were never there. But I had no time to think about it, for the hurricane of ruin was bowling into the hall after me, and if I didn't hurry, I'd be swept off my feet.

I reached the front door and had already pulled it open when something caught my eye – a scrap of paper sticking out of the corner of a book, spinning madly in the wild air. I snatched the book and shoved it in my pocket, then took off through the entrance and down the front steps just as there was an almighty bang and the mansion collapsed in on itself like a pack of cards. I was sent flying into the air, and thudded painfully down on the grit path. I immediately picked myself up and ran, and as I did, the trees that lined the path moved closer together while the hedge at the end grew taller and taller, turning into dense forest. I knew that if I did not reach the hedge in time, before it completely transformed, I was doomed – I would be trapped within the ruins of this enchantment for ever. The hedge seemed impossibly far, but I forced my legs to go faster and my heart to pump harder till I thought it must explode.

And then I heard them. It was like the day I happened upon this place, only in reverse, as a wolf pack in full howling cry came after me. I almost gave myself up for lost; whichever way I went, I was not safe. Behind me, the howling grew louder and, stealing a look over my shoulder, I saw a sight that froze me to the spot. For it wasn't a wolf pack in full cry behind me but a sleigh, drawn by three gigantic wolves – one red, one black and the other white. And standing in the sleigh, cracking a whip and grinning like a death's head, was Old Bony herself. She had come to claim her victim, just as in the old stories. She had saved me from the ruins of the house only so she could enjoy the thrill of the chase, hunting down the human prey she thrived on, and soon enough my head would be another of the skulls adorning the fence posts of her forest estate.

'Bah, you fool, if I'd wanted to do that, it would have happened long ago.' Old Bony reached out a long arm and threw me into the sleigh beside her. Before I could recover my wits, she cracked her whip. The sleigh tilted, the wolves strained, and all at once in a stunning rush of power, we were off the ground and airborne. Rising above the hedge, which was rapidly turning into a tangled dense forest, I glimpsed the forest grabbing greedily at the ruins of the mansion, choking it with thornbushes and creepers and moss. Before my very eyes, Luel's enchanted haven was no more.

I had no words and hardly any thoughts for what was happening, only feelings. It wasn't fear any more that churned in my stomach and prickled at my neck, it was shame. It was my fault that the only thing that had brought Ivan any measure of safety was no more. It was my meddling that had brought the Felix to our door. Yes, I'd broken the spell but that had only made things worse. I had delivered the man I love into the hands of his enemy, and now I was in the hands of Old Bony, for whatever dark purpose she wished.

'Oh you are tiresome, girl,' said Old Bony, breaking into my mind again. 'What possible use are you to me?'

I was stung into speech. 'That, I can hardly tell you,' I said tartly, 'as I have no idea what you want and why you took me from that place.'

'A promise made is a promise kept,' replied Old Bony, 'and I promised the stranger.'

'But why?'

'So she would leave and never return. I only allowed her enchantment in my woods because, like her, I am no lover of sorcerers. But that doesn't mean I wanted her to stay for ever.'

My jaw dropped. 'You *knew* they were here?'

'Of course,' she said scornfully. 'Do you think I do not know whenever a stranger puts so much as a toe in my lands?'

'But Luel never said –'

'Of course not. We all have our pride. I expect I would do the same if I was in her place.'

'But then . . .' A mind-boggling possibility was opening before me. 'But then you must have known I were there when I first stumbled onto their –'

'Whose wolves do you think were after you?' she said simply.

My head was spinning. If Old Bony knew I was there – if she had in fact driven me to seek the safety of the enchanted mansion – then that meant . . .

'It does not mean I cared about the stranger or her nursling,' she said, reading my thoughts again. 'Only that the breaking of the spell must mean they would leave and that I would have my woods to myself again.'

'Well, you have that,' I said sadly. The sleigh lurched and pitched as the wolves began a rapid descent to the earth, apparently following an unseen path down a current of air. There were no more words for the moment as I hung on for dear life, the wind rushing past my ears, my eyes watering from the stinging speed of our descent. In less time than it takes to write it, the earth was rushing towards us, a canopy of trees growing together so densely I thought we must be lost amongst them. But then lights came on below, lights flickering like fireflies, and the trees parted to reveal a way through. We landed smoothly, without a single bump, onto a path lined with skulls glowing like lanterns on poles. I could see the path led to a tall, narrow cottage perched on two long, thin posts like the legs of a giant wooden bird. Surrounding the house was a fence made entirely of bones placed in careful patterns and gleaming like old ivory in the dim light.

I shuddered.

'They were intruders and promise-breakers who deserved all they got,' said Old Bony, reading my mind in her disconcerting way. 'Now get out and follow me.'

I did as I was told, for what else could I do? I was entirely in her power and it was useless to pretend that I wasn't. But all the way along that terrible path, with the empty glowing eyes of those skulls glaring down at me, I felt my heart sinking deeper and deeper and my courage shrivelling with it. I had been rescued from the destruction of the enchanted mansion, but now I had entered the realm of Old Bony, the kingdom of death. How would I ever get out?

'You are impatient,' Old Bony muttered over her shoulder. 'That is your problem, and you must learn to be otherwise. I will help you on your way, for that too I promised. But I never do anything for nothing. That is my rule. You must pay me.'

'How?' I whispered.

'You must work for me for three days and three nights. Do exactly as I say and do not complain once or ask me a single question during that time. In fact, you are not to speak at all. If you do as I say, you can leave and I will help you on your way. If you do not and you break even one of those rules, you will remain here for ever.' She gestured at the bones. 'Do you understand?'

A hundred questions trembled on the tip of my tongue. A hundred questions I swallowed back at once. From the old stories I knew two important things. First, Old Bony was usually a fearsome enemy but, in rare cases, she could prove a surprising ally. You could not predict which; it just happened. And second, she always kept her word *if* you kept yours. I nodded, mutely.

She gave a tiny smile, and I saw that I'd done well not to speak. 'Very well. Come.' Touching the gate, which creaked open with a sound unnervingly like a thin moan, Old Bony ushered me through.

Nineteen

Macabre as its setting was, with the skull-lit path and the fence of human bones, the cottage was surprisingly cosy inside, even if dimly lit and untidy. Unblinking points of light in the dimness soon resolved themselves into the eyes of three large cats – a red one, a white one, and a black one – which purred around Old Bony's legs as she came in.

Old Bony sat herself in a chair by the big stove and lit a pipe while the cats settled down around her. 'Take off your coat and fetch the parcel by the back door,' she ordered.

I did as I was told. It contained nothing more remarkable than some shabby clothes: a large apron, a dress of patched brown wool and some clean but coarse-looking underclothes. 'They're for you,' said Old Bony, in the tone of one granting a great favour, and I couldn't help a small bitter smile as I thought of the beautiful things

I'd been given at Luel's. 'Now put on the apron and cook me supper.' A tremor ran up my spine, as I could imagine only too well the horrors I might be expected to dish up.

But when I went to the kitchen, I discovered a simple basket full of mushrooms, onions, garlic, a bunch of herbs and a knob of butter. Mushroom soup, I thought, with a little inward burble of laughter. What indeed could be more fitting for a fearsome forest witch than a good big pot of homemade mushroom soup?

I chopped and sliced and fried, then I fetched water from the little spring that bubbled out by the back door. All the time I worked, Old Bony smoked her pipe and watched me through half-closed eyes. When the smell of the simmering mushroom soup wafted around the cottage, making my own stomach rumble, the cats sat bolt upright, watching my every move. 'They will have some too,' said Old Bony, when I was ladling the soup into her bowl. 'Set three places for them at the table.'

When it was all ready, the cats sat on chairs at the table, their tails curled around them, and elegantly lapped the soup from their bowls. Old Bony drank her soup noisily, with much slurping, and when she finished she belched loudly, making me jump. I was so hungry by this stage that I felt almost faint, but I knew I must not complain or ask for anything. I watched as they ate and ate till all the soup was gone.

'Now you can wash the dishes and clean the house,' said Old Bony. 'Then go and get some wood for the fire. When you finish that, you can start on the mending.'

There was nothing for it but to do just that. I washed the dishes under their combined unblinking scrutiny, and was about to swill out the water when Old Bony said, 'That will do for your own supper.'

I bit back my anger and disgust and, fetching a bowl, filled it with the dishwater. I closed my eyes and drank it down. It was quite as disgusting as you might expect, and I had trouble keeping it down, the faint taste of mushroom soup sharpening my nausea. But still I said nothing. I washed the dish and put it away, and while Old Bony and the cats snored by the stove, I cleaned the house.

Afterwards, I went outside and found a rickety wheelbarrow by a woodpile. I set off down that horrible path to fetch twigs and small branches. When I spotted a small patch of half-withered berries growing on a bush a little distance from the path, I longed for them as though they were the finest delicacies in the world. But I did not pick them for fear of angering Old Bony. Three days was surely not too long to wait, even if I had to go hungry. You would not die of hunger in three days. Thirst, maybe. But she was clearly not intending me to die of thirst, even if it was dishwater I had to drink.

Back in the house, I went to find the basket of mending. To my dismay I saw it was piled with old stockings as full of holes as colanders. For once in my life I wished I'd paid attention to sewing lessons. I sat there pricking my fingers and wincing as I tried to wield a big blunt needle and rough coarse thread in and out through the many holes, my lumpy repairs looking more like small misshapen potatoes than anything. When I happened to look up at Old Bony, I saw she had woken and was watching me with a little smile on her face, as if she knew precisely what I was thinking – which, of course, she did.

I sat there mending stocking after stocking till it was dark as pitch outside. Yet it seemed that the more I mended, the more unmended stockings there were at the bottom of the basket. As I sat there, thumbs stinging and bleeding from the repeated jabbings of the needle, tears of rage and frustration pricked at the corners of my eyes, but I fiercely blinked them away. How could I weep over such a small thing when it was for my sake that my love had delivered himself into his enemy's hands? My sacrifice was tiny compared to his. I was only bound to Old Bony for three days while he was bound for life. Instinctively, I put a hand to my breast, where the rose petal lay, the only link I had with Ivan.

'You have done enough,' came Old Bony's voice, breaking into my thoughts. 'Put the basket away and have a slice of bread and a glass of milk.'

And there on the table by my elbow was a loaf of bread, as fresh and fragrant as though it had just come out of the oven, though I knew for a fact it had not. Beside it was a pitcher of foaming milk and a glass. The unexpected kindness nearly undid me and it was all I could do not to burst into tears. But I swallowed back both tears and the words trying to escape my lips. I cut a slice of bread and ate it, then I poured myself a glass of milk and drank it. They were both so delicious that I wanted more. But Old

Bony had said only one slice and one glass, so when I had finished, I did not touch them again.

'Good,' she said, 'you are learning.' Old Bony clapped her hands and the bread and milk vanished from the table. She got up and her cats rose too, arching their backs and purring, their yellow eyes fixed on me. 'We ride tonight but you stay here. Whatever happens, do not take one step out of this house while it is night or you will be lost. When day breaks it will be safe. Do you understand?'

I nodded, though in truth I did not really understand. She left then, with the cats, and as I looked out of the window, I saw the skull-lined path light up again, and in that light I saw the cats grow in size and change shape till they were exactly like the three wolves that had brought us here. They *were* the three wolves that had brought us here, I thought, as the sleigh materialised at Old Bony's command and she jumped in. A crack of the whip and they were off, not into the sky but straight into the denseness of the forest, where I soon lost sight of them.

I was alone, with the night pressing against the windows. Everything was very quiet. Though it was not a peaceful quiet but an expectant, breathing silence, as though the house itself was alive and waiting for me to make a move. The wrong move. The move that would see me trapped here for ever as Old Bony's servant. She'd left her ears and eyes behind, I thought with a shiver. This house was an extension of her, and she'd know exactly what I was doing.

Well, if she did, I wouldn't be doing anything wrong. Not snooping in the house. Not looking through her things. Not trying to find a way to trick her, to get out of my promise. No, I would sit here at the table and wait for her return, and try to think about what I would do once my servitude was over and I could set off in search of Ivan. It was only then I remembered the book I'd rescued from the enchanted mansion – the book with the scrap of paper sticking out of it. A scrap of paper I'd recognised, for it had my own handwriting on it: *Till we meet again*. I'd left it there for him when I'd returned home. Now my heart leaped with a wild hope. For maybe, just maybe, he might have written a message on it for me. Or Luel may have. Something that would help me find him . . .

The book was one of the P–T volume of that dull encyclopedia. I leafed through it feverishly. But the scrap of paper was no longer there. No! I could not have lost it! I rummaged desperately in the pocket of my coat but found nothing. I shook the coat, turned it upside down and felt under the lining. Nothing. I wondered if I had dropped it outside when we'd arrived. Perhaps it had fluttered out and was even now lying by the side of the path, glinting faintly in the light from the skull-lanterns. It was so vivid a picture that I was instantly convinced. It could not wait. I had to go out there at once and look for it, for I was sure it contained a message for me.

My hand was on the door handle and I was about to turn it when I remembered what Old Bony had said. *Whatever happens, do not take one step out of this house while it is night or you will be lost.* But I had to. I must . . .

No. I must do as she says, I thought. She was my only chance. I had to stay inside. I had to.

There was a whisper at the door. 'Natasha, oh my Natasha . . .' I froze. It sounded like Ivan's voice. I couldn't shut my ears to the desperate plea in it. I had to get that scrap of paper and read the message he'd left for me. Yes, it had to have been from him, not Luel. For strength, I put a hand on my breast where the rose petal lay, and with the other I reached out for the door handle . . .

I was suddenly jerked back, flung away from the door. Over my heart, the rose petal pulsed against my skin while the voice out in the night whispered and sobbed, and I knew then that it wasn't him but something else – something cruel and watchful, something I must not give in to. The rose petal does not lie. The rose petal was my only true link to him. No, it was our only link to each other. Through the rose petal, I knew he was alive and that it would lead me to him.

I sat at the table, shaking like a leaf, and little by little the desire to rush outside left me. The voice died away and the petal stopped pulsing to lie still and quiet again. It was a test I had passed but I could hardly feel glad of it at that moment, for hearing Ivan's voice had hollowed me with such yearning that I felt only numbness, and time seemed not to exist.

Presently, I stirred. Picking up the book I'd left aside, I opened it and began to read to calm myself, to stop myself from thinking of the presences prowling around the cottage and of the breathing silence of the house. The book was quite as dull as I remembered it to be, and after a short time, I felt my eyelids closing as utter exhaustion began to claim me. Soon the book slipped from my nerveless hands onto the floor, as I pillowed my head upon my arms and fell fast asleep.

Twenty

I woke with a crick in my neck, a furry tongue and a nagging sense that I'd missed something important. I looked around the quiet house. Grey daylight shone through the windows, but I was still alone; Old Bony hadn't returned. The book lay fallen at my feet, and I picked it up and put it on the table, then went to the window and looked out. The bone fence glimmered in the dawn light, the skulls unlit. There was not a sound from outside. I remembered Old Bony's words. *When day breaks it will be safe.*

First things first. I was in need of a good wash and a change of clothes. I warmed up some water in the kettle, stripped, washed, then put on the clean underclothes Old Bony had given me, which were quite as itchy as they looked. I then washed my own underclothes, set them to dry by the stove, put on the shabby brown dress, which was surprisingly warm and soft, and after carefully brushing the dress I'd been wearing, to rid it of the caked mud on the hem, folded it and put it away.

Then I shrugged on my coat and went out into the chill air of morning. I couldn't help a little tremor as I walked out of the house, through the gate and down the path. But nothing ambushed me, nothing moved, nothing made a sound. The forest was perfectly still – unnaturally still – but then, this was Old Bony's realm. I walked up the path, looking carefully first to one side and then the other. It was almost at the very end that I spied it, a glint of white in the undergrowth. The paper was damp and the ink had run a little, but otherwise it was just the same as before. My words, my little drawing and nothing else. Not a line, not a word.

I'd half-expected it to be so but had half-hoped, too, that there would be a message from Ivan. The disappointment of it sat in my belly like a stone as I slowly made my way back to the cottage and the chores Old Bony no doubt would be expecting me to do. Back inside, I laid the paper to dry near the book and set about stoking up the fire, sweeping the house and preparing porridge, for Old Bony was sure to be hungry upon her return. I was hungry too but I made nothing for myself.

Just as I was leaving the porridge to stay warm by the stove, I had an idea. Spies wrote messages in invisible ink or lemon juice. I'd read of such things in stories. To all intents and purposes the paper would look blank, but when held up to candle or firelight, a hidden message would be revealed. What if that was what Ivan or Luel had done?

Excitedly, I went to get the piece of paper. I opened the stove door and held up the paper to the light of the flames. Nothing. I waited for a while and then looked again. Still nothing. Well, I hadn't really expected it, had I? This wasn't some silly spy story from a sensational magazine. This was real and . . .

I suddenly remembered what had happened with the photograph. I fumbled in my bodice for the rose petal, and with shaking fingers, laid it gently upon the scrap of paper. Nothing happened. I waited. Still nothing. This time the disappointment was so profound I felt sick with it. Sadly, I replaced the petal and opened the book at a random page, intending to slip in the paper for safekeeping. As I did so, I glanced down at the page and a word instantly jumped out at me, jolting me so that I almost staggered. For it was not just any word, but a name: Felix.

It was buried in an entry called 'School of Light'. I was now sure Ivan had not just spoken the name by accident. It hadn't been aimed at the crow-man but had been aimed at me! It was the only clue he could give me, and it was the rose petal that had made me see it.

I scanned the entry carefully. The School of Light was not, as its name might imply, some kind of scientific faculty. It was a famous art school in Palume, which had been founded by a woman named Madeleine St Thomas more than fifty years ago.

She is now deceased but her pioneering work on light in art continues to influence a generation of young artists in Champaine. Students are enrolled from the age of thirteen, and come from all parts of Champaine and well beyond.

There have been rumours that the artists of this school use more than natural methods to produce their beautiful effects of light, but allegations that magic is involved are completely baseless. As is well known, the Faustine Empire stringently bans all non-Mancer magic, and a School of Light artist such as Felix Vivian would never have been allowed to enter, let alone win, the inaugural Imperial Art Prize in that country if there was any magic suspected.

The entry ended there. I looked at the publication date in the beginning of the book. The first Imperial Art Festival had been four Christmases ago, according to that item I'd read in the *Kolorgrod Messenger*. The book was published just after that, early in the following year. *Felix Vivian*. He must have been in that newspaper photograph, along with Ivan and the other artists who had travelled on board the Golden Express to the first Imperial Art Prize in Faustina. I tried to conjure up the vanished photo in my mind's eye, to remember all the faces. But it was no good. Apart from Ivan's, the others were a vague blur. I remembered what Felix had said to me: 'We were students together.' If only there was more information in the entry! If only it mentioned other artists of the School of Light!

With a shiver, I remembered the sense I'd had that somebody else looked out from behind Felix's blue eyes – someone who controlled him like a puppet or a ventriloquist's doll – a presence as evil as it was ruthless, as clever as it was merciless. The School of Light . . . one of the Devil's names was Lucifer, which meant 'Bright One, Shining One'. I hastily crossed myself. No, the sorcerer wasn't the Devil. He was a man. Luel had said so. He was a man who had perfected a particularly ruthless brand of powerful magic, which had turned one young man into a slavering beast and another into a hollow shell, a puppet obeying his every command.

And the link was the School of Light. This sorcerer was somehow involved with the school. He could be a painter himself, but he was also someone with power. Perhaps he ran the school, or was an important art dealer or a wealthy patron? Whatever or whoever he was, I would find out.

Something had happened three years ago, something which had caused this man to become Ivan's enemy. Suppose Felix Vivian was a protégé of the sorcerer and had won the Imperial Art Prize through the magical trickery of his master, and that Ivan had found out and threatened to expose them? But while using magic to win a competition was one thing, making an *abartyen* spell-curse was quite another. It was very dangerous not only because it was so difficult, but also because it was magic that was banned everywhere in the world. If discovered, such a spell would land its maker in prison or the gallows. To take such a terrible risk, the sorcerer must have had a very strong motive – much more than the embarrassment of being caught out helping someone to cheat. Ivan must have discovered something much more explosive. The hairs prickled along the back of my neck as I remembered reading my story to Ivan and how he'd reacted. At the time I'd thought he was angry with me, but what if it I'd come to the brink of the truth without knowing it?

Deliberate, calculated murder in the first degree by natural or supernatural means – those crimes were punishable by the death penalty in Champaine and in other places. And such criminals also had their estates confiscated, so their families would lose everything.

I was breathless. Here indeed was a motive strong enough for the sorcerer to not only risk the *abartyen* curse, but to keep looking for Ivan, to make sure the beast-darkness would consume him. Now, the *abartyen* spell had been broken, but it didn't matter, for Ivan was in the sorcerer's hands.

Oh, he will not die, for that would be too easy. Though it was Felix's lips that had moved, they were really the words of that wicked presence behind his eyes. Felix had been turned into a soulless puppet. But not Ivan. There must be a reason why the sorcerer couldn't do it to Ivan . . .

'There is,' said a voice behind me, making me jump. I turned to see Old Bony standing in the shadows. I had not heard or seen her come in, not a whisper, not a glimpse. 'There is,' she repeated, pulling up a chair by the stove, while the three cats slinked out of the shadows to lie at her feet. She looked at me with a teasing glint in her eyes, and I only just stopped myself from begging her to tell me what it was, pleading with her to have mercy on me – on Ivan. But I knew it was no good. I bit down on my lip so hard to stop the cry from bursting out that I could taste blood.

'We've been riding a long time and far away,' she said. 'Fetch breakfast, girl.' I lowered my eyes so she wouldn't see the anger that flared in them and, nodding mutely, went to ladle out the porridge into four bowls. When I returned to the table, there was fine pale sugar in a little silver dish, rich cream in a glass jug, and plump juicy berries in a small basket. Old Bony sat at the table, ladling the goodies onto the porridge for her cats and herself. She looked at me. 'What are you doing, standing there with your mouth open like a great goose? Fetch a bowl for yourself and come and eat with us.'

I did as I was bid, without showing surprise, and ate the sweet, creamy porridge in silence. When all had finished, I got up and washed the bowls, not even blinking as the sugar dish and cream jug vanished. I was then ordered to drag a large tub from the back of the house, fill it with hot water and scrub a big bundle of stained, muddy clothes Old Bony threw at me. It was very difficult to get them clean because I wasn't used to such a task, and my hands were red raw by the time I'd finished and hung the clothes, as instructed, to dry on the bone fence.

Straight after that there was a scrawny, freshly dead chicken on the kitchen table to pluck and gut and make into a soup *and* a pie. Thank heavens I'd helped Sveta do that on more than one occasion so that I was able to do it swiftly and efficiently. After lunch I was allowed a bowl of soup, but the pie was entirely devoured by Old Bony and her felines.

I was then ordered to polish a large set of heavily tarnished silver cutlery that had mysteriously appeared from nowhere and just as mysteriously disappeared once I'd finished. Then Old Bony took out a little flute and commanded me to dance to her tune, all the while mocking me for not being light on my feet. I felt like yelling that it was hardly surprising, for I was so tired I could have crumpled into a heap and slept where I fell. But anger and defiance stilled my tongue, and I danced like a sullen performing bear.

When darkness fell, Old Bony set me to boil thirteen eggs, allowing me to eat one while she and the cats shared the rest. Then once again they left, but not before Old Bony warned me, again, not to step outside before daybreak. I didn't watch them leave this time but sat by the stove with the book and re-read the entry on the School of Light. If only there was more! I took out the rose petal and laid it on the page, but nothing happened. The page didn't flutter to another, the book stayed boringly dense, and after a moment I realised I wasn't going to get any more, because there *was* nothing more. I closed the book and, cupping the petal, brought it to my face to inhale its faint sweet fragrance – the fragile thread that linked me to Ivan and which brought me the elusive but certain breath of his presence from somewhere far away.

'Not for long,' whispered a voice at the door. It wasn't Ivan's this time but Luel's. 'If you don't leave tonight, Natasha, it will be too late. The moon is bright tonight and it will show you a path that will lead you safely through the forest and on your way to us!'

I put my hands over my ears, trying to stop myself from hearing, trying to stop myself from imagining that path. Oh, how I wanted to go and find it, how I wanted to leave this place and begin my search! But I knew I must not; I knew it was all lies.

The voice changed its tone. 'What kind of coward are you, anyway, skulking in the house of bones and meekly doing the bidding of the forest witch like a dumb sheep while my poor lord is tortured and tormented? His suffering is so great and I cannot help him. I am helpless, and that is your fault too, you foolish, selfish child!'

I put my hands over my ears, trying not to listen, but the voice carried on, nakedly articulating my fear and my guilt. 'And what gives you the idea that the forest witch will let you go even when your servitude is over? Whose bones do you think make her fence, Natasha? Whose skulls do you think adorn her path? Why, none other than those foolish sheep like you, who have made the mistake of trusting a wicked being. When your time is up, she will chop you into little pieces and feed you to her wolves, and your bones will join those of countless others who have ventured into her realm.'

I knew it wasn't Luel speaking out there. I knew it was our enemy. By now the sorcerer knew my name, for Felix Vivian would have given it to him, and that meant he could home in on me. I also knew that he wasn't there physically, that it was only his will, seeking and probing for weakness, and that he could not harm me unless I chose it. If I went out into the night, trying to find that path, I'd get lost and wander around the forest for ever and never get out. Unless I went out, he could do nothing. And yet, despite knowing all these things, it was hard to hear that voice speak aloud all those things that troubled me. Only the small, steady warmth of the rose petal against my skin kept me from screaming.

It was a long night, but at length I fell asleep wrapped in a blanket in front of the stove. When I awoke, it was bright daylight and Old Bony was sitting in her chair, smoking her pipe and watching me, the cats by her feet like rag dolls. Dismayed, I scrambled to my feet, dry-mouthed, gritty-eyed, my head still spinning from the restless snatches of dreams.

'What's the matter, girl?' said Old Bony. 'You are looking at me with those great fish eyes. Cat got your tongue?' She laughed heartily at her own joke. I smiled weakly and scurried off to the kitchen corner, but she called me back. 'No, I've had breakfast already; hardly was going to wait for you, lazy lie-abed, now was I? And you have no time to eat. Drink some tea and then warm up enough water for the tub. You have a big job on your hands today.'

Twenty-One

Old Bony had ordered me to bathe her cats, and the task took me well into the afternoon. After the wash, each animal had to be dried in a shawl soft as cobwebs. I then had to make a big beef and cabbage soup for Old Bony and her cats, of which I was allowed a small portion. The exhausted felines fell asleep by the fire with their mistress, and only then could I take a moment's rest.

Looking at myself reflected in the dishwater, I saw that I looked a terrible fright: my hair like a wild blackberry tangle, one eye half-closed from where a claw had caught it on the eyelid, hands and arms so crisscrossed with scratches I might have been mistaken for wearing red lace gloves. My clothes, which I'd not been allowed to change, were steaming dry unpleasantly on my very body. The only part of me that felt any comfort at all was the place where the rose petal lay. But I'd done it and not uttered a word of complaint, asked a single question or spoken at all. Not even so much as a moan had escaped my lips, and I felt a sense of fierce pride and wild excitement. These were the last hours of my servitude. I had upheld my side of the bargain. Tomorrow, I would hold Old Bony to hers.

That thought gave me strength for the rest of the day, through a continuous round of wearisome chores that Old Bony kept devising, as if she was squeezing every last bit of value from me before it was time to let me go. My hands stung and my eyes ached, but I had to keep going.

We had just finished a supper of fried fish and potatoes – this time, I was allowed to sit down at the table with them – when Old Bony wiped her mouth on her sleeve, looked at me and said, 'I am tired tonight, so you will go in my place.' I stared at her, uncomprehending. She gave a little smile. 'Tonight, you ride in the sleigh with my pretties.'

I felt as though my belly had dropped to my ankles as a nauseating wave of fear and despair rolled over me. An exclamation almost burst from my lips but a heroic effort managed to bite it back. I looked at her. She looked back, her eyes full of wicked pleasure. She knew what I was thinking, of course. This was my death warrant. She had intended it all along. The sorcerer had been right. My skull would adorn her path, and my bones her fence. It had all been for nothing.

'Well, that is up to you,' she said, sharply. 'You can refuse. But if you do . . .'

If I did, I would be done for, anyway. What kind of choice was that? None, was the simple answer. None. And suddenly the fear vanished and was replaced by incandescent rage and hatred. So she thought she had me beaten? So she thought she had me broken, and could pick over my poor bones? Well, she could think again. I drew myself up, looked her straight in the eye and nodded.

'Good. One more thing. That rose petal you wear over your breast. You must leave it here.'

I stiffened and instinctively put my hand to my heart. No, I could not do that. It was the only thing that gave me comfort and the courage to endure. It was my only link to –

'Precisely,' said Old Bony, burgling my thoughts as usual. 'You might as well wear a homing beacon.'

I stared at her, remembering the voices of last night and the night before. Ivan was in the sorcerer's hands, under who knew what duress. The sorcerer was very likely to have learned how the rose petal linked us. Yet I hesitated.

'You're going to have to trust me,' she said. 'What choice do you have?'

None, I thought bitterly, as I reached into my bodice and extracted the rose petal. Briefly, I cupped it in my hands and buried my nose in the fragrance, and instantly felt the sting of the scratches on my hands and my eyelid ebbing away. But I knew I had to give it up. With shaking hands, I handed it to Old Bony.

'Good,' she said, and tucked it away in the tea caddy. 'It'll be safe. And so will you.'

I had to believe that. I had to. What choice, indeed, did I have? I got my coat, raised its hood and drew on my gloves. Old Bony fetched her whip from behind the door and handed it to me. 'My pretties know the way.'

Clearly, I wasn't even to be told where I was going. But I said nothing, only nodded. She opened the door and chivvied me out. The cats padded behind me, hardly making a sound. The sleigh sat beyond the gate, waiting for us under the livid glare of the skulls' light. Behind me, I heard a strange breath of air and did not turn for I knew what had happened – the cats were transforming. Keeping my back straight and my legs moving ahead with an effort so great I felt dizzy from it, I walked to the sleigh and got in. An instant later three great wolves loped past, turning to stare at me with cold, glowing eyes. They went to stand in harness, their massive backs blocking any forward view.

I was alone with them, and my only comfort lay behind me, in the cottage. Grasping tightly onto the side of the sleigh with one hand, I raised the whip with the other and cracked it once. Immediately, the wolves took off, straight into the star-studded night sky, so steeply that I nearly fell out of the sleigh.

Eventually, the sleigh levelled out. I soon lost my fear and looked gingerly over the side. We were flying over a vast patchwork of lands – light fields and dark forests, the gentle swell of hills, and rivers winding like thin silver ribbons pricked with the needles of boats. I saw church domes and bulbs and castle towers and fortress walls, the lights of cities and towns, the little huddle of villages, the smoke from thousands, no, hundreds of thousands of fireplaces. On and on we flew, hour after hour, and the exhilaration of it filled me. To speed through the glittering darkness like this, to see our country from the air, was that not a most splendid thing? Who else had ever seen it like this? Old Bony did not mean any harm to me after all. Instead, for reasons known only to herself, she was giving me this gift, this wonderful, unique experience.

Something gleamed in the distance. It was a lake so vast it looked like an inland sea. I knew what it was – the Northern Lake, named after its location at the border of the northern lands. Beyond it were the frozen salt marshes and the strange grey forests of the north, with their hollow, crooked trees, home to a swarm of strange creatures. This was the realm of fearsome shapeshifting *feya* shamans and witches.

I shrieked as the wolves plunged, sickeningly fast, towards the lake. No wonder Old Bony had insisted on my leaving behind the rose petal, my only form of protection. This had been her intention all along – my death by the freezing waters of . . .

Bang! Crunch! The sleigh landed so hard my teeth rattled and my head jerked back. When I recovered my scrambled wits, I saw we were on some kind of rock shelf, only just a little bit bigger than my sleigh. I hadn't seen the rock from the air because it was the same colour as the water. Now what? I stared at the wolves. But they stood stock-still, staring straight ahead.

I gingerly climbed down from the sleigh, hoping the wolves would not take off and leave me marooned in the centre of the lake. But they remained still. I looked in all directions. There was nothing but water. I looked down. It was just a rock, bare and smooth as a skull. Not a stick, not a blade of grass.

There had to be a reason why we were here, and it was up to me to find it. I felt under the sleigh, but found nothing. Warily, I looked around where the wolves were standing. Still nothing. Cautiously, I walked around to the end of the rock, where it jutted into the water. Nothing . . . and then I saw it.

At first I thought it was just a flaking in the rock. I'd noticed it only because the rest of the rock was so smooth. But when I ran my hand over it, I felt a kind of hinging. I levered the rock up to reveal a little hollow underneath. And in the hollow, there was nestled a little tin box.

Gently, I lifted it out and held it in my hand. The weight told me there was something in it. I longed to open the box, but the past three days with Old Bony had taught me wariness. Old Bony had sent us here. Therefore, the tin belonged to her, and she would not look kindly upon me interfering with it. So why send me? I looked at the wolves. Their glowing eyes looked back at me calmly.

I thrust the tin box into my coat pocket, got into the sleigh and cracked the whip. Immediately, the wolves rose. We flew back over the water, back towards the southern shore of the lake, on and on till the eastern sky began to change from a silvery black to rose, then to vermilion, orange to gold, as dawn began to break.

By the time we landed back on Old Bony's path, the sun had risen in the sky and the light of the skulls had gone out. The wolves in front of me vanished, and in their place were the cats stalking disdainfully in front of me. As I followed them back to the cottage, I thought a little hysterically that their raised tails looked exactly like question marks.

Old Bony was waiting in her chair by the fire. 'You got it.'

I nodded and, taking the box out of my pocket, handed it to her.

'What are you giving it to me for?' she said crossly.

I stared at her dumbly.

'It's yours, fool. Why else would I send you to get it?'

I shrugged.

'Open the box,' she said with a small smile.

The lid was stiff and I had to struggle with it a little. But at length I got it open and stared at what was revealed there: a cheap comb, a neatly folded pocket handkerchief, and a round tin a quarter full of tiny pastel-coloured tear-drop-shaped sherbet sweets, the sort you can buy at any fair. Nonplussed, I looked at Old Bony.

'The stranger left it for you,' she said.

Luel had left it for me? Again, I looked at Old Bony for answers.

'You may speak now.'

'What is it for?' I asked. My voice sounded strange in my own ears, for I had not spoken aloud for three days and three nights.

'She didn't say. That is for you to find out.'

'But surely you must be able to . . .' I bit down on the rest of the sentence. 'Why did Luel ask you to put it on the rock?'

'She didn't. That was my doing,' she said. 'You couldn't have it till your time was up, and it had to be kept safe.' She reached into her apron pocket. 'She left this as well.'

It was a folded sheet of paper. I fumbled it open and saw a single line written there. *Lilac Gardens, Palume.* A twist of anger went through me. Luel must have intended me to follow them at once. She had left this and the box with the witch three days ago and in all that time Old Bony had breathed not a word. I had lost three days.

'You did not. You gained them,' said Old Bony, calmly. 'You had courage, spirit and intelligence to spare. What you lacked was self-control and patience, and that lack would have brought you undone very swiftly. Now you have them.'

I restrained the sharp retort that rose to my lips. 'With your permission,' I said politely, 'I should like to be on my way as soon as possible. May I take a little food and other necessaries for my journey?'

'You may,' replied Old Bony, 'and I suppose you'll be wanting this too.' She reached for the tea caddy and took out the rose petal.

I looked at it. I longed to hold it. Without it, I had no link to Ivan. I swallowed hard. 'I think it had better stay in your safekeeping,' I murmured. 'If I am to get to Palume safely, the sorcerer must believe I am still here.'

A flicker of surprise crossed Old Bony's face. She smiled. 'Quite right. You have learned much. I give you my word it will be waiting for you.' She tucked the rose petal back into the tea caddy, and as she closed the lid I felt a sharp pang of regret pass through me. 'Now, then, you spoke of necessaries,' said Old Bony briskly. 'I suggest you get them ready. And you may take this.' She clicked her fingers.

I gasped, and it wasn't at the sight of the loaf of bread and hunk of cheese that had appeared on the table, welcome as they were. The tapestry bag I'd lost in my entry through the mirror was also sitting on the table, a little battered but otherwise whole. I unclasped the handle and looked inside it. There were all my belongings, safe and sound. So this, too, she'd hung on to without telling me! But I could hardly feel angry with her now. 'Thank you,' I said. 'Thank you so much.'

Old Bony shrugged but looked as pleased as her sharp little eyes would allow. 'There's one more thing,' she said, lifting a hand to her head and yanking out a single hair. 'This is my gift to you.'

'Oh. Er, thank you.' I took the strand of hair gingerly.

'Keep it safe,' she said gravely. 'It can go through walls and pierce metal and stone. But it may only be used once, so use it wisely.'

I nodded and carefully laid the hair and the slip of paper inside Luel's box. I packed the food and the box in my bag and looked at Old Bony. 'I will leave now, with your permission.'

'You have it,' she said. 'My pretties will show you the way out of the forest. Then head to the Lodka river port. Once you are there, ask for "the wanderer". Say the forest lady sends her greetings. Can you remember that?'

'Yes,' I said, a little dazed by these cryptic instructions, but knowing better by now than to ask too many questions. 'Lodka, wanderer, forest lady greetings. I'll remember.'

'And best if you keep quiet about your history and your intentions, even to friends. For it won't be just yourself you put in danger, but also them.'

'I will keep it to myself. I promise.'

'Good. Go then,' she said. 'Go with my blessing. You are a girl of brave heart, and it will guide your way.'

If she had been anyone else, I would have kissed her on the cheek. But she was Old Bony, the fearsome forest witch. And she'd made my life a misery for three days and three nights. So instead I bobbed my head respectfully. 'Thank you, lady of the forest. I will never forget you.'

'I'm certain you won't, my girl,' said Old Bony, with a great cackle of laughter, and I knew I'd struck the right note.

If the cats felt any sense of outrage at being asked to act as guides for a mere clumsy human, they showed no sign of it. We made the two-hour journey in total silence apart from the occasional crackling of a twig under my foot.

When we reached the edge of the forest, beyond the fields that butted up against it, I could see, rising in the air, the yellow-and-white bulbs of a village church. I had no idea where exactly I was, but Old Bony had said to head for Lodka, so it must be in that general direction. Lodka was a long way south of my own home; I had obviously come out of the forest in a very different direction from the one I'd come in. Either that or the geography of the witch's realm was utterly unlike the country outside.

The cats left me there, and I set off across the fields, towards the village. Upon reaching it, I soon found the place where the Lodka-bound coach picked up passengers.

There was an hour to spare before the next one arrived, so I sat on a bench, and after eating some bread and cheese, took out the box Luel had left for me and extracted the slip of paper. *Lilac Gardens, Palume.* It made as much sense as the first time I read it; that is, not a great deal. That was clearly where I had to go, but for what purpose was still not clear. Was it to meet Luel? To see Ivan?

And why had Luel left me those other things? I took each out in turn, but could see nothing particularly special about them. I peered closely at them and saw that each sweet bore a faintly imprinted letter. That wasn't unusual, though. Cautiously, I touched one to the tip of my tongue. There wasn't even a tingle. The sweet tasted inert, like chalk. 'Useless,' I murmured, disappointed, and was about to replace it in the tin when I realised something. I'd not said 'useless' in Ruvenyan. I'd said it in Faustinian. I remembered that word from my childhood, from the tutor who used to fling it at us. *Nilos*, she'd tell us, you're all *nilos*! What on earth had possessed me to say that now?

An extraordinary idea bloomed in my mind. Once again I put the sweet to my tongue, only this time I kept it there a little longer before removing it. 'Strange, it's really strange,' I murmured, and that also came out in Faustinian.

I picked up another sweet, touched it to the tip of my tongue and said something that I didn't understand at all, in a language I didn't recognise. I tried another. 'Yes,' I said, and this time it was my own language. I picked another, and now there I was saying something in a language I recognised, though I knew very few words in it. It was Champainian.

I peered at each sweet in turn. Yes. There was no mistake. 'F' must stand for Faustinian, 'C' for Champainian, 'R' for Ruvenyan and 'A' for Almain, probably. Oh, Luel, I thought excitedly, bless you, bless you! A tin full of instant language – one of the most useful gifts I could ever have hoped for! With these I could not only understand and make myself understood in Champaine, but I could easily disguise my own Ruvenyan origins perfectly.

Though I must not do it yet. They were calling all passengers to the coach. It wouldn't do to make people suspicious. I put away the sweet tin in the box, closed it and put it back in my pocket. The comb and hanky most probably had their own secrets. But I'd have to wait to find that out too.

Twenty-Two

The journey to Lodka was perfectly uneventful, and before dark, the coach was disgorging its passengers at an inn by the port. Lodka is a big port and there was a perfect crowd of boats at the harbour, all sorts of crafts, from graceful skiffs to lumbering fishing boats, elegant passenger steamers to workaday barges loaded with goods of all kinds. Could Old Bony have meant a boat when she said to ask for 'the wanderer'?

I went to the harbourmaster and asked. 'The *Wanderer*?' he echoed, and opening a great ledger, ran his finger down a list of names. 'Ah, yes. Here it is. *Wanderer*. It's in port at the moment. It's a Faustinian barge, out of Ashberg. Carries old clothes and other used goods.'

I was puzzled. How on earth would Old Bony know a Faustinian barge-captain? 'Who's the *Wanderer*'s captain?' I asked.

'Young man named Andel. Ashberg native. But he's got a Ruvenyan girl with him. Don't know her. She's not a local. You'll have to hurry if you want to catch them. They're due to leave any moment.'

When I found the *Wanderer* it was already moving away from the quay. I waved my arms and shouted at the barge's occupants – a very tall, broad young man at the tiller, and beside him, a dark-haired young woman. 'Please stop!' I yelled. 'I bring greetings from the lady of the forest!'

Light broke into the woman's green eyes and she smiled, revealing a flash of sharp white teeth. 'Then you must come on board,' she shouted back, and the barge edged close enough for me to jump on.

When I was safely on board, the girl held out a hand. 'You are most welcome, friend of the lady of the forest. I am Olga, of the family Ironheart.'

Ironheart! The famous clan of werewolves! That explained why Old Bony knew her. I'd never imagined meeting one from that celebrated family, and I suddenly felt very shy as I shook her hand. 'Er, good evening, Lady Ironheart. I am so very honoured to –'

'Don't be silly,' said Olga crisply. 'And don't call me "Lady". I'm just Olga. And this is my man, the famous Captain Andel.' And she shot him a proud, loving look.

'Really, Olga, you must stop flattering me,' said Andel, laughing. He had a soft, rather charming accent when he spoke Ruvenyan. He shook my hand. 'Welcome aboard,

Miss. Any friend of Olga's is a friend of mine.' With a twinkle in his eyes, he added, 'But may we perhaps know the name of our charming guest?'

I could feel myself going bright red. 'Oh, sorry. I'm . . . Sveta Popova,' I said, using my mother's maiden surname as a precaution.

'Well, Sveta,' said Olga, 'we are very pleased to meet you.'

'And I you.'

'Is the lady of the forest well?'

'She is in fine form.'

Olga nodded. 'She doesn't change, that one.'

'I don't suppose she does,' I said.

'Do I know this mutual friend of yours?' said Andel, quizzically.

'No, my love, you do not. Not yet, anyway.'

'But she knows about me, or at least about the *Wanderer*?' said Andel. 'Otherwise she would not have sent Sveta.'

'You are quite right, my darling,' said Olga, and squeezed his hand. 'All of us forest-people are of interest to its lady. That is how it is.'

'Then I suppose I have to hope this grand personage doesn't think ill of a simple barge-captain hobnobbing with an Ironheart,' he said lightly.

'Oh, she isn't grand, just powerful,' Olga replied, smiling. 'And she doesn't interfere unless she must.'

'I'm relieved,' said Andel, with a touch of irony. 'But now, Sveta, tell us – where are you bound?'

'The seaport,' I said promptly. 'And there, to board a ship bound for Champaine.'

'Ah, you have a long journey ahead,' he said discreetly, not asking me why I wanted to go there. 'Well, we can take you as far as the port at the river mouth. From there you can find a vessel that will take you across the sea. Will that do?'

'Oh, yes. Thank you. Thank you so much.' I fumbled in my bag. 'I can pay and –'

'Please put your purse away,' said Andel, a little sternly. 'You are amongst friends here, lady of the forest or no lady of the forest.'

I coloured. 'I'm sorry. I did not mean to cause you any offence.'

'None taken,' said Olga briskly. 'Now then, Sveta, how about we leave grumpy Andel to his tiller and go sort out your sleeping quarters. Then we can have a good brew of hot tea?'

'Sounds wonderful,' I said.

As I followed my new friend to the cabin of the barge, I thought how very different she was to how I'd imagined a werewolf to be. I'd imagined darkness, brooding, bestial silence and sudden rages. Not this frank, open-hearted girl, quipping lightly with her lover.

I hadn't expected the warm book-lined cabin either, or talking companionably with Olga over excellent tea and honey cakes, as the barge chugged peacefully down the river, with Andel at the helm. To my relief, Olga did not probe me for my history but spoke happily of her own. And what an extraordinary story she had to tell!

I listened with bated breath to her account of how she'd met Andel during a dangerous adventure in the Faustine

Empire. That was the first I had heard that things were beginning to change radically in the empire, for I took little notice of international news in my country fastness, and the news was still so very brand-new. And I learned that my new friends had had an important hand in those momentous events, and that as a result, the young werewolf and the simple barge-captain had very high connections in the Faustinian imperial family.

'But it's not what Andel and I care about,' Olga said. 'It's that we made true friends with whom we shared so much, and whose happiness mirrors our own.'

'That is so beautiful,' I said, deeply moved, and longed to tell her my own story. But I knew Old Bony hadn't issued her warning lightly; and the last thing I wanted to do was to endanger the happy crew of the *Wanderer*. Olga looked at me quizzically but she did not question me.

A little later, when Andel came in, I managed to bring the conversation round to general talk about Palume, and then to what really preoccupied me. 'You have a lot of books,' I said, gesturing to the shelves. 'I wondered if you had any about art in Champaine?' I added swiftly, 'You see, I worked for a painter back home and I thought I might try to get a similar job in Palume. But I mostly know about art in Ruvenya, and it would be good if it sounded like I knew what I was talking about in terms of art in Champaine, too.' How smoothly and plausibly the lies tripped off my tongue, I thought, slightly disgusted with myself.

'Excellent idea,' said Andel, smiling, 'but unfortunately I don't have a specific book on the art of Champaine.

However, I did pick one up a little while back about art in general, and it is bound to have an entry on Champaine.' He walked over to the shelves and pulled out a rather shabby book inset with a sepia plate of a painting showing a city scene. *Modern Art and Artists*, its title read in Faustinian. 'For a book on art, it's not very useful, I'm afraid. There are only a few pictures and they're not even in colour. But it's only about five years old.' Andel flicked to the index. 'I'm sorry, there's no specific entry on Champaine. But I can see Champainian names amongst the artists, so if you like I can –'

'Would you mind if I had a look myself?' I asked, trying not to sound too eager.

'Oh. You know Faustinian, then?'

'Only a little. I'm no good at speaking it but I had a Faustinian tutor as a child and she made us read endless things,' I said quickly, 'so I can read it a lot better than I speak it. Plus I have a dictionary I can consult if I get stuck.'

'A Faustinian dictionary?' said Andel. 'But I thought you were going to Champaine?'

'I am. I've got a Champainian phrasebook, too. I just brought the Faustinian dictionary in case I decided to go to Faustina at some stage,' I gabbled. 'It's the one I had when I was a child.'

Olga and Andel looked at each other. 'Well,' Andel said, 'if you need any help translating anything, just ask. And you can keep the book if it's useful.'

'Thank you so much,' I said hastily. 'But please, I'd like to give you something in return.' I rummaged in my bag and brought out the encyclopedia volume.

To my surprise Andel's eyes widened. 'Olga,' he exclaimed. 'Did you see this?'

Olga glanced at it, then at me, noting my baffled expression. 'Andel's got almost a complete set of that encyclopedia,' she said, getting up and pointing at one of the furthest shelves. 'Only that one was missing.'

'Well, that's marvellous,' I said, sincerely relieved that at least I could do something, however small, for them. 'I'm so pleased.'

'So am I,' said Andel, grinning. 'Now, it's getting rather late. How about some dinner?'

After a simple but excellent meal of fat sausages, potato mash and caraway-flavoured cabbage, I pleaded tiredness and went off to bed. Olga had made a cosy little nook for me in the cargo hold, where she'd rigged up sheets to create a makeshift tent, made a comfortable bed out of soft old clothes and provided a big fur coat for a blanket. It was quite dimly lit in the cargo hold, but they'd given me a lantern, and its soft golden glow made my little nook feel even more homely. Settling in amongst the bedclothes, the fur draped across my lap, I took out the art book and the dictionary, leaving the tin of sweets to one side. I wanted to try to translate what I needed without the help of the sweets first, for I had no way of knowing how long their effect might last, and it would be rather awkward if I should still be speaking Faustinian to Olga and Andel tomorrow morning.

I scanned the index of *Modern Art and Artists*, looking for names I recognised. Felix Vivian was there but only as a mention (the book dated from the year before the inaugural prize). In fact, he was mentioned only in the context of his father, one Richard Vivian, and, agonisingly slowly, jumping from book to dictionary, I managed to decipher the whole entry, discovering that Richard Vivian was:

a noted painter of landscapes. Messir Vivian's work occupies an honoured place in the annals of Champainian art and he is also well recognised beyond, especially in Almain, where he holds such an honoured place that he has been given that country's Distinguished Artist Medal. Once closely associated with the circle of disgraced Almainian artist Timon Gelden, a noted early patron, Richard Vivian is now the Vice-President of the Fine Art Academy of Champaine, while his son Felix is a promising artist and member of the Palume art movement, the School of Light.

Could Richard Vivian, Vice-President of the Fine Art Academy of Champaigne, be the sorcerer? It was possible. He held power in the art world, his son knew Ivan and there was that association with the School of Light. But would a father really turn his own son into a puppet – a soulless tool? It didn't make sense.

I decided to look up the entry on the School of Light. Most of it was a discussion of artistic techniques, which I only half-understood. But there was also a list of the school's more 'prominent' young artists, excluding Felix Vivian who at the time must not have been considered 'prominent', only 'promising'. They were all young, most in their early twenties, but a few were even younger. That was four years ago, of course, so Ivan would only have been about seventeen.

In my notebook, I wrote down the five names that seemed to correspond most closely in age to him: Sebastien d'Roch, Gabriel Fontenoy, Gaetan Theodorus, Charles Gauvain and Thomas Mandon. All five had already had their first exhibitions at the time, and were considered to have glittering careers before them. Apart from that, the entries noted that all five had quite privileged family connections: Gaetan Theodorus's father was a well-known society painter, Sebastien d'Roch would inherit a large baronial estate, Charles Gauvain's aunt owned one of the biggest stores in Palume, Gabriel Fontenoy's godfather was a celebrated explorer, and Thomas Mandon's older sister was a bestselling novelist.

I stared at the five names, wishing the book had included photographs. Sebastien, Gaetan, Gabriel, Charles, Thomas – which was Ivan's real name? I had no way of knowing right now. But at least I had names to start my inquiries in Palume, as well as the Lilac Gardens, whatever they were.

It took me an age to fall asleep that night and seemed like I'd slept no more than a few minutes when I was jerked awake by a bump and a clanking, scraping noise outside. Going up on deck, my eyes still gritty and my limbs like lead, I discovered that it was bright daylight and that we'd arrived at the river-mouth port of Stereki.

Against my rather weak protestations, Olga and Andel packed some food for me and then Olga escorted me off the barge, to point out the place where I might take the shuttle omnibus that conveyed travellers to the seaport on the other side of town.

'I hope you find what you are looking for,' she said, as we parted with a warm handshake. 'For I see in your eyes there has been much sorrow and trouble, and I would wish on you the same happiness and good fortune we have.'

'Thank you,' I murmured, 'thank you so much for everything and for . . . for not asking me any questions, when you had a perfect right to.'

'Bah,' said Olga lightly, 'no-one has any right to force others to bare their heart.' She took an envelope out of her pocket and pressed it into my hand. 'By the way, Andel wanted me to give this to you. No,' she said, when my eyes widened, 'don't open it now; wait till you have a moment to yourself.'

'I don't know what to say,' I said.

'Then don't,' she said, smiling. 'There's one more thing I have to say. The difference between good magic and bad magic is that the first fits itself to you, and the second tries to fit you to it. Remember that and you won't go wrong.' She smiled at my disconcerted expression. 'Don't worry, I don't know all your deep dark secrets. Only, there is a smell of magic about you, and I know that smell, even if my darling Andel doesn't. Now, hurry up or you'll miss the bus.'

'You are both so very kind,' I babbled. 'I will never forget you.'

'You better not,' she said teasingly. 'We'll certainly be expecting news of you by and by.' After a final wave she was gone, leaving me shaking my head and smiling.

As the bus rattled through the streets, I opened the envelope to discover that my extraordinary friends had given me a final gift far more valuable than the couple of banknotes I'd half-expected. Instead, there was an official-looking passport document on thick paper, in the name of 'Sveta Popova', complete with a most creditable facsimile of the Ruvenyan double-crowned lion seal. In my agitated single-mindedness, I hadn't even considered how I was going to pass the Champaine port authorities' check. Now I was even more glad I had at least repaid them a little, even if it was with that dull book.

At the seaport, I soon found a merchant steamer bound for Boucal, the Champainian port closest to Palume. I spent practically all of my money on the passage, but I could not worry about that, not when I was finally well and truly on my way.

Twenty-Three

The least said about the next couple of days, the better. I had never been on an ocean-going ship in my life, and it was not a pleasant experience. As soon as we were out of the harbour and into open water, I began to feel queasy. By the time we were a couple of hours away from land, my stomach was heaving and I was miserably, atrociously sick for the rest of the day and night and some of the next day. It was only during the last few hours of the voyage that I felt normal again, and after a thorough wash and a light snack, almost human.

Profiting from a moment when I was alone, I took out Luel's box and looked at the comb and the handkerchief. They must have some purpose. Rather gingerly, I took out the comb. It seemed like nothing more than an ordinary comb. But then the sweets had looked like ordinary sweets until I had tasted them. Perhaps, like the sweets, the comb had to be put to use for its purpose to be revealed. I raised it to my head and warily began to comb my hair.

And as I did so, there, spinning softly down into my lap, was a delicate silk flower – a little pink rosebud so finely made it looked like the real thing. Another rake of the comb and there was another silk flower, a pale blue peony this time. Hmm. Silk flowers were the sort of thing you pinned on a fine hat or a ball gown. And these looked like the very best, most expensive sort, imported from Faustina, where they were a traditional handicraft. But what use were they to me?

Next, I unfolded the handkerchief and shook it. Before I even had time to put it to my nose, tumbling out of the folds came a miniature case in cream morocco leather. I opened it and found it contained a beautiful little manicure set made of filigree silver and mother-of-pearl. And inset into the lid of the box was a tiny inscription that read 'Made in the Faustine Empire'. I stared at the manicure case and the flowers as the germ of an idea came into my mind. These things were giving me a hint: not only must I change my identity, I must change my nationality.

Sveta Popova would do till I disembarked. But it wasn't safe to continue with this name afterwards, or to be associated in any way with Ruvenya. The sorcerer's spies were sure to be looking out for a Ruvenyan girl. But I didn't feel I could pass as a Champainian in Champaine; I would too easily be recognised as a foreigner. I should become Faustinian.

I needed a new name. What better than to take as a surname that of our old Faustinian neighbour, the *kaldir*

Dr ter Zhaber? And for a first name, why not Alexandra, my middle name? I knew it was also used in Faustinian. So I would be Alexandra ter Zhaber. Easy to remember, easy to fit into.

Now for my cover story. Who was Alexandra ter Zhaber, and why was she in Palume? Let me think – yes, Alexandra is an orphan seeking her only living relative, her father's sister, Aunt Hilda ter Zhaber, who's lived in Palume for decades and has worked as secretary to several artistic families in the capital – families associated with the School of Light. But Alexandra doesn't know the present whereabouts of her aunt, which is why she has to go around making inquiries. My imagination sped on, clothing the bare story with all kinds of details, so that within a few minutes, Alexandra felt like someone half-real, like a well-drawn character in a book. All that was needed now for Alexandra to step out of that book and become real was to take one of Luel's language lozenges – the one marked 'F'. But that I could not do until we had safely arrived in Boucal.

We finally docked there the next morning. It was raining, and disembarking in the midst of the mud and bustle of the port, in a crowd of noisy passengers, I attracted just as little attention from the officials as I had hoped, with my document hardly even drawing a glance before it was stamped. Clutching my holdall, I walked not towards the railway station, where most of the passengers were heading, but into the ramshackle alleys behind the port. There I might be able to accomplish my identity switch, safe from prying eyes. I also hoped to find a pawn shop where I could sell the manicure case, for I did not have enough money to buy even a third-class ticket to Palume.

I settled on a quiet spot in a sheltered doorway and nervously opened the tin of sweets. I had no idea if these lozenges would work in the way I hoped, or how long the effect would last, *if* they did at all. Still, I had to try. With my heart banging against my chest, I picked an 'F' sweet from the tin, and quickly swallowed it before I could think twice.

At once, I felt my brain spasming and my thoughts becoming as shapeless as rags. In the next moment, a tingle started at my feet, running all the way through my veins, like the fizziest, sharpest sherbet, fast as quicksilver, right up through my throat and into my head, ears, eyes and tongue. Then my mind cleared, brilliantly, in the same way a landscape jumps into view when sunlight pierces fog.

Words bubbled to my lips. Faustinian words. Most wonderful of all, not only could I speak them, I understood them completely, instinctively, as though I'd been born to them. Excitedly, I took out *Modern Art and Artists* from my bag. Yes, I could read it perfectly now, without any need of translation. It felt completely natural!

I was about to replace the tin of sweets in the box when a thought struck me. I might speak Faustinian like a native now, but I wasn't in Faustina. I was in Champaine. And if I was to make any kind of headway in my investigation, if I was to get by in this country at all, I needed to be able to speak at least some of the language. But I did not need to be word-perfect in it, just have young Alexandra ter Zhaber's reasonable grasp of it, learned in the schoolroom.

After a little reflection, I took out a 'C' lozenge, broke it in half and swallowed it. A smaller version of the previous effect coursed through me, and when I opened my mouth, Champainian words came out, a little distorted and misshapen with a distinctive Faustinian accent, but recognisable still. Now I was all set, linguistically speaking, as long as the effect of the sweets lasted. I had no way of knowing how long that would be. I'd just have to wait and see, and if there were any sudden lapses when I was not in a position to take another sweet, then I'd have to pretend to be deaf and dumb.

By dint of walking further into the town, I soon came across a pawn shop. Its dusty display window was crammed with all kinds of exotic but shabby goods, obviously sold by desperate travellers like myself. The owner, a thin little woman with a sharp nose and even sharper eyes, snatched the manicure case from me, examined it carefully through a magnifying glass, and then named a sum that was surely a miserable fraction of what the piece was actually worth. But I pocketed the two grubby banknotes and handful of loose change she'd given me without demur.

'That coat of yours, it's lined with fox, isn't it?' she asked, giving me a sidelong glance.

'Yes.' Shabby though it might look now, it had once been of good quality.

'Well, if you want to sell that too, I can give you a little more. Or maybe you can pick something in exchange.'

Why not? I'd already noticed how much milder the weather was here than it had been at home. So instead of money, I exchanged my heavy coat for an almost-new grey woollen jacket with black velvet trimmings, as well as a hat and gloves to match.

Retracing my footsteps, I headed back to the railway station, where I bought a third-class ticket to the capital. The next train wasn't due for another couple of hours, so I went looking for a bathhouse and there spent one of the banknotes on a complete session. After a blissful soak in a hot tub, I had my hair washed, cut to shoulder length and dyed, transforming my normal chestnut to an almost-black dark brown. My eyebrows were plucked into a different shape and my skin rubbed with an ointment that would add a little colour to my winter-pale skin. Meanwhile, my dirty clothes had been laundered and dried, so that when I got dressed again, they felt almost as new. I would have loved to change into the red cashmere dress, but it was too fine for a third-class passenger. Finally, I bought a hairbrush, a mirror and a hairnet from a shop near the bathhouse, and a savoury hot pie from a bakery. Thus equipped, revived and transformed, I set off back to the station.

Though the effect of the language lozenge hadn't worn off, I kept the tin of sweets in my pocket so I could quickly pop one in my mouth if necessary. Just as I had no idea how long the lozenges' effect would last, I also did not know how many times I could use the rest of Luel's gifts.

And whilst I still had money, I preferred to leave them for a time when I might really need them. I smiled a little bitterly to myself as I thought this, for the old me, impatient and curious, would not have been able to resist trying out that magic again and again. Old Bony was right – I had learned self-control.

Twenty-Four

The train chugged through the sodden countryside, halting at stations in villages and small towns. We were passing through fine farming country, and many of the passengers looked like farmers in their best clothes. There was a holiday atmosphere to it all, and I soon found out why when my closest bench-neighbours told me everyone was on their way to the annual Palume Show, which was opening that evening. They were a friendly couple with work-worn hands and neat but old-fashioned clothes, who introduced themselves as the Gerards. According to them, the Palume Show was the biggest agricultural show in the whole country, if not in the world. They planned to stay with their only daughter, Finette, who worked as a milliner in the big city and who they were very proud of.

Then they wanted to know about me, so I used the opportunity to practise my cover story. When they discovered I didn't have a place to stay, Madame Gerard said,

'We have a cousin, Madame Pelty, who runs a cheap but most respectable pension on Argent Lane. I'm sure she'd find space for someone recommended by the family.' She scribbled something on a slip of paper and handed it to me.

'This is so very kind of you,' I said.

'You look about our Finette's age,' said Messir Gerard, gently, 'and we wouldn't like to think of our little girl all alone with nowhere to go.'

I was deeply touched by their concern, by the ordinary kindness of total strangers who, like Olga and Andel, had helped with an open heart. 'Thank you,' I said softly. 'Thank you very much.' And slipping the paper into my pocket, I added, 'I wonder if by any chance you might happen to know where I might find the Lilac Gardens? Are they in the centre of the city?'

'Haven't heard of them, dear,' said Madame Gerard. 'But then we so rarely venture to the city and there are so many parks there.'

'There's an information kiosk for travellers in the central station, where we arrive,' said Messir Gerard. 'I'm sure they'll be able to help you.'

Soon the lights of the central terminus came into view, and our train drew in at the station with a great hiss of steam and a clanking of wheels. Just before we alighted, I impulsively fished the silk flowers from my bag and presented them to the Gerards. 'A speciality from my country,' I said, 'and a small return for your kindness.'

'No, no, you do not need to do this,' protested Madame Gerard. 'It was a pleasure to meet you, my dear.'

'A real pleasure,' echoed her husband, 'and no need for any return.'

'I can just see these on one of your daughter's new hats,' I said, 'can't you, Madame?'

Madame Gerard looked longingly at the flowers. 'Yes, but –'

'But nothing! Please, I have brought more of these with me, and it would make me so happy if you might accept them.'

'Why, then, you must take them, Pauline,' said her husband, 'for it would not do at all to refuse a gift given in such good heart.'

So she accepted them, with many thanks and a beaming smile, and they both gave me a hearty kiss on both cheeks, the Champainian style. We parted the best of friends, and as I headed off to the information kiosk, leaving the Gerards to wait for their daughter in the station tea-room, I felt more hopeful than I had at any time since that terrible day when Ivan had vanished.

But the dandyish man at the kiosk, who'd been busily brushing his brilliantined moustache upon my approach, was not nearly so sympathetic. After I asked my question, he looked me up and down and said sharply, 'There is no such park in Palume, Mam'selle.'

'But I was told –'

'Then you were misinformed,' he retorted.

'Oh,' I said. 'Maybe there is a map I could –'

'Mam'selle,' he said, drawing himself up, 'it is my job to know every bit of the map. I repeat, there is no such park in Palume. That does not mean there is nothing called Lilac Gardens.'

'I don't understand.'

'Lilac Gardens is not a park or a public garden, Mam'selle, as you seem determined to believe,' he said, with some asperity. 'It is an establishment.'

'I – I beg your pardon,' I said lamely, not sure why I was apologising to this puffed-up popinjay. 'This establishment . . . what it is, please?'

'It is an art gallery, Mam'selle. A rather smart one,' he said, looking me up and down again, as if to say I could not expect to be allowed anywhere near such a place.

But I cared not for what he thought. Looking calmly back at him, though my pulse was racing and my legs felt weak, I said, 'How may I find this, please?'

In answer, he reached under the counter and produced a map. 'Buy one of these and I'll mark it in for you.'

I handed over a couple of coins and he marked the place in red ink. 'It is too far to walk. You must take a cab.' He raised an eyebrow. 'Or an underground train, if you don't have the money for a fare.'

'Thank you,' I said, and smiled. 'You've been most helpful.'

The startled, baffled expression that flickered over his face was priceless. It would take him a moment to work out if he'd just been insulted with irony or if I was simply a foolish foreigner who hadn't understood she was being patronised. Either way, it would annoy him, and pay me back a little for his rudeness and disdain. Once, I thought as I walked away, I would not have been able to stand up to someone like that.

⚘

If it hadn't been dark by then, I'd have ignored the popinjay's advice and made my way to Lilac Gardens on foot, to save my money. I'm good at reading maps, and from it I'd worked out that Lilac Gardens was most likely about a thirty-minute walk away. But it was night, and though the streetlights were on and I had a map, I was in a foreign city about which I knew little. I didn't know, for example, which areas were safe to go in alone at night, and which weren't. It was likely that Lilac Gardens, being a rather smart area, was not situated in a bad neighbourhood, but I couldn't be sure. And in any case, I wanted to get there quickly, so I took the underground train.

Like the ocean voyage, this was another first for me. Though my supposed home city of Faustina also boasted an underground railway, Byeloka most certainly did not. I soon got used to it as it did not seem much more different than an ordinary train, only smaller and noisier, the sound magnified in the tunnels.

Emerging from the underground station and into the street, I looked at my map under a streetlight. The gallery should be only three blocks away. I started walking, becoming aware of the quiet here, after the noise of the underground and the bustle of the station. It was a residential area lined with big houses set back behind high walls, and though there was adequate lighting, there was something about the place that made me feel uneasy. I soon realised what it was – there were no other people around; my footsteps were the only ones ringing on the cobblestones. Occasionally, a vehicle drove past, almost silently, as if coachmen must come with greased wheels, and horses with the light step of ghosts in order to venture into this hushed place.

The image made me shiver. I took a hold of myself. I was letting my imagination run away with me. There was nothing wrong here – this was just a wealthy area, and wealthy people don't walk because they can afford to have the best vehicles money can buy. Still, I quickened my step and, reaching the right crossroads without incident, turned into the lane where the art gallery should be.

It was there all right, housed on the ground floor of a tall, narrow grey stone house. Unfortunately, though, Lilac Gardens was closed. A curtain was drawn across its big bay window, so I couldn't even peer inside. But a notice informed me that it was owned by Messir d'Louvat and that the gallery was merely closed for the preparation of an exciting new exhibition that was set to open soon. Underneath was a date and a time – this Saturday at midday. The day after tomorrow.

I looked up at the house. All the windows were dark, and no-one seemed to be home. There was no point in lingering. If I was to be sure of speaking to someone, I'd have to come back the day after tomorrow.

Luel had given me the name of that gallery for a reason. I'd half-hoped I'd find her there. But it was now obvious that was not her intention. Perhaps Messir d'Louvat was the sorcerer. With that name, not only was he clearly an aristocrat, and thus likely to be wealthy, he was also an art dealer. And art dealers, aristocratic or not, were powerful – as far as artists were concerned, they could make or break careers. And occasionally they were also linked to not very savoury people. A few years ago there'd been a scandal in Byeloka concerning a prominent dealer who'd been hand in glove with art thieves and had been sent to prison for it. What if Ivan had discovered that d'Louvat had done something like that and had threatened to expose him, not knowing that the dealer had sorcerous powers?

With ifs and buts you might put Byeloka in a bottle, as Sveta would say. I was letting my imagination run away with me. But there had to be some connection between Ivan and Lilac Gardens, or Luel would not have sent me there. Perhaps I would find out if I turned up on Saturday.

Halfway back to the underground station, I thought I heard footsteps behind me. I turned my head, but all was quiet and there was not a person in sight. Still, I had an unpleasant feeling of being watched, and it wasn't until I was hurrying down the stairs to the busy platform that my heart rate began to return to normal.

Twenty-Five

I'd consulted the map and seen that Argent Lane, where the Gerards' cousin had her pension, was on a line that branched off from the one I'd been on. Arriving at the right station a short time later, I soon found my way to Argent Lane. It was a short, narrow street, and Madame Pelty's pension was halfway down. The lady herself proved to be a sharp-tongued, round person with a gimlet glare, which softened considerably when she read Madame Gerard's note.

'We're pretty full due to the show,' she said, 'but I do have a little attic room I could let you have, to tide you over till another room is freed up.' And she named a sum that was so modest I thought I hadn't heard right.

'Thank you, I'll take it for the week,' I said, producing my banknote.

She looked at it carefully before putting it away in the pocket of her apron. 'That'll be enough for half-board, breakfast and an evening meal, as well as the bed and warm water for your ablutions. No bathroom here, but there's a respectable bathhouse a couple of streets away. No visitors in the room, and no noise at night either. Or any other time, in fact.' She looked at me sharply. 'Are you a musician?' she barked.

'Er, no,' I said, bemused.

'Good. Faustinians often seem to be musicians, for some reason. Violinists, frequently. Glad you're not one of them. Can't abide those screechy things.' She pointed at my bag. 'That all your luggage?'

'Yes, Madame.'

'Good. Can't abide mountains of luggage, either. Right, then, come in. I'll give you a jug of water so you can freshen up, and you can go straight on to the room. Can't miss it. It's the only attic room without any junk in it. Now, dinner's in ten minutes. But you weren't expected, so you'll have to make do with soup and bread in the kitchen tonight.'

'No problem, Madame,' I said faintly, and followed her into the house.

❧

The attic room was very small and the furniture rather basic, but at least it wasn't cold. The room was up against the chimney, and heat from the fires downstairs had been rising into it. I unpacked, washed my hands and face, then went downstairs to the kitchen, as instructed.

The cook was a youngish woman who seemed friendly enough but whom I could barely understand, for she had an accent I hadn't heard before. 'She's from the south – they all talk as if they have mouths full of cake,' the kitchen-maid whispered to me as she ladled out my leek and potato soup, so thick and tasty it was like a meal in itself. 'But you get used to it after a while. And you're from Faustina, I hear. I read in a magazine yesterday about the romantic engagement of your Crown Prince. Wonderful story, isn't it?'

'Yes, it is,' I said a little dazedly.

'Oh well, we don't have Crown Princes here, but we still have amazing stories, don't you think?'

I nodded, my mouth full of leek and potato.

'Like about Mam'selle Durant. Imagine, it said in the paper she never once gave up hope, but then she must be used to it I suppose, what with her mother dead long ago and her father always being away in those foreign places. I'm sure I should go to pieces, would you?'

I had not the faintest idea what she was talking about. But I nodded, wisely. 'Most likely.'

'They say he's pretty ill; well, brigands wouldn't be thinking of your health, would they? Our President said it was an outrage and ... oops, the boss is looking this way, I'd better get on with my work. Oh, by the way, my name's Claire.'

'Alexandra,' I said, smiling. We shook hands, and she darted off to her work.

Shortly afterwards, I went up to my room. My long journey was really taking its toll, and I longed for bed. Undressing clumsily in the light of the one candle I'd been given, I could hardly keep my eyes open. Even though the mattress was a bit lumpy, the pillow a little thin and the covers rather worn and frayed, I fell asleep as soon as I hit the pillow, and slept dreamlessly all night.

 ❧

I awakened to weak sunlight and the cooing of a pigeon sitting on the windowsill.

Today I would start going around the houses of those five young men. If I'd not been so dazed last night, I might have pumped Claire for information. She sounded as if she had all the gossip on tap. Well, I could always try this morning.

First of all, though, I needed to test my language. 'Good morning,' I said to the empty air, 'and how are you?' Yes, I was still speaking quaint Champainian, with that Faustinian accent. But was it my imagination or did it sound a little more halting than before? So I tried something a little more complicated, and was left searching for words, with Ruvenyan breaking through from underneath. The effect was obviously wearing off.

So now I knew that the sweets lasted about twenty-four hours. I counted the number of F and C sweets I had left. Six of the first, six and a half of the second – just under a week's supply.

My hands felt clammy and my breath fluttered in my throat. A week, that's all I had. And where was Luel? Why hadn't she contacted me in any way? What was going on? Oh, if only I had the rose petal with me! Old Bony said it put me in danger but now I wondered if that was really true. At least it would have led me directly to Ivan. I could have coped with anything then. I would not feel so discouraged when thinking of everything I had to do, alone, far away from my family and everything I had known.

Oh, my poor mother. I had promised Sveta I would let her know I was all right. And I had completely forgotten! I had in fact not thought of my family at all in the last few days. How shameful. I must remedy it as soon as possible. The post office would be my first port of call. I counted the rest of my money. I would have enough for a telegraph, but remembering the last time I'd sent one, I hesitated. Because you had to order telegraphs specifically and a copy was kept of them, they were too easy to track down. A letter would be slower, but cheaper and much safer, as I could just post it in the box amongst a heap of other mail. I tore a page out of my notebook and wrote some brief words.

Dear Mama, dear sisters,

This is to tell you I am safe and well. People are very kind and I am hopeful everything will work out. Please don't worry about me. I am fine and staying in a good place. I will write to you again soon.

With all my love,

Your Natasha.

There. It would reassure them whilst not giving away too much in the unlikely event the sorcerer discovered it. I folded the letter and put it in my purse. I'd buy envelopes and stamps at the post office.

I washed from head to toe in some warm water, put on the red cashmere dress, and went down to breakfast in the dining-room, where the other guests were already gathered. They were older than me, mostly middle-aged and elderly couples, except for a family with small twin boys who kept remarkably quiet. I was the only foreigner, but after polite introductions they soon lost interest in me. As Madame Pelty had said, they were mostly country people up for the show, and their talk was of livestock and crops and the weather. I was left alone to my bread and butter and weak coffee, wishing there was creamy sweet porridge, fried eggs and strong tea instead. Breakfast was a poor meal in Champaine, it seemed.

On my way out a little later, I poked my head in at the kitchen door, intending to find Claire the kitchen-maid. But I was told by the cook that the girl wouldn't be at work today as she'd been laid low with flu. So out I went into the bright day.

Like most people, I'd seen images of Palume in magazines and books – its famous bridges and elegant streets, gold-domed theatre topped with a flight of bronze angels, charming restaurants, splendid department stores, decorated underground stations, and the grand presidential palace. I'd always suspected the reports were overdone, and last night the darkness had hidden the city's true beauty. But now, though my mind was intent on other things, I couldn't help noticing how lovely it was.

The main post office was a rather splendid building, too, and it was crowded with people, much to my satisfaction. The harassed clerk who served me was much too busy to even look up when I asked for three envelopes and international stamps. He just threw them at me, calling out 'Next!' as soon as I'd paid for them.

I posted my letter, keeping the other envelopes and stamps in my purse, and headed to the room where the address directories were kept. Unfortunately, they were grouped into city districts rather than by surnames, though each district volume did list the names of residents in alphabetical order. So it took me quite a while to track down the five names I was interested in: Fontenoy, Gauvain, Mandon, d'Roch, Theodorus, plus a sixth, Vivian.

I wrote down all the addresses in my notebook. At least the Theodoruses and the Mandons lived in the same district, but the others were scattered here and there. The Vivians, I learned, lived in the same district where Lilac Gardens was situated. Though their address was at the opposite end of the district from the art gallery, the disagreeable discovery made my skin prickle as I remembered the unease I'd felt last night, and again I wondered if Felix's father could be the sorcerer.

No, I told myself stoutly, for even if he was and his spies were out, they'd not have recognised me. I looked and sounded quite different from when Felix had seen me and I had not carried the rose petal with me, so there was nothing to link me psychically to Ivan. Indeed, ever since I'd left it behind at Old Bony's, I hadn't felt him near me at all. I didn't want to linger on that thought, for if I did, I'd become frightened and sad, and I couldn't afford to be. I couldn't even afford to think about Ivan too much. I had to simply concentrate grimly on my plan, as though it was all that existed, as though I was in a vacuum. Not a lover, not a daughter, not even a friend; just a person with a job to do. If I allowed my feelings to get the better of me, all would be lost.

The district where the Theodorus and Mandon families lived was the closest to the post office, so that was where I started. By now it was midday and the restaurants and coffee shops in this lively area were starting to fill up, and because the day was so bright, with a touch of coming spring, there were even people sitting at little pavement tables outside. But the street where the Theodorus family lived was an oasis of quiet; not the uneasy quiet of the area around Lilac Gardens, but peaceful and relaxing.

The Theodorus family occupied the first and second floors of a four-storey apartment house made of elegant grey stone, with decorated white balconies. Clearly, painting the ladies and gentlemen of Palume society did not make one a pauper. I rang the doorbell, and was confronted by another supercilious dandy, this time in a footman's uniform.

'All members of the public must go to the back door,' he coldly informed me.

'Forgive a foreigner's ignorance, sir,' I said humbly. 'If you will direct me to where I should go, I'll be very grateful.' Over his shoulder I could see the grand entrance hall and a row of portraits, two of which especially caught my eye. They were of the same young man, but by obviously different hands.

The footman noticed the direction of my glance and shot me a suspicious look. 'You need to go down there,' he said, pointing to a side alley. 'Understand?'

'Yes, sir, of course. Excuse my rude staring,' I said. 'I could not help noticing those very fine paintings. They must be by great masters indeed.'

'They are,' said the footman, unbending just a little. 'By the Messirs Theodorus, father and son. Family portraits, you understand.'

'Oh, yes,' I breathed. 'In my country it is said that the name of Theodorus rides as high as the stars. Is that – is that the younger Messir Theodorus in those paintings?'

'It is indeed. Messir Gaetan. One's a self-portrait he painted last year, the other was painted by his father. They are reckoned to be most striking,' said the footman, complacently.

'That they are, sir. It must be wonderful to work for such great gentlemen,' I said, fearing I may be laying it on a little thick.

But I needn't have worried for the footman preened himself a little and said, 'It is. But then the family only ever hire the very best-quality persons.'

I only just restrained an incredulous laugh. I bobbed my head and said, 'Please forgive me for keeping you talking so long, sir.'

'Not at all. Now, there's your way to the back door. And in future, remember, in this country ordinary folk go to the back door. It is only guests and people of importance who may use the front.'

'I'll remember, sir. Thank you,' I murmured, feeling an overwhelming desire to kick him in his self-important behind. Of course I did no such thing but scuttled round to the side alley, pretending to head for the back door. As soon as I heard the front door close, I sidled out again and took off in the opposite direction. I had no need of any more inquiries at the Theodorus house. I had learned all I needed to know and could now cross Gaetan off my list.

The Mandons, brother and sister, lived about five minutes' walk away. Their house was rather smaller than the Theodorus residence, and the fresh-faced maid who answered the door was also nowhere near as expensive-looking or superior as the Theodorus's footman. Upon being told I was a journalist who wished to interview the 'very talented Mandons' for a Faustinian magazine, the maid told me quite readily that Messir Thomas and Mam'selle Anne were out lunching in the Blue Bird, 'as is their custom'.

'Oh, yes, the Blue Bird, that famous place where artists and writers gather on Blue Street,' I said cunningly. 'Even in Faustina we have heard of this.'

'Oh, no, it's not Blue Street,' corrected the maid, just as I'd hoped. 'It's on Luna Street.'

'Of course. I'm just confused,' I said with a rueful smile. 'Well, thank you for your help. I will return later. When do you expect them back?'

'Not for a few hours. But you may leave a note if you like.'

'No, it is fine. I will come back later.'

'I will tell them to expect you, Mam'selle . . .?'

'Ter Zhaber. Mam'selle Alexandra ter Zhaber of *The Mirror Magazine*,' I said glibly. 'Thank you. And good day to you.'

'And to you,' she said, sounding just a little puzzled, as if she was beginning to wonder what all that had been about.

If Thomas Mandon was out lunching with his sister, it was unlikely he was Ivan. Still, it didn't hurt to check, and so I headed for Luna Street and the Blue Bird with a brisk step. On the way I passed a bookshop and saw, displayed in the window, several volumes of Anne Mandon's latest bestseller. And next to them, to my delight, was a charming portrait of the blonde, blue-eyed writer, displayed on a small easel, with the initials 'T.M.'. Thomas Mandon had painted his sister's portrait, thus making my job a good deal easier.

The Blue Bird was only a few blocks away. It proved to be one of those small wood-panelled restaurants with stained-glass windows, of which Palume seemed to have more than its fair share, and it was crowded with mostly young people chattering and laughing. I could not see all of them properly from the street, so I went in and ordered a small coffee, to consume while standing at the counter. I sipped the liquid slowly, scanning each table till I finally spotted Anne Mandon's unmistakeable features. She was sitting at a table at the far end of the room with a group of young men, one of whom must be her brother, to judge from the strong family resemblance. There could be no doubt – Thomas Mandon was not my Ivan.

Now there were three left. I was hungry by now and the next closest address – Charles Gauvain's – was a fair walk away. I bought myself a slice of onion tart from a bakery – the cheapest thing I could find – and ate it while sitting in a nearby park dotted with statues and fountains. I was just shaking the crumbs from my lap and getting up to go when a familiar voice hailed me from behind. It was Madame Gerard, arm in arm with an auburn-haired young woman wearing a pretty little hat. The hat was trimmed with something I recognised – the silk flowers.

'Alexandra!' said Madame Gerard, beaming. 'I thought it was you! What a good surprise! I am most pleased to see you!'

'And I you, Madame,' I said sincerely. 'How is the show? And Messir Gerard?'

'Both good. Louis is at the show again today, meeting up with his old army cronies. But tell me, my dear, did you manage to get a room at Emilie's – I mean, at Madame Pelty's?'

'I did, thank you. It is a very pleasant place to stay.'

'Oh, good. And what news of your aunt?'

'None yet. But I am hopeful I will find her soon.'

'I too. Oh dear, how remiss of me,' she exclaimed, looking almost comically dismayed. 'Here I am completely forgetting my manners. Alexandra, my dear, may I introduce you to my daughter Finette?'

'How do you do?' I said, and shook Finette's hand.

'Very well, thank you.' She smiled. 'It is very nice to meet you and to have the opportunity to thank you as well.' She pointed to the flowers. 'They are so beautiful and are of such wonderful quality. I've never seen finer, and in our shop we get a lot of these from Faustina. Which firm made it?'

'Oh, just a small firm called . . . called Luel,' I gabbled. 'You will not know it because, er, Madame Luel, the owner, is a seamstress who used to work for my family, then she set up this business. Only a year since.'

'I see. Maman told me you brought more of them with you,' said Finette, with a questioning tone in her voice.

'Yes, that is so,' I agreed cautiously.

'Then might you perhaps consent to bring some to the shop where I work? I know my employer, Madame Ange, would love to see them and buy some if, of course, they are indeed for sale.'

'Why, yes, of course,' I said eagerly. This was an unexpected opportunity and I did not intend to miss it. 'When would you like them by? I have left the goods in my room of course but I could bring them to the shop later on today, or tomorrow if that is more suitable.'

'Later on today will be perfect,' said Finette. 'I just had the morning off to be with Maman and I am going back to the shop at two. Perhaps if you might call around three or four?'

'Very well, I will bring a good selection,' I said.

'I look forward to it very much,' she replied.

I parted company with them soon after, pleading an urgent errand, and hurried as fast as I could back to Argent Lane. On the way there, I bought some tissue paper and a cardboard box from a stationer's, for I'd need to pack the flowers so they wouldn't crush.

Twenty-Six

With my door safely bolted, I sat on the bed with the comb. I pulled it once through my hair and down tumbled a lovely spray of golden mimosa mixed with jasmine, set against a backing of silver lace. Twice, and there was a tiny bouquet of rosebuds of an unusual shade between orange and pink. I hesitated. Rashly, I'd said I'd bring a good selection. But I had no way of knowing how many more the magic would give me. It wasn't like with the sweets, where I could see at a glance how many I had left.

Still, nothing ventured, nothing gained. So I combed my hair again and this time into my lap tumbled a perfect shower of miniature flowers, everything from violets to geraniums, daffodils to lilies, bluebells to pansies. And rosebuds of red, white, gold, mauve and pink.

Hastily, I lay the comb aside, hoping that the sudden bounty didn't mean the comb's magic was exhausted, the way a stressed plant might produce a rush of flowers or fruit just before dying. I had no way of knowing that except by running it through my hair again and that I was certainly not going to do. At least now I had more than enough to take to Finette's shop, and could leave a few behind as well, just in case.

I carefully made my selection. I'd take the spray of mimosa but leave the rose bouquet behind. And I'd take three or four of the individual rosebuds, as well as several other types of flowers. The rest I'd leave for another day. I wrapped the selected flowers in tissue paper and laid them gently in the box, all except for one, which I pinned to my hat. Then I crept out of my room with my precious cargo, down the stairs and into the street, without being spotted by anyone.

The millinery shop was a good distance from Argent Lane and I did not want to run the risk of crushing my parcel under my arm on a long walk, so I spent the last of my coins on a ride on the underground train. I'd have to hope that Finette was right and that Madame Ange did love the flowers, or I'd be in something of a pickle till I could get the handkerchief to conjure up something for me – only *if* it would, of course. From everything I'd ever read, it's foolish to have faith in that sort of *feya* magic, for it is unpredictable and can stop working every bit as easily as it started.

More than ever I wished Luel would contact me. Things would be a lot less uncertain if she were with me. Old Bony had said she'd 'followed her nursling' – which meant she had gone in search of Ivan. She had not been the sorcerer's target; it was Ivan who was in danger from him.

So where did that leave Luel? She had been able to keep Ivan safe, hidden away, but had been powerless to break the spell-curse. Now that Ivan was in the sorcerer's grasp, was she also perhaps helpless and unable to rescue her lord, able only to watch him from a distance? That must be it. Luel was in hiding. She didn't even know I was here, and I couldn't find her. Once again, my doubts about leaving the rose petal behind resurfaced. For not only was it my link with Ivan, it also allowed me to speak to Luel. If I'd had it, I might have been able to reach her through a mirror. But that way was closed to me now, leaving me quite on my own.

The simply named *Madame Ange, Milliner* was a beautiful shop, with white carpets, gilded mirrors and crystal chandeliers, and the company's airy, filmy creations poised on stands, like sculptures in a gallery. Madame Ange herself was a tall, graceful woman with silver hair stylishly piled on her small head, wearing a simple yet elegant dress that set off the beauty of its pearl-grey silk. She looked the epitome of the legendary Palume elegance, and her manner was of that natural politeness that is a mark of true elegance, beside which the superciliousness of the self-important dandy was shown up for what it really was – the mark of a fool. It was not for Madame Ange to have me sent round to the back door; nor for her to treat me with anything less than absolute courtesy, and that was obviously true in her relations with her staff, too. Fortunate Finette, to have found employment in such a place!

Just as the young woman had predicted, her employer loved the flowers. Madame Ange delicately turned them over in her hands, her eyes alight. 'This is the work of a true artist,' she murmured. 'I've never seen anything quite as perfect. And yet Finette tells me this person isn't even a trained flower artist but used to be a humble seamstress.' Madame Ange looked at me.

'She trained herself,' I said hastily. 'I used to watch as she'd practise.'

'One can practise and practise, but if one does not have the gift, the result would be competent and nothing more,' Madame Ange said coolly. 'And these are extraordinary, worthy to be worn by princesses. Does the imperial family of Faustina not know about Madame Luel?'

'No,' I said. 'You see, it is only new, her business, and she is most modest. It is I who suggested to bring some of her creations to Palume.'

'Hmm,' said Madame Ange thoughtfully. 'Have you shown these to anyone else?'

'No, Madame. Not yet.'

'Good.' She turned to Finette. 'The hats for the President's wife and daughters,' she said, 'for the garden party. Fetch them.'

'Yes, Madame,' said Finette, shooting me a happy glance.

So that was how I sold my entire stock, which would be destined to adorn the hats of the Champainian Presidential family. Madame Ange gave me a fair price for the flowers, not that I knew the going rate for such things, only that my purse was fatter with banknotes and that I had enough to tide me through quite a way ahead.

'If you are in contact with Madame Luel, tell her I will buy everything she cares to send,' Madame Ange said as she paid me. 'Indeed, I'd like to make an exclusive contract with her, if that would be agreeable. Our clientele here is very influential in all walks of life, and it would be well worth her while.'

'Thank you, I will tell her,' I said a little faintly, hiding a smile at the thought of the *feya* becoming, of all things, an exclusive Palume hat-trimmer.

Finette saw me off into the street, and as we shook hands, she said, 'My mother would like to invite you to the restaurant one evening, before she and Papa return home. They thought perhaps this coming Tuesday evening. We will come and fetch you from Madame Pelty's. Would that be agreeable to you?'

'Oh, yes. Thank you. You are all so very kind.'

'No, not at all. It was your generosity in giving my mother your beautiful flowers that will earn me a bonus this month,' she said, smiling. 'Madame Ange is just delighted with me for having asked you to come today.'

'Then I am very pleased indeed to have helped,' I said warmly.

'Oh, by the way, Maman mentioned that you had been asking where Lilac Gardens was. She thought it was a park. But it's –'

'An art gallery. Yes, I found that out. So you've heard of it?'

'Oh, yes, of course. But only because of the painting.'

'What painting?' I asked, confused.

'The one where the model was wearing one of our creations,' she said. 'The painting was called *Summer Morning*. Madame Ange created the hat specially for it.'

'So *Summer Morning* was exhibited at Lilac Gardens?' I asked.

'Yes, after it won the competition. That was before my time. I was still at home then.'

A funny feeling tingled up my spine. 'What competition?'

Her expression was a little puzzled. 'The Imperial Art Prize, of course. The very first one.'

I stared at her, suddenly feeling cold. 'The one Felix Vivian won?'

'Yes. I thought you'd know the name of the painting, as you're from Faustina.'

'I . . . I had forgotten; I was pretty young when it won.'

'It's true Felix Vivian's done nothing since,' said Finette. 'You see, I think *Summer Morning* was his masterpiece, and when it vanished, his heart broke and he just could not take the strain and –'

'It vanished? What do you mean?'

'It was stolen from Lilac Gardens about a month after it won the prize. Madame Ange said it was the perfect crime: there was a guard on it, it was supposedly impossible to steal, and yet it vanished without a trace. Some say magic must have been involved.'

'What do you think?'

Finette shrugged. 'I don't know. It's possible. On the other hand, maybe it was just clever thieves. I'm sorry, Alexandra, but I have to get back to work. Thank you,

232

again, and I look forward to seeing you on Tuesday evening with my parents.'

'Yes, I look forward to it too,' I said cheerfully.

As I walked away, my mind was in a whirl. What I had just learned had put a completely new light on things. That's why Luel had sent me to Lilac Gardens, because that was where a brazen theft had occurred – the theft of a valuable, prize-winning painting. What if it was an inside job? And Ivan had found out? Something startling came to me then and I nearly gasped aloud.

Old Bony had said there was a reason why the sorcerer could turn Felix into a soulless puppet, but not Ivan. And now I knew why – Ivan had resisted and Felix had not.

Felix had allowed himself to be taken over. Not because he was afraid or weak-willed – but *because he was striking a bargain*. I suddenly felt sick and had to sit down quickly on a nearby stone bench. *Oh, he won't die*, Felix had gloated. *That would be too easy*. That was the voice of his master, the voice of the sorcerer. And the fate of that poor fleshy puppet would be the fate of my love, because he had willingly delivered himself into the sorcerer's hands.

Terror shook me, and a pit of black despair seemed to open at my feet. Who did I think I was fooling? I couldn't save Ivan. I wouldn't get to him in time. How paltry my little triumphs had been so far, how useless my investigations! I'd gotten no closer to Ivan and I had no idea where Luel was, I was living on borrowed time in a foreign city and was scaring my family back home. What good was I to anyone or anything?

I took a hold of myself. I really would be no good to anyone or anything if I thought like that. Ivan had delivered himself into his enemy's hands, yes, but before that he had resisted so fiercely that only the worst spell could vanquish him. And even after he had endured three terrible years as a monster, the darkness getting worse with each day and threatening to swamp him, he had resisted. He had fought hard to preserve his spirit, clinging fiercely to the last shreds of his humanity. I could not – would not – believe that that resistance, tempered and toughened by those terrible years, would have now disappeared like snow in the sun.

Dashing away tears, I stood up. I had a job to do. And do it I would, even if hell itself should open before me. There was no point in dodging the question and trying to get at things sideways. No, I would not go back to canvassing candidates for Ivan's identity. I had to confront the evil head-on. I had to go back to Lilac Gardens and demand to be let in.

❦

The art gallery was still closed when I arrived, the street just as quiet. But I could see lights on in the windows above. Someone was home. I banged on the front door, loudly, but there was no reply. Looking up, I saw a curtain twitching and a face appeared in the window: a mean face, pinched and narrow.

'Open up!' I yelled in my thick accent. 'Open up at once!'

The face vanished. A few moments later, the door opened. A man stood there, the owner of the pinched face. The rest of him, thin and stoop-shouldered, with a few lank dark hairs clinging to a domed skull, was no more attractive. But he was smartly, expensively dressed, and in his small black eyes was the expression of one used to command. This was no servant. This was the master of the place, Messir d'Louvat himself.

'How dare you make such a commotion in my street!' he sneered. 'I don't take on women artists and never will, and whoever told you that this performance would attract my attention is going to get a letter from my lawyer. Now vanish at once before I take it into my head to give you the lesson you deserve!'

Thunderstruck by this baffling speech, I could only stare at him.

'Get going before I change my mind!' he hissed, and was about to close the door in my face when I stepped adroitly past him.

'No,' I said, pushing the door open, 'it's not going to be as easy as that.'

'What do you think you –'

'Shut up,' I growled, advancing on him. 'I've found you. And you're going to do as I say.'

'What?' He backed away, fear flickering over his face, and it made me feel good.

'Not so sure of yourself now, are you, d'Louvat? Not like the last time.'

'What?' he repeated weakly. 'I don't know what you're talking about. What last time? I've never clapped eyes on you before.'

I laughed. 'Right. But hear this – what you did to Felix Vivian, you're not going to do to the man I love.'

His eyes widened. 'Eh?'

'I won't allow you to,' I said, a little uncertainly now. Something was wrong. He wasn't reacting in the way I had expected.

He looked at me for a moment, then his face cleared. 'Oh, I see. You're dez Fomer's floozy! I told that fool yesterday not to bother me again with his daubs; they're never going to get anywhere and neither is he. What he does might be good enough for Ashberg or whatever tin-pot little place you come from, but this is Palume. You need to be special to make it here, and he isn't, not by a long shot. And what happened to young Vivian back then was not my fault. He had a brain fever, but then he was never strong, even his father said that and he should know, so I will not have these absurd accusations bandied about by a –'

'Shut up,' I said wildly. 'Just shut up.' Nausea was churning in my throat. I'd made a mistake. This wasn't the sorcerer.

'No, I will not,' he said, drawing himself up. 'You go home and tell your boyfriend that not only can he forget about Lilac Gardens, he can forget about any other gallery in Palume too. I'm going to get the word out that . . .'

But I wasn't listening. There was a feeling crawling up my spine, a feeling like the other night, when I felt as though I was being watched. It wasn't coming from d'Louvat. It was coming from behind a door just beyond him. I could feel it, waves of it, searching me out . . .

'What's behind that door?' I said, cutting him off in full flow.

'Eh? That's the gallery, and if you think you're going to . . .'

But I had already pushed past him, and opened the door.

I opened the door to a big white room, an exhibition room. It was quite bare, with no furniture and no pictures hanging on the wall. And nobody there at all. But the feeling I had of being watched was stronger still.

'Don't you dare . . .' came d'Louvat's fretful voice behind me, but I took no notice. I walked through the room to a door at the far end, and tried it. It was locked.

'Open it,' I said.

'What? You must be –'

'Open it,' I hissed, grabbing the art dealer by his lank hair and yanking so hard that he squealed. 'Open it or I'll show you what we do to crooks in my country.'

'You wouldn't dare,' he said tremulously, but he took a key from his fob pocket and put it in the lock, turning it. 'You're a journalist, not dez Fomer's floozy, aren't you?' he said, looking at me with an ingratiating expression. 'Who told you? It was supposed to be a secret and . . .'

I ignored him and stepped through the open doorway into another room, another exhibition space, smaller than the first but also bare. Except for one thing. Halfway up the far wall was a set of golden brocade curtains, drawn closed. The feeling intensified in me. The watcher had to be hiding behind those curtains.

'Look, I'll give you an exclusive. But only if you keep quiet till tomorrow,' said d'Louvat desperately, as I walked over, snatched the curtains aside and saw . . .

A painting. I'd never seen it before – not as a painting, that is. And yet I knew it. For it showed a sunny walled garden, where climbing white and pink roses rambled on the walls, as well as the more exotic blooms of mimosa and jasmine. There was a little white wrought-iron table and chair in the garden, and a young woman sat there with her back to me. She had a pretty, filmy summer hat on her head, her black hair in long loose ringlets down her back, and her dress was a flurry of pale pink ribbons and snow-white tulle of the same delicate shades as the roses.

It was the exact scene I'd seen in my dream, at the enchanted mansion. Only that had been taken from life, and this was a version in brushstroke and paint. Beautifully, even exquisitely rendered though it was, there was a quality to it that made me feel uneasy, even beyond the fact I'd seen it in a dream.

'*Summer Morning*,' said d'Louvat, and his voice had changed, softening into what could almost be called love. 'Isn't it beautiful?'

'Mmm,' I murmured.

'He was always a competent painter, Felix Vivian. But this – well, who would have thought he had such genius in him? No-one expected him to win that prize, that's for sure. Sebastien d'Roch or Gabriel Fontenoy or Gaetan Theodorus were much more likely contenders, in most people's opinion, including mine. And theirs! But Vivian's work came out of nowhere. He kept it under wraps till the big day and triumphed.' Messir d'Louvat shook his head. 'Hollow victory though, you might say.'

'What do you mean?'

'Well, there are those who say madness enhances talent, but that's sentimental tosh. Madness destroys talent. And he's never done anything worthwhile since.'

'Felix Vivian is mad?'

'Let's say he's touched. Never been quite the same since his breakdown after the painting vanished. Though he had that spell in the asylum, which at least set him back on his feet. That's where he started painting crows.'

'Crows?' I echoed, with a shiver.

'Yes, it's become his thing. Dull as ditchwater and no artistic merit whatever,' the art dealer said scornfully, 'but it keeps him calm, I suppose. Travels all over the place painting the wretched things. As if a crow in Faustina was any different to one in Palume.' His gaze returned to the painting. 'Anyway, what really matters is that this has returned to us at last. It may be Vivian's only work of genius, but most artists would die happy knowing they'd created it!'

'How – how did you get it back?'

'It just turned up on the doorstep. Maybe the thieves had an attack of conscience. Who cares? It came back, that's what matters.' There was no enmity in his voice now. He seemed genuinely happy.

Shaken, I stared at the picture. When I'd told Ivan what I'd seen in the dream, when I'd asked him if it was his dream or memory, Ivan had put his head in his hands and said, 'God forgive me. Yes, you are right.' Why had he said that? I couldn't understand it. Surely he hadn't stolen the picture out of artistic spite? No. It had to have something to do with the girl. I remembered my feeling that something bad had happened to her. I remembered Rosette in my story. With an effort, I said, 'The girl in the picture. Where is she now?'

'Mam'selle Durant? Why, she's at home with her father. There's double cause for celebration at the Durant residence, of course.'

Durant. I'd heard that name before, and recently, too. Durant. Yes. Last night Claire had mentioned something about a Mam'selle Durant's father being rescued from brigands and becoming very ill. 'I hope he's getting better. It must have been very worrying for her, to wait so long for news of him.'

To my astonishment, d'Louvat winked. 'Makes a good story for the press, I agree. Truth is, she'd given him up for dead and got on with her life long ago. She's a sensible girl.'

Sensible be damned. I thought she sounded cold-blooded.

'Funny thing, isn't it,' he went on musingly, 'that he turned up out of the blue pretty much at the same time as the painting. There was a rumour flying around at the time that he'd been involved in the theft, as revenge for Vivian winning the prize.'

'Why would Messir Durant want to do that?' I asked, confused.

'Eh?' He stared at me. 'What's Messir Durant got to do with it? I'm talking about Gabriel Fontenoy.'

All the blood rushed from my face. I gasped. 'What? It's him . . .?'

'We don't know yet if it was Fontenoy who took the painting or why it came back when he did,' said d'Louvat, misunderstanding me. 'And we can't ask him any questions about it for quite a while, because he's still unconscious. It's lucky his care has been taken in hand by the most eminent brain physician in the land, Dr Golpech, the same man who cured Vivian, and who I understand from Durant has devised a revolutionary new treatment to try to cure Fontenoy.'

My knees buckled. 'Oh my God.'

'What on earth's the matter?' he said, alarmed.

'Nothing. I just . . . The address,' I managed to say. 'Where is the Durant residence? I must . . . I must speak to them.'

'They don't like journalists,' said d'Louvat. 'You'd not get past the first . . .' He saw my expression and shrugged. 'It is in the Tricorn district, but if you think you . . .'

But I'd stopped listening, and fled.

I took a cab this time. 'I'll give you double the fare if you get me there quickly,' I gasped to the driver.

'It's a fair trot from here, but I know a back way that'll be quicker than the boulevards, which will be choked at this time of the evening,' the cab-driver said unflappably. He was as good as his word, and as we sped through the backstreets I felt as though I were hovering in some strange nightmarish state of numbness, my mind repeating the same things over and over, my feelings fogged and frozen.

Ivan's real name was Gabriel Fontenoy. He was in the Durants' house, where a girl he'd dreamed about during his long ordeal lived. A girl who, according to Claire's newspaper article, had never given up hope, but who, according to d'Louvat, had long ago given him up for dead. A girl he'd probably been in love with. A girl who had a prior claim on him and who even now was probably at his bedside, hoping that he'd recover, while he lay insensible, at the mercy of a brain physician who had supposedly cured Felix Vivian. A brain physician. *The absolutely perfect cover for a sorcerer.*

I had to warn them. Whatever it cost me, I had to tell them the truth. I had to make them understand that whatever lies the doctor was peddling, the young man was in the gravest danger from his attentions. At least he wasn't in the asylum, like Vivian had been. So there was some hope. But I had to make the Durants realise that they had to help him. I had to help defeat Dr Golpech, whatever it took, even if it broke my heart to think it might be Celeste Durant whom Ivan – no, Gabriel – would turn to afterwards.

Gabriel. He was still Ivan in my heart and in my memory. I saw him in those last moments, in the mirror, his lips murmuring my name, his eyes full of such love and grief. The memory tore at me. I could never stop loving him. But when he was safe, when he was recovered, who would he choose? Me or the girl he'd loved before, with whom he shared a history, a home, a language? If I really loved him, all I should want was his happiness, even if it didn't include me.

The Durants' house was huge, set behind tall, imposing gates in a distant part of the city, where houses with gardens were the norm. The cab-driver let me off outside the closed gates, and as I paid him, he said, 'I hope you have an appointment. They don't let just anyone in.'

'I have an appointment,' I said firmly. 'I'm from Madame Ange, the milliner. I have to show Mam'selle Durant some new designs. It's all been arranged.'

He raised an eyebrow. 'I see. Very well. But it's a long walk back to the centre and cabs don't often ply the streets here. Would you like me to wait for you, just in case?'

'It's quite all right,' I said. 'Thank you.'

'As you wish.' He lifted his hat. 'Goodbye, Mam'selle, and good luck.' And with that the cab left at a brisk trot, the sound of the horse's hooves ringing on the cobbled pavement till they had turned the corner and disappeared.

I glanced up and down the street. Nothing stirred. I looked up at the house and could see the lights were on. Taking a deep breath, I reached for the bell on the gate, and rang.

Twenty-Seven

The peals of the bell had only just died on the air when a big burly man came striding out of the shadows towards me.

'No-one admitted without appointment,' he said. With his large frame, huge hands and small, watchful eyes, he looked like a formidable guard dog, even had I not glimpsed the knife at his belt. The Durants were clearly expecting some kind of trouble.

'There was no time to make one,' I said, trying to keep my voice calm. 'I'm on an urgent errand.'

'The doctor told us the fresh medicine supplies wouldn't arrive till tomorrow morning,' said the man sharply.

'Oh, I'm not from the doctor,' I said quickly, thinking that at least I knew now that the doctor wasn't actually here. 'I've come from Messir d'Louvat. From Lilac Gardens art gallery.'

'Why didn't Messir d'Louvat come himself?'

'Because he's had to go to the police. There was a break-in at the gallery.'

The small eyes widened. 'What?'

'Please, let's not waste time. I must speak to the Durants at once.'

'Wait here. I will fetch Messir Durant,' the man said, and he strode off.

He returned shortly after, with another man. Tall, distinguished-looking, with light brown eyes in a tanned, strong face, thick pepper-and-salt hair and a neatly trimmed beard, he looked to be in his forties and wore a well-cut tweed suit. He surveyed me appraisingly. 'I didn't know d'Louvat had such a charming young assistant.' His voice was mellow and deep.

I coloured. 'I'm not his assistant, Messir. My name is ter Zhaber, Alexandra ter Zhaber, and I'm just hired help for the exhibition tomorrow.'

'By your accent, you're Faustinian,' he said, sharply.

'Yes, Messir, I am. And I'd just arrived at Lilac Gardens on Messir d'Louvat's request, to start getting things ready, when he came rushing out in a terrible state.'

'It was a break-in, you say?'

'Yes. Someone got into the gallery and . . .' I shot a meaningful glance towards the imperturbable guard. Durant understood.

'Remy,' he said, 'please open the gate and let the young lady in. We will need to discuss this in private.'

Remy reached over to the gatepost and pressed something. There was a hiss of released steam, the heavy iron gates swung open, and I walked through, the gates shutting behind me with a hollow clang.

I'd done it. I was in. Now I had to somehow persuade the Durants to let me see Ivan – Gabriel. I could not bear to tell them my story until I had seen him with my own eyes, and proved to myself that he was alive.

'Apologies for the reception,' said Messir Durant, as we went up the stairs and into the house, 'but we are living in strange times, and I've told Remy to be careful.' He ushered me into a large, well-lit hall and down a long corridor hung at intervals with striking, light-filled photographs of exotic lands, animals and people. I remembered reading in *Modern Art and Artists* that Gabriel Fontenoy's godfather was a celebrated explorer. But what the book hadn't said was that he was also a talented photographer, for the bottom-right of each picture was signed 'Edmond Durant'.

He turned, saw me looking at them, and smiled. 'You like my photographs, Mam'selle?'

'Oh, yes. They are most interesting.' I pointed to a picture of a magnificent white wolf captured in mid-pounce. 'And dangerous to take, too!'

'Oh, well, you just have to know what you're doing,' he said with a shrug.

'It must be an interesting life you lead, Messir,' I said.

'Oh, yes, it is,' he said, 'but then I have never been one for the little life. Adventure and risk and discovery – that is my lifeblood. Staying at home and doing the things everyone else does has always bored me.'

We had arrived at a quiet, book-lined study. Durant motioned me to a chair, and after closing the door, sat behind the desk. Above the desk, I noticed, was a rather formal oil portrait of a young woman with a small child on her lap. His wife and daughter, presumably. There were also a couple of other paintings: one of a house set in a woodland scene, the other a still life. Though they were quite small, almost miniature, they drew the eye at once, with their vivid, striking composition.

Durant shot me a sharp glance. 'Now then, Mam'selle, what's this about a break-in at the gallery?'

I smiled winningly and took my notebook and pencil out from my bag. 'I have to tell you, Messir, that was only a pretext.'

'I beg your pardon?' He stiffened, his eyes now cold.

'I mean, Messir d'Louvat told me you didn't like journalists, but I had to ... take the opportunity to to see if I could –'

'You're a journalist?' he echoed, cutting me off.

'Yes. I ... I work for a small ladies' magazine in Faustina, called *The Mirror*. I'm supposed to be covering some fashion stories, but I –' I put on my sweetest smile – 'well, to be frank, Messir Durant, I heard a rumour about the show at Lilac Gardens and couldn't resist going there. Messir d'Louvat wasn't very happy at first, but he allowed me to see the painting, in the end.'

'I can see that he might,' said Durant, raising an eyebrow. 'You have a most persuasive manner, Mam'selle. So you saw *Summer Morning*. What did you think of it?'

'It's beautiful,' I said sincerely. 'Really beautiful.' I gestured at the other paintings. 'I notice you have some fine pictures here, too. Are they also by Felix Vivian?'

'No, they are by my godson Gabriel.' A little tremor went through me. 'Except the portrait, of course,' he went on. 'That was painted well before his time.' He gave me a searching look. 'Now, Mam'selle, this article of yours. What is it you want to know about *Summer Morning*?'

'Actually, Messir,' I said hastily, 'I was very much hoping to interview your daughter about how she feels now the painting's been found. You see, if I'm to get this story into *The Mirror*, I have to look at it from an angle my editor might like, you understand?'

'Ah, of course, a woman's angle,' he said with a scornful smile. It stung, but I pretended to take no notice.

'Precisely,' I said brightly. 'Your daughter's story would inspire our readers. It's so romantic – the story of the daughter of a famous explorer, who inspires a beautiful painting, and whose long-lost love returns from the dead!'

'It's a bit late to break that story,' he said impassively. 'It's been in the magazines already. I'm sure people are quite tired of it.'

'Oh, no, Messir. Readers can't get enough of it. And my angle will be different. I know people will love it. Please, if you would just allow me to speak to Mam'selle Durant, I would be most grateful. I am trying to make my name, do you see, and this would help so much.'

'Oho, an ambitious little minx,' he said. 'Well, then, if I give you permission, you must promise to show me your story before you print it.'

'I promise, absolutely,' I said fervently.

'Very well. You may speak with Celeste. But I warn you, she may be a little short with you. It's been quite an ordeal for her, all this.'

'I will be very diplomatic and discreet, Messir, I promise. You must have been very happy to have your godson return safely.'

'I was more than happy,' he said quietly. 'I can hardly express what a joy it was to know he was alive, even if he is not well.'

'Yes . . . and what about the treatment that Dr Golpech is using? I heard it was very . . . radical.'

'Golpech knows what he's doing,' said Durant brusquely. 'His methods are unorthodox but I trust him. He'll do the best for Gabriel, I know. Lucky my godson had the sense even in his disorientated state to make his way to Golpech's surgery, or we might have lost him there and then.'

I stared at him. 'I don't understand.'

'Golpech found him on his doorstep one morning. He was in a terrible state, and Golpech only got a little from him before he lapsed into an unconsciousness he hasn't come out of yet.'

'But how –'

'How did he get there? We don't know yet. We're making inquiries.'

I nearly told him then, but thought better of it. I had to see Gabriel. 'I understand Dr Golpech runs an asylum,' I said, 'so why –'

'Why isn't he being looked after there? My dear young lady, he is my godson. He is better off here. Besides, he needs complete security and quiet and we can provide that here much better than in that noisy place.'

'And Dr Golpech agrees?'

'I didn't give him the choice,' he said impatiently.

Thank heavens for the arrogance of the rich and famous, I thought. It had given Ivan a slim chance. 'Do you expect to –'

'Look, I don't have the time for more questions.' He rang a little bell, and a servant appeared.

'Please take Mam'selle ter Zhaber to my daughter's rooms,' Durant said. 'Tell Celeste I have given my consent to an interview.' He turned to me. 'You have ten minutes, Mam'selle, no more. We are expecting the doctor in half an hour and you will have to leave well before that.'

'Of course, Messir. I will, I promise. Thank you so much.'

'Yes, yes,' he said absently. I could see he'd already dismissed me from his mind. If he only knew, I thought as I followed the servant, if he only knew my real story, he'd soon change his tune! But now was not the time to tell him.

Both times I'd seen Celeste Durant – in the dream and in the painting – it had been from behind. I'd never seen her face. Now I saw she was as exquisite as a porcelain doll, with a mass of jet-black ringlets framing an oval face of flawless peaches and cream, big blue eyes under a long curling sweep of black eyelash, her lips a pouting pink, a flash of pearl-white teeth visible within. She wore a silk dress that matched the colour of her eyes and showed off her figure to great advantage, and I immediately felt utterly plain and frumpish beside her.

Then she opened her mouth and the spell was broken. 'So you want an interview. Why should I give you one? I've never heard of your magazine. And I don't care for Faustinians.' Her voice was petulant, dismissive.

'Please, Mam'selle,' I said humbly, though inwardly I seethed at her tone, 'I would be so honoured if you would let me ask you questions. You are the model for a painting that is really famous in my country. And yes, it is beautiful, but it hardly does you justice.'

Her face softened. 'Why, that is very kind. Is it true?'

'Sorry?' I said, thrown.

'That Felix's painting is famous in your country?'

'It certainly is. It is a great work of art. But more importantly, it captures the very light of your beauty. In fact, in Faustina, the subject means more to people than the artist, you know.' The flattering, lying words felt unbearably slimy on my tongue, but they did the trick. She beamed.

'So I am famous in Faustina?'

'Oh, yes, Mam'selle, you are. And now, with the painting back and the return of Gabriel Fontenoy, you will be even more famous. It is not just your beauty people will focus on. It is also the inspiring story of your womanly courage. Please allow me to tell it.'

I felt nauseous even saying such things. But she was obviously delighted.

'Oh, very well,' she said, with an unconvincing attempt at casualness. 'If you remember this is my story, not his,' she added.

'Excuse me?' I said, confused.

'Oh, it's Gabriel this and Gabriel that; it's as if they forget that it was me who suffered the most!'

I gaped at her. She saw my expression and snapped, 'Well, it's true. I was the one left behind – to wait and wonder. How do you think that felt?'

My belly was churning. I wanted to slap her till her ears rang, to yell, 'Do you have any idea, you selfish cow, what poor Gabriel has gone through?' But it would have been pointless. She didn't know. And even if she had, it would hardly have penetrated her self-absorption. I decided instantly that I didn't want to tell her the truth.

I said smoothly, 'I can understand how difficult it must have been for you. And now, too, when you have to keep watch at his bedside and help the doctor to –'

'Do you think I am some kind of servant?' she said haughtily. 'I most certainly do not help the doctor. I wouldn't even if the doctor would want me to, which he doesn't.'

My heart was racing. 'I've heard that the treatment advocated by the doctor is quite radical.'

Celeste shrugged. 'He says it's the only way to pull Gabriel out of whatever brain fever he is in. Though there hasn't been much progress so far.'

'Is it possible – would it be possible – to see him?'

It was her turn to stare. 'What? You want to see the doctor?'

'No, not the doctor – Gabriel Fontenoy.' I hurried on. 'Just for background, you understand. It makes such a difference if one can write at firsthand. I would of course be focusing the article about how hard it is for you, remembering what he was, and now what he is – hoping against hope that he will get better, but feeling discouraged at times, saying if only –'

'Mmm. I like that,' she said. 'That's a good way of putting it. Very well. No harm showing you, I suppose. Just a quick glimpse, mind. Dr Golpech is due soon and I'm sure he would be tiresome about it if he knew.'

I nodded. Yes, I'm sure the good doctor would be tiresome about it, I thought. 'It must have been quite a shock,' I said, as I followed her out. 'I mean, when you found out about Messir Fontenoy turning up on Dr Golpech's doorstep.'

'Yes, of course it was a shock. We don't know exactly how it happened because he didn't get time to tell the doctor before he passed out; he had only managed to say he'd escaped from his kidnappers and that they were Ruvenyan.'

'What?'

'Yes, outrageous, isn't it! Our President is, of course, outraged that such a thing could happen on our own soil to one of our citizens, and he's sent a stiff letter to the Ruvenyan Ambassador, who denies all knowledge of it, the liar. But what can you expect from such a barbarous country?'

Anger rose in me but I tamped it down firmly. 'You say it happened on your own soil? Do you mean . . .?'

'Yes. He was in Palume when it happened. Back then we thought that he'd just gone off in a huff. He'd been behaving badly ever since Felix won that prize. He was jealous of him winning, but angry too that he hadn't even known I'd been sitting for him. Felix said it had to be a secret because he knew Gabriel would be jealous.'

My heart lurched unpleasantly. 'About how he vanished – didn't you suspect something had happened to him?'

'No. He took off one day without a word. His old nurse went with him. I couldn't stand her. She always stuck to him like glue. She was one of the reasons we didn't worry at first. Later, when we still heard nothing from him, Papa hired an investigator. But we discovered nothing.'

'What about his nurse?' I asked.

'What about her?'

'You said she always stuck to him like glue. Where is she now?'

'The kidnappers most likely killed her. How should I know? She's unimportant, anyway.'

I took a deep breath. 'Don't you think it's odd that the kidnappers never asked for a ransom from Gabriel's family?'

'Gabriel's an orphan. His parents died when he was twelve, in a boating accident. They had no money, and Papa is his godfather, so that's why he took him in and let that ghastly old woman stay here.'

'But why wouldn't they ask your father for a ransom, then?' I persisted.

'Who knows what goes on in the heads of people like that? Stupid as well as barbarous. Maybe they just wanted a slave. I've heard they still keep slaves in Ruvenya.'

'You are mistaken,' I said tightly. 'And in any case, that's hardly a credible motive.'

'Who knows?' Celeste shrugged. 'All we do know is that they took Gabriel and held him captive until he managed to escape.'

She was remarkably incurious, I thought. But then I suppose self-centred people usually are. Nothing matters unless it relates directly to them.

We had reached another wing of the house, which did not look as if it was used by the family. There was little furniture and what there was of it was shrouded in dust-clothes. We went down one corridor, then another and finally down a small flight of stairs to another level, through another set of doors, till at last we came to a room that was completely dark. However, it was a quality of dark I could not understand, until I touched one of the walls and discovered it not to be plaster or brick, as you might expect, but a smooth slippery surface that reminded me of glass.

'Papa normally uses this room for his photography,' came Celeste's voice out of the darkness. 'Other people have darkrooms; he has a light-room.' I couldn't see her – I couldn't see anything – and yet I was aware of something just beyond us, a faint emanation that made the hair on the back of my neck stand up.

Light came on, suddenly. I gasped. For we were standing in a kind of antechamber, looking through a glass wall into the strangest room I had ever seen. It was made entirely of glass. The wall we were looking through was clear, but the other three were translucent interlocking panels, each panel imprinted with the black outline of an image – faces, flowers, animals, landscapes – in a style that was like a shadow of the photographs I'd seen in the hall, as though the walls were giant photographic negative plates. But strange as it was, that wasn't what drew my eye and caused the breath to thicken in my throat.

For in the middle of the glass room, illuminated by a silver light that shone down from the top of the chamber like an eerie artificial moon, was a plain wooden bed.

And on the bed lay a young man as pale and still as though he were a stone effigy in a church. The impression was reinforced by the silver mesh skullcap that covered the top of his head, and the drape of the bedcovers, which under the eerie light, appeared like carved stone. His eyes were closed, and the light bleached everything of its true colour, so that even the rich tones of his red-brown hair were faded. In that strange glass bubble, surrounded by those weird negative images, it was as though he were floating between reality and dream, and for one dazed, terrifying instant, I thought I *was* dreaming him, and that I must soon wake up.

Twenty-Eight

After only a moment, my heart jerked back to life, my blood tingling, my limbs shaking with the thrill and grief of it. Oh dear God, it *was* him. It was Ivan. Gabriel. My love. After all my long search, there he lay. So close yet so far. I yearned so much to touch him I thought I must faint from the fierce pain of it. As if from a great distance I heard myself say, 'Are you sure he's breathing?'

'Of course. See the cap? It monitors his breathing. If he wasn't breathing, it would go black. It also keeps the flow of *antirentum* irrigating his brain,' Celeste said, in the tone of someone repeating a tedious lesson.

'*Antirentum?*'

She waved a hand. 'It's Dr Golpech's brand-new medicine. A miracle cure, he calls it.'

'That's very ... interesting. A miracle cure! I think our readers would be fascinated to know more about it.'

'Well, I don't know any more than what I've told you already. It's all very hush-hush.'

'I see. Mam'selle, it's a most extraordinary room. How do you get in? I see no way in or out.'

She pointed to a spot on the wall, which to the casual eye looked simply like a slight imperfection in the glass. 'I press my thumb to that and the door opens. You can't see it otherwise, because it seals perfectly. Only if you have the right thumbprint can you get in. And only three people have that: Papa, the doctor and me. It's one of Papa's inventions. Don't ask me how it works.'

'That's amazing,' I said, sincerely impressed. 'Does that mean that no-one else can go in?'

'Only if they're accompanied by one of us three.'

My pulse raced. 'Can I go in, with you? I would very much like to look a bit closer at the . . .'

'No,' Celeste said firmly. 'The doctor's due any moment. We'll have to go now.' And she reached out to the light lever on the wall.

'No,' I said desperately. 'Please don't turn it off yet. I need to take it all in.' I couldn't tear my eyes away from him, from where he lay so still. I couldn't bear the thought of what was happening in there. I had to get in there, I had to – whatever it took, whatever it cost. If I could only get in, I thought wildly, I could save him. Somehow I'd get him out of the room that now seemed like nothing so much as a gigantic glass coffin.

'Right, I think you've seen your fill,' Celeste said impatiently. 'The doctor will be here soon, and you'd better not be seen around here; he doesn't like people gawking at his patient.' She pulled the light lever down, plunging us into darkness once more.

But I'd had an idea. An idea born of desperation and longing. As we went out of the antechamber, I said, 'Listen, I can pay you to let me in. I can pay you well.'

Celeste laughed. 'My father's one of the wealthiest men in Champaine. I have all the money I need.'

'I didn't mean money,' I said. 'I meant something much more unusual.'

'What?'

'Something rare and amazing, which no-one else in Palume will have and that everyone will envy, I can guarantee you that.'

'What is it?' she snapped, her eyes alight with sharp curiosity. 'You must tell me.'

'I can't tell you, or it won't work.'

'Something magical?' Celeste said, her eyes narrowing. 'Papa doesn't like magic. He says it's dangerous, and he doesn't want me to have anything to do with it.'

If he only knew he'd let in the worst sort of magic with Golpech, much worse than anything he could have seen in far-off lands, I thought. What would he say then? 'Yet he invents a light-room that can only be opened by a thumbprint. That's a kind of magic, some people would say.'

'He'd say such people are stupid. He'd say that's just pure science,' Celeste said, and the scornful way in which she spoke told me I was in with a chance.

'But you don't feel the same way about magic as he does,' I hazarded.

'I don't see why I can't try it. Everyone else does! People I know have their fortunes told and buy little love philtres and have been given amusing magical baubles, like my friend who has a ring that changes from diamond to ruby to emerald in a flash, or another friend who has a pair of silver shoes that make her a perfect dancer. Where's the harm in that?'

'Where indeed?' I echoed.

'This thing you have – is it like that?'

'Very much so, only better. None of your friends could have anything like it.'

'I want to see it,' Celeste said, her eyes alight with greed.

'I don't have it on me,' I lied. 'I'll have to fetch it first. But it's worth waiting for, I can promise you that . . .'

'You better be right,' she said, and I knew then that she'd taken the bait, 'because if it isn't, I'm going to have you thrown out and thrashed into the bargain, do you understand?'

'I understand,' I said impassively. What did I care about her threats? She was less than an ant to me. Even the thought that she'd once been in Gabriel's dreams mattered not a jot any more. All that mattered was the knowledge that my love was here and that come hell or high water I was going to get him out of that glass coffin and bring him back to true life.

'Don't come to the front door. There's a walled garden at the back of the house,' she said. 'You can reach it from the next street. Come to the garden door in –' she looked at her watch – 'in three hours' time, at ten o'clock, and I'll let you in. Understood?'

'Perfectly.'

Shortly after, Celeste had the servant escort me out, and I left the house without seeing Messir Durant again. I could only hope that between now and ten o'clock he wouldn't find out what his daughter had promised to do and tell the doctor; I could also only hope that in that time Celeste would not change her flighty mind. And most of all I hoped that my gamble would pay off, and Luel's gifts would not let me down.

I had no need to go back to Argent Lane, for I had the box in my pocket. But I couldn't stay too close to the Durants' house whilst the doctor was in the vicinity, in case somehow he got a whiff of the magic. So I walked away from the house, down one street after the next until finally I came to a little fenced park on the edge of a square that had a tall clock in its centre. The park was deserted and not very well-lit; I didn't feel very comfortable being there, but I didn't have much choice, for this kind of quiet residential area offered very little in the way of public spaces where I might have passed unnoticed amidst a crowd. No little cafes, no shops, no theatres, just this empty, shadowed bit of greenery, benches and a couple of statues of historical figures, caught in a moment of action, like stone photographs.

Stone photographs . . . I shivered suddenly, thinking of Gabriel, lying under that weird silver light in that strange glass room, and how I'd thought he looked as still as stone. What *was* that poison coursing through his veins? What was it doing to him? *A miracle cure* – the Durants might think the aim was to heal Gabriel, but I knew it was not. Something terrible was being done to my love's mind, something which would turn him into a puppet, like poor Felix Vivian – a puppet that the sorcerer Golpech could work through, for his own purposes. Felix Vivian was a pawn now, a soulless tool, but he had once been a good painter. A more than good painter. *Summer Morning* showed that, quite clearly.

My skin prickled as something struck me. An artist's picture is like a writer's story: it carries a voice. *Summer Morning* had spoken to me. It had made me uneasy. And it wasn't just about coming face to face with the scene in my dream. It was something about the painting itself, some disturbing quality. And even *before* I saw the painting, I'd felt it. I'd felt a presence. Something watching me. Something whispering in my mind. Something that disturbed me, that raised the hairs on the back of my neck. What if it was the same thing as when I had looked into Felix Vivian's clear blue eyes and seen another presence? What if *Summer Morning* also had a presence behind it? For what if Felix Vivian had not naturally evolved from a good, competent painter into one of magical, unusual genius, but had instead made a dark bargain with a sorcerer?

It made a dreadful kind of sense. If Gabriel had found out the secret behind *Summer Morning*, and threatened to tell the authorities, then that might have been enough motive. Because a spell that enslaves your spirit is regarded with great horror, and its creator would be

263

severely punished, in the same way as the creator of an *abartyen* spell. Perhaps it could even explain the theft of the painting: Golpech himself tying up loose ends, removing it from sight while he searched for Gabriel, who had inexplicably vanished after the *abartyen* spell was cast. Luel had thwarted him there, by whisking her lord away . . .

Luel. Where are you, Luel? I need you! I took the box out from my pocket and looked at the things within: the comb, the handkerchief, the tin of sweets and Old Bony's single hair.

I took out the handkerchief and said, 'This is for Celeste,' and shook it. Instantly, to my delight, into my lap shimmered a gauzy blue scarf threaded with gold embroidery in the shape of flowers with tiny jewels in their centre. It was enchantingly lovely, exquisitely made and absolutely covetable.

I took up the comb. 'Again, for Celeste,' I said, and ran it through my hair. A flower swirled down at once, only this time it didn't fall softly, like the silk flowers had. No, it fell with the weight of stone, for this flower was carved out of a single piece of white opal with shifting colours inside it like the fires of the earth.

These were gifts for a rich girl, not the humble pretty things I had received. Magic that fitted its recipient . . . Which would Celeste prefer? I had to give her the choice. The tin of sweets would be of no interest to her, I was sure. But it was probably a good idea for me to take some more, for though I was still some way from the twenty-four-hour deadline for each, it was better to be on the safe side. I swallowed half a Faustinian sweet and half a Champainian one, and then I had to somehow endure the three hours till I could return to the Durant residence. I paced round and round that wretched park more times than I cared to count, each strike of the clock making my heart beat faster.

I was in the street at the back of the house well before ten o'clock. The stone wall of the garden faced me: it rose steep and high, and was topped by jagged bits of broken glass that shimmered under the moon like lethal icicles. There was a door of metal, set tightly into the wall, and firmly locked. Any idea I might have entertained of getting back into the Durants' house over the wall – if Celeste did not keep her promise – quickly faded away. As for going through the front door, well, there was still Remy to get past. And after that, Celeste's father. And if she had told him what had happened, I'd never be allowed in again. How ironic that it was in his house that the darkest sorcery was being practised, under his very nose!

I could tell him the truth, of course. But I hesitated. To him, Golpech was an eminent doctor and someone to be trusted, who was trying to make his godson well. And me? Well, I was a liar who had entered their home under false pretences, who had inveigled his airheaded daughter into showing me the glass room and who sought to corrupt her with promises of magic. *I* would look like the enemy, not Golpech. No, I had to rely on myself and my own resources.

I paced up and down, up and down, waiting, waiting for what seemed like another age before I heard the lock rattle and the door open silently on oiled hinges.

'You're here,' Celeste said unnecessarily. She was wrapped in a magnificent cloak with a sable-lined hood. In the moonlight her porcelain face glimmered in the shadow of the dark fur.

'Yes. Has the doctor gone?'

'Left half an hour ago. And Papa's gone to bed. All's quiet. Did you bring it?'

'Of course.'

'Then show it to me now,' she ordered, 'before I take you any further.'

I took the gauzy scarf out of my pocket and held it in one hand, with the opal flower in the other. 'Choose.'

'What? I don't understand. Are these what you've brought me? I thought . . .'

'Have you ever seen anything quite like these?' I said, interrupting her. 'Look at them closely.'

She did, and I saw her eyes widen as she took in the little jewels on the embroidery, and the flash of colours deep in the opal. 'No, I haven't seen anything like them. But my father is rich and he goes to exotic lands. He could probably find me things like this somewhere.'

'No,' I said, shaking my head, 'he most assuredly could not. For no human hand created these. They have come from pure *fei* magic.' *Fei* was *feya* in the tongue of Champaine.

'How . . .' Her eyes were huge now and her tongue was unconsciously passing over her lips.

I had taken the handkerchief and comb out of the box and put them in my pocket before I came into the garden. Now I pulled them out. I handed her the comb and said, 'Comb your hair.'

'What? With this cheap thing?' she said with great scorn.

'Trust me. Do it and you'll see,' I said, struggling to keep my voice steady, and hoping with all my heart that the magic wouldn't forsake me.

It didn't. As Celeste ran the comb through her hair, something that flashed a brilliant white fell out of her black ringlets and dropped at her feet. She picked it up and uttered a cry of sheer delight. 'Oh, how beautiful!'

It was a brooch shaped like a white daisy, carved from a single large pearl, each petal rimmed with tiny diamonds that gleamed in the moonlight. She looked at me, her eyes aglow.

'I told you,' I said cheerfully. 'You've never seen anything like it.'

Luel was here, I thought. Nearby. Working her magic in secret, for reasons best known to herself.

I looked around quickly, but there was nobody in the walled garden except Celeste and me. There was nowhere Luel might hide, only bare trees, a still fountain and some moss-eaten old statues. The garden didn't look much like the one in *Summer Morning*, not at this time of the night or the year, but it was still clearly the setting. If Luel was about, then she was keeping herself invisible and . . .

'What about the other?' Celeste's voice made me start. 'Eh?'

'So I've seen what the comb can do. What about the handkerchief? I want to see what it can do,' she said impatiently.

'Shake it then,' I said, handing it to her and taking back the comb, 'and you'll see.'

Celeste shook the handkerchief – and there was a pair of the prettiest, softest dancing slippers you ever saw, in pale blue satin with golden buckles. Taking off her own shoes, she slipped them on. 'Why, they fit me perfectly,' she said in wonder.

'Of course. That's how magic should work,' I said. 'It fits you perfectly. If it's good magic, that is. But bad magic makes *you* fit into *it*. There's the difference.'

She stared at me. 'How do you know so much about it?'

'Oh, you get around, in my job,' I said hastily. 'You hear things.'

'Where did you get these from?'

'They were given to me as a gift. That's all you need to know.' I took back the handkerchief. 'So – now you've seen what each can do, which do you choose?'

She shot me a sideways glance. 'Both.'

'What?'

'I want both,' she said levelly, her eyes narrowed. 'Or I don't let you in.'

My heart sank. 'But that's not what we agreed to.'

'You either do as I say or you don't go in. And then I'll go to my father and tell him you've been trying to bribe me.'

I looked at her. Her eyes glinted with a nasty light. I knew that if I thwarted her she'd do just as she said. But

I also knew that the need to possess the magic had taken a powerful hold of her mind so that I was still in a strong position. I didn't really want to give Celeste both things, but more than anything I wanted to get into that room. 'Very well, you can have both.' She stretched out an eager hand, and I took a step back. 'Wait a moment. One now, the other *after* you've let me into the room and not interfered.'

Celeste stared at me suspiciously. For a moment I feared that caution would overcome greed. Then she nodded, and held out her hand again. 'Agreed. If you throw in the shawl and the opal rose too.'

I shrugged. 'As you wish.' I gave her the handkerchief, and she pocketed it, scooped up all her things, and gestured for me to follow.

As we went back through the dark, silent house, down long corridors, I was attempting to fix the way in my head. I needed to try to understand the layout of this house in case anything went wrong – her father awakening, the doctor returning, servants prowling about – and I had to hide till we could get into the glass room. But nothing happened, and soon we were back in the dark antechamber. Celeste pulled down the light lever and the room sprang into view. Ivan was as motionless as before, but it seemed to me that the helmet shone with a much brighter glow.

'Did the doctor increase the dose of *antirentum* by any chance?' I asked.

'Yes, he did. What's it to you?'

'I'm just interested. Now, are you going to open up or not?'

'Impatience,' she snapped. 'Why you think it's so interesting to stare at someone lying there like a log, I can't imagine.'

That she could describe the man she had grown up with, that she was supposed to be in love with, in such a way sent a shiver of repulsion down my spine. Cold selfishness like that was a form of madness, I thought, a soul-sickness. Felix Vivian might be a hollow shell because of black magic, but Celeste was hollow by nature, without any help from sorcerers.

'I don't suppose you can,' I said tightly. 'Now, if you want the comb, enough delay.'

Celeste snorted and pressed her thumb to the knot in the glass. Instantly, the panel in front of us slid open and we stepped through. As soon as we were inside, the panel closed behind us, sealing us into a quiet, still space that felt completely cut off from outside. For the wall we'd just come through had an odd feature: from the outside, you could look through it, but from the inside it was completely opaque, and the other walls with their interlocking image-imprinted panels dazed the eye so that you could not see through them either. And the light made you feel as though you'd stepped into another world, of moonlight and shadows and shifting images – a cold, timeless box of light floating somewhere yet nowhere.

'There,' she whispered. 'You've got what you wanted. Now give me the comb.'

'No,' I said, my eyes fixed on the still figure on the bed. 'Not till I'm ready.' I started to walk towards the bed.

'What are you doing?' she said uneasily.

'No interference,' I said tightly. 'Remember?'

'You can't go near him,' she snapped. 'It isn't allowed. Come on, get out.'

'Shut up,' I said brutally, rounding on her. 'You think that's all the magic I have, those baubles I gave you? If you interfere, I've got something much more powerful, something that is very dangerous indeed.'

Her eyes widened with shock. 'I don't believe you.'

'Really?' I said, pulling Luel's box out of my pocket, and taking out the tin of sweets. 'You see these? Just one of these is enough to cause a storm of poison gas that will overwhelm you at once. Not me, mind, just you.'

Her lips were white. 'No . . . you can't . . .'

'You want to test it?' I asked, holding up the lozenge in my hand. 'You've seen the magic of the other things. You really want to test this one?'

She shook her head. 'Who . . . who are you?' she whispered. 'What do you want?'

'I'm someone who can make things very unpleasant for you,' I said brusquely. 'And as for what I want, it is that you go and stand over there –' and I pointed to the wall we had come in through – 'turn your back to me and put your fingers in your ears. And don't you dare move till I tell you to. Understood?'

If looks could kill, I'd have been stone dead. But I didn't care what she thought or how she looked, only that Celeste did as I'd told her. And she did, without another murmur.

I approached the bed, breathing hard. Oh, he was so still, so very still. Even this close to him, his skin had that waxwork look of the dead, his features fixed into an expression of bland impassivity.

I held out a trembling hand and gently touched his forehead. It was icy cold, and the chill of it went right through me. Under the bedclothes he wore a plain shirt and loose trousers of soft pale cloth. I put my head to his chest and I could just hear a feeble pulse, but slowed down so much it was as though his heart hardly beat at all. But on the crown of his head, the skullcap pulsed gently, and I saw that what I'd taken for silver mesh was in fact a network of very fine clear glass tubes, through which a silvery liquid flowed, with a whispery, sinister sound. This must be the *antirentum.*

More than anything, I wanted to tear that horrible thing off his head. But something stopped me; an uneasy feeling that if I did that right now, when he was unconscious, it might hurt or even kill him. I had to find some other, more gentle way of getting through to him. His spirit was there, I had to believe that. I had to believe I wasn't too late.

I bent down to him and kissed his cold forehead. I kissed his closed eyelids. I kissed his motionless lips. And each time the touch of him on my own lips was like the burning of ice, but I did not flinch. Then, holding his hand, I put my mouth close to his ear and whispered, 'Wake up, my love, wake up. I've come for you. I love you, please wake up.'

The simple words came hard. They hurt, for I was struggling against a cold so deep the breath was freezing as it left my lips and the words shattered like ice in my throat. But I forced them through, repeating them again and again, as if they were a magic formula, a talisman against the fear that was invading me with every moment that passed.

Then I felt my breath getting warmer, warming not only my words but the space around his ear. Then, to my incredulous delight, a faint blush of colour began to appear in the lobe of his ear, then the top, then the skin near it. All at once, so close to him, my lips brushing his ear, I caught a very faint scent, so faint I thought I was imagining it. It was a scent that brought tears to my eyes and made my heart pound, for it was the shadow of a sweetness I knew with a thrilling tingle of the blood.

Then his eyes opened – those beautiful, limpid grey-green eyes. Clasping his hand, I cried joyously, 'Oh, you've come back, you've come back . . .'

But the words died on my lips as I saw the bewildered expression in his eyes as he looked at me, without a hint of recognition. Pulling his hand away from mine, he whispered weakly, 'Who are you?'

Twenty-Nine

His words stabbed me to the heart, and this time I did flinch. But I should have expected it. I should have known that the sorcerer's poison would have already worked its way into Gabriel's mind, through that abominable silver cap. Fighting back a grief-stricken panic, I said very quietly and gently in Ruvenyan, 'It's me. It's Natasha.'

Something flickered in his eyes, as if a memory was trying to struggle up through layers of forgetting. But then it was gone. He looked up at me, bewilderment giving way to anxiety. 'I'm sorry. I don't understand what you said.' He spoke in his own language, Champainian, his voice still a little weak but soft and musical. 'Yet somehow I feel as though I ought to know you,' he went on. 'Am I in a dream? A nightmare? Please, tell me.'

I was trembling all over. I longed to hold him, to kiss him and never let go, the longing so strong it ached like a sharp physical pain. But I knew that if I tried to touch him too soon I would only frighten him.

I said heavily, and in my accented Champainian said, 'No, this is no dream, Gabriel.'

'Then where am I?' he faltered, his gaze flickering around the room, and once again there was no hint of recognition in his expression.

'In the light-room of your godfather's house in Palume, on Dr Golpech's orders.'

I heard a slight sound behind me and, looking over my shoulder, saw that Celeste Durant had turned around and was staring at us. Gabriel saw her too. Shock flared in his eyes as he tried to sit up. I instinctively put an arm around his shoulders to help him, and the silver cap pulsed once, brightly. I was jolted back, as though from an electric shock. Gabriel fell back on the pillows, all expression leaving his eyes as he slipped almost instantly back into that deathly sleep.

'He knew me.' Celeste's voice came to me as though from a long distance. 'He knew me. You saw that, didn't you?'

Oh, yes. I had felt the sharp pain of that realisation. He had recognised her at once, not me. But I wasn't going to let the knowledge overwhelm me. 'I did. And if you want that to happen again, you must tell your father the silver cap must come off and your house must be barred to the doctor from this moment on.'

'Are you mad?' she cried. 'Why would we want to do that?'

'Don't you understand? The so-called miracle cure is all about keeping him in that half-state. The *antirentum* is wiping his memories, gradually and ruthlessly. It is starting with the most recent, and if it keeps going, soon he will not know you either; he'll know nothing at all, he'll cease existing in every way that matters. He will be a hollow shell.' My eyes filled with tears as I looked at him. *Death would be too easy*, Felix had said.

'You *are* mad,' Celeste said blankly. 'Quite mad. To speak about Dr Golpech's treatment like that when it's the only thing that will help Gabriel to –'

'Think of Felix,' I interrupted. 'Think of what happened to him.'

'What do you mean?'

'That was Dr Golpech's work, too.'

'What was?' Celeste said faintly, and I saw the foolish girl had no idea what I was talking about.

'Surely you have noticed he's not like he used to be?'

'Who? The doctor?'

Could anyone really be so dense? 'No, Felix Vivian.'

'So? That was quite different. Felix wasn't kidnapped – he just went crazy,' she said, with a chilling carelessness. 'Anyway, I've kept my side of the bargain. You must keep yours.'

'Only on one condition,' I said. 'I must stay here.'

Celeste stared at me in disbelief. 'Are you –'

'Mad? Yes, very probably,' I rejoined harshly. 'But that's what I want. And if you want what was promised, you have to agree.'

'If the doctor finds you here –'

'I don't care about that.' And I didn't.

'If I tell Papa –'

'But you won't,' I hissed, 'because if you do, you'll lose all those gifts I gave you, everything will vanish in a puff of smoke. If you say nothing, think of all the pretty things you can conjure up for yourself!'

I watched as the covetous gleam returned to her eyes. 'They're bound to find you in the morning,' Celeste retorted.

'Let me worry about that,' I said. 'Just remember this: say nothing, and it will all be yours, always. Tell anyone – anyone at all – and everything will vanish at once.' I was talking nonsense, making it up as I went along, for in truth I had no idea how long the magic might last. But it didn't matter. Celeste didn't know of my ignorance. All I needed was to buy a little more time, to try again on my own. Tomorrow morning, if I failed, they'd find me. But it didn't matter. Whatever happened, I'd be here with him, beside him.

Celeste shrugged. 'Very well. If you want to be so stupid as to spend the night here, that's your lookout. Now give me the comb.'

'I'll throw it out to you as soon as you open the door and leave,' I said. 'Not before.'

Celeste glared at me. 'How do I know you'll do as you say?'

'You don't. You'll just have to hope I do.'

'You're a real hard-hearted shrew, you know that?' she exclaimed. But one look at my face told her I wasn't going to respond. With a theatrical shrug, she went over to the wall and put her thumb to the knot of glass. The panel slid open, and she stepped out. Just before the panel closed again, I threw the comb through the opening, straight at her. She caught it, and the last glimpse I had of her before the door sealed shut was the look of triumph on her face. In the next instant I knew why – the light abruptly went out and I was left in total darkness.

Thirty

No, not quite total darkness, for a faint silvery glow still gleamed in the blackness of the room. It was the mesh cap. On my hands and knees, I groped my way towards the bed. Once I reached the end of the bed, I slowly rose from my hands and knees. I felt along the bed till I reached the other end. The silver glow of the cap was illumined Gabriel's face in a strange, ghostly light. I touched him, very lightly, careful not to touch the cap. His skin, I noticed, was getting chillier but not all the warmth had left it yet. Squatting on my haunches, I whispered, 'I'm here, I'm still here, I'll never go away . . .'

Gabriel shifted a little then, and I had to draw back in case I inadvertently touched that evil cap. But I was happy, for the fact he had moved at all showed that the power of the *antirentum* potion had not yet sunk its tentacles deep into his brain.

I crept closer and began to speak again. I spoke of the time I had first stumbled out of the blizzard and into his life. I spoke of my feelings when I first entered the mansion, and the fear of that first encounter with him as an *abartyen*, the conversations with Luel, the dreams, the way I had begun to understand that he wasn't the monster he seemed to be. And as I went on, gradually, without even noticing, I slipped out of Champainian and into the language of my heart, my own mother tongue. As the words flowed from me, I could see colour beginning to return to his skin once more, and though his eyes stayed closed, he shifted restlessly and gave a long sigh.

'That story I told you – the story I wrote – of Rosette and Robert and the white rose?' I said softly. 'You told me an editor would say it wasn't quite finished. Well, I've thought of how it must end. Shall I tell you?' I continued. 'Robert smelled the white rose, and its scent brought Rosette back to him. It brought hope back to his frozen, broken heart. And when he opened his eyes, oh when he opened his eyes, it was Rosette he saw before him, not her ghost, not her shadow, but the living girl, warm and loving. She opened her arms to him and he went into them, and then, hand in hand, they walked away, into a land where all dreams come true and happiness is for ever.'

I came to a shuddering stop. Gabriel had opened his eyes and was looking at me. I could see memory stirring deep in his eyes. I knew what I had to do now, though it would hurt me unbearably. 'I dreamed your dream in the mansion,' I said in Champainian. 'I saw Celeste – I saw the girl you loved, the girl you recognised as soon as you woke. I saw the painting Felix had done of her. It's come back, you know, that painting. It's come back and it's hanging in Lilac Gardens and . . . Oh!'

His hand had suddenly shot up, and he seized my wrist. 'No,' he said, 'don't.' His eyes were wild. 'Speak to me like you were before. I don't understand the words, but they fell like gentle rain. Not like this. Please, speak to me like you were before.' Trembling, he dropped my wrist now, and though I did not understand why my words had so troubled him, I understood that I must do as he asked.

I switched back to Ruvenyan. But I was only just a little way into telling him how we had parted at the mansion when Gabriel stopped me suddenly. 'I should know these things. I should understand these words. I did once, didn't I?'

I looked at him. His eyes were shadowed by fear, his Adam's apple bobbing convulsively in his throat. I said gently, in his own language, 'Yes. You did.'

'I wish I knew again,' he cried. 'Oh, if only I could remember.' There was helpless pain in his voice, and it cut me to the quick. Then something struck me – a wild, almost mad hope. Language and memory go together. We had known each other in Ruvenyan. What if . . .

Feverishly, I pulled out Luel's box from my pocket. I took out the tin of sweets, praying desperately that amongst the language lozenges would be one I'd overlooked – the one I needed. I fumbled the tin open and stared.

For when I had last looked in, there had been several sweets. Now there was only one. It was white, embossed with a letter in red. *R.*

My skin prickled with a thrill of awe. I took out the sweet and, holding it between thumb and forefinger, said quietly, 'This is Luel's doing.'

'Luel?' Gabriel repeated, sounding a little puzzled. 'I think I know the name. 'Wait. Yes. I do. She's gone. Where has she gone?'

'I don't know,' I said. 'Not yet. But she always watched over you, she always tried to keep you safe. Will you – will you trust me?' I held out the sweet to him.

He looked at me. 'Yes,' he said. 'I will ... I do.' He opened his mouth, and very gently, I placed the sweet on his tongue. I saw it fizz as soon as it touched his flesh, and then it vanished.

An extraordinary expression came over his face. 'I can see more clearly,' he said wonderingly. 'Is that what ...' Then he stopped, his eyes wide.

'You spoke in Ruvenyan,' I said happily.

'Then tell me again,' he said, 'tell me what you told me before, when I could not understand. Please ...'

I felt almost hollow with disappointment. I had so hoped that as soon as he knew my language again he would know me. I started again from the beginning, and as I spoke this time I could see a change coming over his face. His features hardened, his lips tightened and his nostrils flared. To my horror I saw a fierce amber gleam light up deep in his eyes and I knew that my imprudence had done something terrible – that the memories of his life as an *abartyen* were stirring inside him once again and thrusting him back into that darkness.

'Forgive me, I should never have started, I should have waited, I . . .' My throat thickened with tears, choking off the words, my eyes filling with the stinging water of sorrow and guilt and lost hope. I looked away so he wouldn't have to see, wouldn't have to feel anything he didn't have to, and I wished with all my heart that I could change what I'd done.

And then he spoke. Softly, wonderingly but clearly. 'Natasha. Oh, *daragoya maya*. Oh, my darling, my sweet Natasha, please look at me.'

My heart stilled. I could not speak. I could hardly breathe. I turned my head and looked at him. And what I saw in his face then was something I knew I would never ever forget, not if I lived to be a hundred, and it flooded me with a thrilling, dizzying warmth from the top of my head to the tips of my toes.

'I remember the scarlet rose in the snow at your feet,' he said, his voice shaking with urgent emotion. 'I remember the white rose of your story, I remember your sweetness and bravery and beauty. I remember everything but I know, too, how unworthy I am of you. Natasha, why do you ask me to forgive you when it is I who is so –'

'Hush, *daragoy moy*, my darling.' I picked up his hand to kiss it, but he gave a kind of groan and pulled me down to him instead, and we were kissing passionately, tenderly. My limbs were melting, my senses reeling with his closeness, his warm male smell, the taste of his lips on mine, my heart singing with happiness. Then through my delight I saw the silver cap flash, and I cried out in warning. But he lifted up a hand and carelessly pulled it off and threw it across the room, where it shattered on one of the panels. At once, the silvery liquid inside ran out onto the negatives imprinted on the glass, so they glowed with a light that illumined the whole room before dying away again.

Gabriel sat up, smiling a little at my astonishment. 'That's better. A good deal better.' He pulled me to him again and kissed me long and lingeringly. Then, holding me away a little, he said tenderly, 'You gave me a name, *daragoya maya*, when I could not tell you mine. Do you still want me to be Ivan, or could you get used to Gabriel now?'

'Oh,' I said, blushing, 'I could.' I'd thought before I could only *think* of him as Gabriel, not *feel* him in my heart, but everything was different now. Everything had changed. 'Gabriel,' I said shyly, trying out the sound of his name, which was softer in Ruvenyan. 'Gabriel, I love you.'

He laughed joyously and drew me to him. 'And I love you, Natasha, my beautiful girl, flower of my heart ...' Time vanished as we lay in each other's arms, holding each other tight, breathing in the smell of each other's hair and skin, our hearts pulsing together.

Presently he said, 'Natasha, my darling, we should get out of here. I used to be able to open this door; let's see if I still can.'

In one fluid movement he got off the bed, sweeping me up with him. There was no sign at all of the weak, trembling figure he had been as, hand in hand, we felt our way to the glass knot on the exit wall.

'Open sesame,' he said, lightly pressing his thumb against the knot. Nothing happened. He tried again but still nothing. 'It must have been changed. I should have expected it.'

'It doesn't really matter now, my love,' I said cheerfully. 'So what if we're still here in the morning? Once we tell your godfather what the doctor was really doing . . .' I trailed off as I saw the grim expression on his face.

'Oh, Natasha, it isn't poor old Golpech we need to beware of,' he said quietly, 'but someone who was once dear to me, who I trusted absolutely.'

'Celeste?' I said, confused. 'But I thought –'

'Not Celeste – her father. My godfather. The great man, Edmond Durant.' He bit off the words.

My scalp crept with horror. '*He* is the sorcerer? But why would he do this to you? I don't understand.'

'Better you don't,' he said in a low voice. 'It's our only hope now.'

'What do you mean?' I said wildly.

'If you don't know, then he might still spare your life,' he said, looking at me with that same expression of loving sorrow that I'd seen back home, in the mirror.

'No,' I said sharply. 'I am not going to let you do that again. We are getting out of here together.' I spoke more confidently than I felt.

'If only we could,' he said heavily. 'Oh, if only Luel was here –'

'You have Luel to watch over you, but I have Old Bony!' Fumbling for Luel's little box, I extracted from it the single strand of Old Bony's hair. *It can go through walls and pierce metal and stone. But it may only be used once, so use it wisely.* Well, the wall was glass, not stone or metal as she'd said, but I knew the time was right to use it. I pressed Old Bony's hair against the knot.

Nothing happened for a moment except that, under my fingers, the strand of hair grew stiff as wire and hot as a coal. I dropped it with a yelp and it fell at my feet, where it instantly vanished. All at once a rumble started under our feet and there came a high humming sound. The panel shuddered wide open, the glass instantly crazing into a spider's web of cracks.

'Quick, before it all comes down on us!' Gabriel grabbed my hand, and we ran through the opening of the antechamber and into the corridor outside, just as the light-room exploded in a lethal shower of broken glass behind us. Now the whole house must be aroused.

We were halfway down the corridor when Gabriel stopped. 'Can you hear that?' he whispered.

'What?'

'Listen.'

'But there's nothing to . . .' And then it struck me. That was precisely it. There were no sounds of pursuit – no running feet, no shouts, no slamming doors. Nothing. It was eerily quiet.

Our eyes met. 'Maybe they just didn't hear . . .' I faltered.

'Oh, I doubt that,' Gabriel said grimly. 'And we can't go out this way. That's what he'll expect, and he'll be waiting for us. But I know another way out.'

Halfway down in the other direction was a door, and behind it, some steps. 'There used to be a tunnel that leads from the cellar to the back garden,' Gabriel said, as we headed down. 'It's our only chance.'

It was a real rabbit-warren of a cellar, with storerooms leading off each other in a seemingly endless series. In one, there was a shabby old greatcoat hanging on a hook, and scuffed gardening boots underneath. We stopped long enough for Gabriel to fling on the coat and pull on the boots, before hurrying on.

At last we came to a small locked door set into the wall a little distance off the stone floor. Gabriel kicked it open, and we climbed through the doorway into a long dimly lit passage that ended in what looked like some sort of grating, beyond which lay only darkness. The tunnel!

'We're nearly there,' I cried in relief. 'We're nearly there!'

'Perhaps,' said Gabriel calmly. I glanced at him and saw he was very pale, his eyes very bright. He took my hand. 'Are you ready?'

'Yes,' I said. If he wouldn't show fear then neither would I, I thought as we sprinted down the passage, towards the grating. Now was not the time to get scared, to conjure phantoms, to imagine that something was following us – something unnatural and horrible. The hairs on the back of my neck rose. I wanted to look back but I dared not.

We finally reached the grating. The bars were heavy, but desperation lent us strength and we soon pushed the grating open and scrambled through into darkness. Gabriel slammed the grating shut behind us, and we sped hand in hand down the dark, musty-smelling tunnel, heading towards the faint light we could see at the end.

Closer, closer. The darkness was ebbing, the light getting stronger, brighter. Stronger. Brighter. Dazzling.

It was so blindingly dazzling we had to throw up our hands in front of our faces.

And then the light moved into the darkness of the tunnel and took shape. There was no doubt as to what it was. And yet still I could not believe the evidence of my own eyes as the huge white wolf loped rapidly down the tunnel towards us.

Thirty-One

It moved with animal grace. It made no sound and had no smell, and its eyes shone fixedly. Its gaze held us rooted to the spot, while it advanced with its eyes glowing and tongue lolling, its shining fur sparkling at the edges with tiny pinpricks of light. And then, as it came closer, I could see the walls of the tunnel through its body, as though it had no real form but was some kind of projection.

'It's not real, Gabriel,' I said wildly, hardly knowing what I was saying. 'It cannot hurt us . . .' I went to take a step forward.

'No!' Gabriel shouted, pulling me back. 'You don't understand. Don't touch it. Don't look at it. Close your eyes.'

'It's a bit late for that,' said a deep, mellow voice. It seemed to come directly from the wolf's shimmering jaws. The creature was so close now I could see its terrible teeth and I knew that, whatever it was, it would kill us. Panic flooded through me. 'Luel! Luel!' I screamed in blinding terror. 'I know you're here somewhere. Why have you abandoned us?'

The wolf suddenly halted. 'You really want to know?' it said. 'Why, then, so you shall.'

And moving so swiftly that I could not even see how it was done, it appeared behind us, herding us like sheep towards the end of the tunnel. Gabriel took my hand, and I held it tight. We did not speak for there were no words to say. My outburst had gained us a few moments, but we both knew that's all it would be.

We emerged from the tunnel into the walled garden, and there under the moonlight, the wolf's shape shimmered and faded, though it still hung in the air like a pale shadow. It hovered by the side of the man who sat at the wrought-iron table, amusement crinkling his eyes and twitching his lips.

'Oh, what a pleasant surprise,' he said. 'If it isn't the intrepid girl reporter from the non-existent Faustinian magazine, hand in hand with the family renegade.' He crooked a finger at me. 'Come here, my dear.'

My hand slipped from Gabriel's. My feet started to move. I struggled to stay put but I could not.

'Please,' Gabriel cried in his own language. 'If there is any human feeling left in you at all, let her go. She knows nothing.' If I could not stop moving, Gabriel could not move at all, except for the features of his face, which were contorted with hatred and fear.

Messir Durant's gaze flickered lazily over Gabriel, but he did not reply. 'Well, well, my dear,' he said, as I drew near, 'I have to hand it to Luel. She still had a trick or two up her sleeve, didn't she? Pity she can't enjoy knowing she helped you fool me, if only for a while.' He gestured behind him. 'You wanted to know why she has abandoned you? Look over there.'

I looked over to where he pointed, and the last hope left me.

Five statues in the garden. Five moss-eaten marble statues yet only four niches. I noticed that one statue had simply been shoved in at the end, as though it had been an afterthought. And no wonder, for though the others were the kind you usually see in gardens – nymphs and fauns – this one looked like one you might see in a graveyard. It was a mourning figure of a little old lady, hunched over with her hands over her eyes, as if she were weeping. I knew her at once. But it was Gabriel who spoke first. 'How?' he said. 'How could you do it? She is a *feya*.' And there was the same bleak hopelessness in his voice as there was in my heart.

The sorcerer smiled and turned to me. 'He is referring, of course, to the idea that a *feya* cannot be spellbound by a mere mortal. True enough. She cannot be *compelled*. But if she freely allows it to happen, that is quite another thing.'

'You made her a promise,' said Gabriel wildly. 'You promised her my freedom in return for her binding. Didn't you?'

'Why, yes, I believe I did.'

'Then you must do as you promised,' Gabriel burst out. 'You must, or you will be cursed.'

He laughed. 'Cursed? What childish notions you have! There she is, stone. There you are, trapped. Nothing you can do can change that.'

No, I thought, looking sadly at the statue that had once been poor Luel. She could not help us now. And I had given away or used all her gifts. I had used Old Bony's too. We had nothing left.

Then, quite suddenly, I remembered the feeling I'd had hours before, when I had met Celeste in the garden. I had felt Luel's presence then. And I had repeated Olga's words to Celeste, telling her that the difference between good and bad magic was that the former fitted you, but the latter tried to bend you out of shape. Yes, I had used everything I'd been given. All except one thing – the tin box.

I could feel the shape of it in my pocket, pressing against my thigh. Dropping my hands to my side, as though utterly dejected, I positioned my left palm over the shape of the box. I pressed, very gently, hoping against hope that I was right.

I don't know what I expected. But it was certainly not what actually happened. For at that very moment, a familiar voice came floating through the garden. 'Papa? Are you there?'

A startled expression flooded the sorcerer's face. He made a rapid pass with one hand and the wolf-shadow disappeared. Another movement of his hand and my throat seemed to close up, my tongue stilled. Edmond Durant got up quickly, just as Celeste came into view. Wrapped in a velvet robe, with her glossy hair in a net, she looked a little dazed, as though she had just emerged from sleep. 'Why are you out here, Papa?' she complained. 'It's cold . . .' Then she saw me and Gabriel. Her eyes widened in shock. 'Gabriel? You're awake?'

'Yes, Celeste. I am,' he replied gently. 'Wide awake now.'

Celeste looked in confusion at her father, and I realised in that moment that the girl had no idea what was happening, nor who her father really was. 'But Dr Golpech said the cure would take a long time.'

'Then I guess he was wrong, sweetheart,' said her father uncomfortably. 'Now, why don't you just go inside and . . .'

But Celeste wasn't listening. She looked at me, then at Gabriel. 'You know her,' she said, bemusedly.

'Yes,' he said, still in that gentle voice. 'I do. She is the girl I love.'

'Oh. Right.' She absorbed the information without a flicker of emotion. Gabriel's eyes met mine. And I understood then that what I'd taken for grief over lost love was actually a kind of protective pity.

'Papa, I don't understand,' said Celeste, fretfully. 'Why are they out here in the garden with you? Felix wouldn't say.'

Gabriel gasped. But before he could speak, Durant cut across him. 'Felix is *here*?' His voice sounded calm but the expression on his face belied it.

'Yes. That's what I came out to tell you,' Celeste said, with a hint of asperity. 'He wants to speak to you. He said I'd find you in the garden.'

Baffled, I looked at Gabriel. He looked back with the same confused expression. He had no idea either.

'Well, tell him to wait,' snapped Durant.

'But he won't, Papa. He says it's urgent, that he must see you, or he'll tell what he knows. What does he mean?'

Hope flared within me again. The sorcerer would have to deal promptly with this unexpected new danger. If he left us here we might get away. But he did nothing of the kind. Visibly controlling his anger, Durant remarked, 'I can't imagine what he thinks he means, but you know what Felix is like. Gets in a flap over nothing. Very well. Tell him to come out here.'

Celeste nodded.

'But you stay inside,' he continued. 'You hear?'

She shrugged. 'Why would I want to be out here, anyhow?' Her gaze slid over us, without interest or expression. 'It's cold and I want to go back to bed.'

'You do that, my dear,' her father said quietly. 'And sweet dreams.'

As Celeste wafted back across the garden and towards the house, Gabriel turned to Durant. 'It's over, Edmond. If you don't want to be destroyed, go now. It's your only chance.'

For half a heartbeat, Durant stared at him, looking as astonished as I felt. Then he laughed. 'You fool. Do you think you can bluff me? *Me*?'

'Felix is turning on you. You know what that means.'

'It means he'll be destroyed along with you,' said Durant lightly. 'Most satisfying symmetry, I'd say. Ah, here he is. Now we are all together. Isn't that nice?'

I turned to see Felix approaching, alone. He was wearing evening dress, as though he'd just come from a ball or the theatre, but his expression was wild, his face pale. He did not look at us, but only at Durant. Without preamble, he said, 'I remember now. It's come back.'

'My dear boy,' said Durant, casually holding up a hand and halting him where he stood, 'what's come back? Your wits? Your will? Somehow I doubt it.'

Felix's eyes did not waver. 'You bound me.'

'Willingly, as I recall,' said the sorcerer lightly. 'Didn't I give you exactly what I promised? Fame? Adulation?'

'You only let me have it for a short while,' muttered Felix. 'And then you had him –' and he pointed at Gabriel while still looking at Durant – 'steal my painting.'

'Ah, there I must protest,' said Durant. 'That was not my doing at all. Indeed, it was I who got that painting back for you, when I destroyed that old witch's magic. Yes, that's right. It was her. Luel took the painting. But then she always did everything her dear boy wanted. Isn't that right, Gabriel?'

Gabriel did not reply.

'He was jealous of you, Felix,' Durant continued. 'You were right. He didn't win that prize. You did. He didn't touch my daughter's heart. You did. No wonder he tried to destroy you. He is your enemy, you know that.'

Felix's eyes turned to Gabriel.

'Don't let him do this, Felix,' Gabriel said quietly. 'Not for my sake. Think of Celeste. Think what's it's done to her.'

'But she wanted it, too,' said Felix dully. 'She wanted to be famous.'

'But she didn't understand,' said Gabriel sadly. 'She isn't made that way.'

'My daughter never did have much imagination,' said the sorcerer, smiling. He did not seem in the least put

295

out by the exchange. 'And the little she had troubled her. Better it should live in the painting, along with Felix's poor excuse for a spirit. Those fools at the School of Light and in Faustina have no idea. They think that enchanted paintings can be spotted easily. But then they had never seen anything like this one. People look at *Summer Morning* and see a great love story – the love of a painter for his lovely muse. In art, it might live for ever. In life, it was a weak, poor thing, and doomed to failure. It's a kindness I did them both, really.'

Gabriel's face darkened. 'You are a monster,' he growled.

'Actually, I rather fancy that was you,' said Durant cheerfully. 'A beast for three years. That's bound to have an effect. Mind you, I could hardly have done it if the beast hadn't been slumbering inside you all the time.' He looked at me. 'Don't you know, my dear, that your beloved could revert at any time? Just look at that nasty violent light in his eyes. Oh, I grant he had a good deal more spine than Felix. He's riven by dark passions – rage, hatred, jealousy, pride, recklessness, all roiling inside him. That's what he's really like and one day you would have found that out to your cost. Oh well, it's all academic now.'

Durant made a pass with his hand and the shimmering wolf reappeared. Another movement of his hand, and Felix was pulled towards the wolf as if he were on strings, his eyes wide in mute, disbelieving horror.

'No!' shouted Gabriel. 'Don't do this, Durant. What threat is he to you?'

'You've changed your tune,' said Durant calmly.

'I was wrong. He was never going to fight you. He can't. In the name of God, Edmond, he has been your faithful servant. Have mercy.'

'How very touching,' said the sorcerer. 'He pleads for his enemy. But what use to me is a tool that has gone rusty?'

Felix looked at Gabriel, and into his eyes came an expression that struck me to the heart. There was hopeless sadness in it, and bitter shame. I saw his lips move, trying to speak. I thought I saw him form two words: *Celeste, forgive* – But he got no further, for the sorcerer's hand moved again, and Felix crumpled as though he'd been felled, his eyes rolling back in his head.

As we watched in horror, Felix's body seemed to fold in on itself, to shrink, change shape. Before our very eyes, he turned into a thin, bedraggled crow with dull, filmy eyes. The bird struggled up, hopped a few steps, twitched, then fell sideways. Blood appeared at the corners of its eyes. It twitched once more, then lay quite still.

'That *was* mercy,' said Durant, kicking the crow's body aside. 'A quick death, no lingering agony. For you, I'm afraid, it will be different –' Durant's hands moved rapidly so that the wolf grew bigger and brighter, hovering beside him like a giant guardian. Or a familiar. A sorcerer's familiar, in the shape of a white wolf. But not like Old Bony's feline familiars. Those had been solid things, real albeit weird. This was different. Images flashed through my mind. A row of photographs. A white wolf caught in mid-pounce. A room of light. And a thread of memory: a macabre little newspaper story, casually seen, almost instantly forgotten. Until now. *A man devoured by a spirit-wolf called up by a northern shaman . . .*

My tongue moved. My throat unblocked. 'I know where you got the spirit-wolf – from a northern shaman,' I said.

The sorcerer's hands stilled. He turned his head to look at me. 'Well, well, well. The little Ruvenyan is full of surprises. You're right, my dear. But only in part. The shaman – Byelfin – he didn't give it to me. He couldn't. Oh, he had power. He knew the ways of shapeshifters, and it was from him I learned the beast-spells. He said I was the best pupil he'd ever had. And he was very good, in his way. But his understanding was limited, as was his power.' Durant was warming to his story, and I held my breath, hoping the pleasure of it would be enough to distract him for a few moments at least. I caught Gabriel's glance, trying to telegraph to him to stay quiet, and saw in his eyes that he understood.

'Byelfin had no notion of the world outside his little patch,' Durant went on in a reminiscent tone. 'Indeed, he feared and hated it. He lived in an unchanging world bound with rules he had never tried to challenge. He had no notion how new, modern methods could be used to radically transform ordinary magic into something much more powerful. Yet it is true that it was when I was with him that my great inspiration came. It was his reaction to the very mention of a camera that gave me the germ of the idea.'

Another piece fell into place in my mind as I remembered something about the customs of the north. To the northern shamans and witches photography was not a benign thing, an attempt to record a moment of time; it was attempted robbery – a theft of the spirit. Unsuspecting travellers had been killed for just carrying a camera, let alone trying to take a photo. It was probably why the man in the newspaper report had died. 'Most people think it's just superstition,' I said, 'but you understood it was not.'

Durant raised an eyebrow. 'Quite right. Their hatred of photography is based on an instinctive understanding. Light in the lands of the northerners is not what it is elsewhere. In summer their nights are white, in winter their days are black, in autumn their dawns are filled with rainbows, in spring there are lightning storms that last for hours. Unique. Strange. Unbelievably potent. So for them a photograph isn't just a photograph. It takes on the strangeness of the light, which is the very magical spirit of those lands. It captures it. It is that light which the shamans and witches bring into themselves, like living cameras. It is that which they turn into their spirit-guardians, like living photographs – wolves, bears, birds.'

His words had an eerie poetic quality, which resonated uneasily with me. I thought of my flight in Old Bony's sleigh. Of deep lake waters. Of frozen salt marshes and grey forests. Of the weird, shifting light of northern skies. It was there, in an island on the Northern Lake, that Old Bony had chosen to hide Luel's box . . .

Instinctively, my hand reached for it. My heart thumped. I could not look at Gabriel. I could not let him see what was in my eyes. For now I had to take the biggest risk of my life. 'But *you* don't do it that way,' I said quietly.

'It is not your own spirit mixing with the light. That is too great a risk, for a shaman can be killed if his spirit is captured while in animal shape. Indeed, that is exactly how you disposed of your old teacher so he could tell no tales. He trusted you. It was easy for you to ambush him.'

Durant smiled a wintry smile. 'You are quite right. Byelfin was limited, as I said. He lived in a world where pupils did not turn on their masters.' He shook his head a little sadly. 'You are a clever girl. It is almost a pity that you have to –'

'You don't risk your own spirit. Instead, you take the spirit of others – human and animal,' I went on, as though he hadn't spoken. 'With humans, you must have an agreement, even if they don't fully understand. But with animals, like the white wolf you tracked and captured in the north – that's not needed. You used spells to hook its spirit – Byelfin's spells, twisted out of shape. And then you funnelled it through the camera. You fix it for ever in your photograph.' I looked him straight in the eyes. 'You told me you did not like to live the little life. But that is precisely what you are doing. You are not a great sorcerer, Messir Durant. You are a thief. Just a common thi–'

The wolf pounced, its eyes glowing into mine with a wild, murderous hatred; it was like looking into the deepest pit of hell. A breath of fire and ice enveloped me whole, and I felt the flesh dissolving from my bones and my veins seizing and sparking, squeezing my heart in a fist of fury till I fell to the ground and knew no more.

Thirty-Two

I'm struggling up through deep murky water, into a thick, clinging grey fog. I can't see anything. My eyelids are pressed down as though they are stone. I've died. I must be in the afterlife . . .

'There she goes again, thinking she's died. What an imagination that girl's got.'

'Lucky for us all that she does, my friend.'

I know those voices.

I'm wandering in the fog again, for how long I do not know. Then out of it comes another voice. I strain to hear it.

'She's stirring. She's awake.'

I know that voice too. I want to reach out to touch him but I cannot. It is as if I am made of marble.

'Not yet,' says the light voice.

'Be patient,' says the harsh one.

He takes my hand. His hand is warm so I know he cannot be dead. Does that mean I am not? My hand lies in his, cold, inert, heavy. I can feel words in my throat and tears in my eyes, but the words cannot rise and the tears cannot fall.

I feel the touch of his fingers tracing the outline of my face. The fog thins. I feel the touch of his lips. On my forehead, ears, eyes, lips. His lips are so soft, but mine might as well be made of stone. The fog thins some more and I can now see his shape, but oh, so far away. Despair fills me, the fog rolls in again and I am alone, wandering in greyness.

'Leave her,' says the harsh voice. 'It is not yet time.'

'Our friend is right, my lord,' says the light voice. 'You must let her rest.'

No, I want to say, no, it is not rest I need. I need him to keep hold of me, to not let me go.

'I will not let her go,' Gabriel says, and it is as though he has heard my thoughts. A tingle begins in me, deep down. 'I will never let you go,' he breathes. 'Never.'

He isn't far away, as I feared. But close. So close! The tingle is growing. Growing.

'You remember, my love, when you told me you thought the scarlet flower against the snow was like a living painting?' he whispers, and there is a slight shake in his voice, as if he is trying to hold back a smile, though a smile mixed with tears. 'Well, there is such a painting now. My first in a long, long time. I've called it *Scarlet in the Snow*. And I do so need your opinion on it, so you really must wake up.'

The tingle flushes through my veins, itching, roaring, and quite suddenly the fog rolls away and my eyes fly open. I gasp and look straight up into my lover's anxious face and, without a word, reach up to him.

Time disappears as we hold each other tight, my head against his chest, his mouth on my hair, breathing in each other's smell and warmth, feeling our hearts beat so close they might as well be one. 'You said something about wanting my opinion . . .' I murmur happily. And without another word he lifts something up from beside him.

My breath catches. It is the most beautiful painting I have ever seen, though it is so simple. It shows a snowy garden under a pale blue sky, framed in a window – a snowy garden where a glorious scarlet rose blooms on a bush, like a living ruby. It is just as I saw it and yet not, for on the same bush blooms another rose – a white one. They are twined together, and it seems to me as though I can smell the double fragrance of the flowers, a fragrance that goes directly to my heart.

'I know I've been out of practice for a long time,' Gabriel says, a little uncertainly. 'And that shows. I'm not sure even that it's finished – it probably still needs –'

'No . . . Oh, Gabriel. It's just that . . .' I struggle to express what I feel. 'It's as if I am in there, looking through that window with you. It's so perfect, so beautiful, I have no words for it.' And all at once, the tears that wouldn't fall start flowing.

Gabriel puts down the painting and catches me in his arms again. He dries my tears and kisses my eyes and says, with a little laugh in his voice, 'Now there's a reaction any artist would relish.'

'Just as long as you don't get a swollen head,' I say, smiling.

'Me? God forbid!' He laughs, before a little cough sounds. 'But, my darling, I was forgetting we have company.'

I emerge from the shelter of his arms to see Luel and Old Bony regarding us with calm patience, from two chairs on the other side of the room.

'Good day to you, child,' they say in unison.

I smile a little shakily. 'Er, good day to you, too. I am glad to see you both, though I do not understand how any of this is possible or where we are or how long I've been here.' I look around at a charming wood-panelled room I do not recognise, through a window beyond whose glass is half-familiar, sunny woodland.

Old Bony crosses her arms. 'As to how long you've been here, that's quickly told. Five nights.'

'Five nights!' I echo in astonishment.

'The poison had got into you,' Luel explains, 'and already sent your spirit wandering. It took time and our combined efforts to bring you back. As to where we are, that is also swift to say. It is the old Fontenoy house, deep in the heart of the woods outside Palume. Gabriel was born here, but it was shut up when his parents died. Now it lives and breathes again.'

I remember now why the landscape seems so familiar. I had seen it in Gabriel's miniature painting, hanging in the study at the Durant residence. I can't help a little shiver at the thought of that place. 'It's over, Natasha, quite over,' Gabriel says, putting an arm around me.

Luel then chimes in hastily, 'And as to explanations, my child, they will be lengthy, so I propose that they wait. You should first get up and have something to eat. I'll order herbed chicken and cream cakes.'

'Tush, my friend,' says Old Bony. 'What the girl needs is strong hot tea and creamy porridge, not your fancy table.'

I smile at them both. 'I should like hot tea and herbed chicken – that would be the finest thing, don't you think, Gabriel?'

'Or perhaps creamy porridge and cakes?' says Gabriel, mischievously.

'Whatever it is, let us have plenty of it,' I say pertly, and he laughs and kisses the tip of my nose.

'There's a girl after my own heart!'

As Luel had promised, the explanations came later, when we were all sitting comfortably by a roaring log fire, replete after a large meal that had filled a table end-to-end. The two old *feyas* had competed mightily in the production of this hilariously varied meal, and it must be said they also ate the lion's share of it.

We talked for hours, and so it was that I learned that when you use a strand of Old Bony's hair, she feels it. And how at the same time the rose petal she had kept safe for me jumped in its box like a living thing. She had known then that something was wrong and had tuned her *feya* ears to listen out. But even then she might not have come to our aid if I hadn't spoken of the white wolf, a child of the forest, twisted and tortured, and of the fate of the old northern shaman. Guided by the homing beacon of the rose petal, Old Bony had woven a spell of speed and invisibility, and had swept off at once in her sleigh. Like an avenging fury, she had swooped down from the night sky and into the Durants's garden. I heard then how a strand of Old Bony's hair instantly released Luel from her stony prison, and how together the two *feyas* cast a powerful spell that turned the white wolf against its master. The sorcerer had not stood a chance.

'Torn to shreds and vaporised,' said Luel, with grim satisfaction.

'Not even a bone left to adorn my fence,' said Old Bony, with a rather terrible smile.

And the white wolf whose spirit had been enslaved and perverted? It had vanished at the same moment, reduced to a pile of ash, which Old Bony returned to its home so that its spirit could finally find rest.

Though his ultimate fate made me shudder, I could not find any pity in my heart for Edmond Durant, for the long list of his victims cried out for justice, and justice was what he had got. And if his daughter was now fatherless, she had in truth, as Gabriel said, not had a real father for a long time.

'You see,' Gabriel said, 'I was a real orphan but I had the memory of my parents' love for me. But Celeste was an orphan in all but name, for her mother died long ago and the closest she ever got to her famous father was in the pages of newspapers and magazines. Though she never lacked for anything materially, her heart was hollow as a honeycomb. And though I never loved her in the way you thought, I grew up with her and I do care what happens to her. Luel made a spell that night that would convince the whole household that my godfather had left unexpectedly for one of his trips abroad. Later, news of his death abroad can be circulated. That way, Celeste is spared the shame and disgrace of the truth, and she can hold up her head in society. And Luel says that the spell on her died with the man who cast it, so she will be back to normal.' He gave a little smile. 'Celeste's kind of normal, that is. I am glad, Natasha. I want her to have a chance to have a life as happy as it can be. Do you understand?'

'Of course I do,' I said softly, and kissed him. 'And I love you all the more for it.'

I heard then how Luel had bent over the crumpled body of Felix – the sorcerer's death had broken the crow-spell – and had found a very faint pulse. Old Bony was minded to leave him to take his chances but Luel wouldn't hear of it. 'His last thoughts were not for himself and that was why his heart did not give out,' she said, 'and I was not about to just leave him.' So they took him to Dr Golpech's house, left him on the doorstep and rang the bell.

'Golpech had nothing to do with Edmond's crimes,' Gabriel said. 'He was just used. That story of my being found on his doorstep was just that – a story. Golpech was told by Edmond that I'd been found unconscious in a squalid dive in the city, that it was obvious I'd been living a shady life under an assumed name and that for this reason it was best if people thought I'd been kidnapped by foreign bandits. Golpech agreed because Edmond helped to fund his researches, so he was hardly going to ask too many questions. He was happy to have someone to experiment on with that *antirentum* of his. It's supposed to clear bad memories. Perhaps it will help Felix.'

They went on to tell me the story of how the white wolf had come to be. Potent as a shaman's spirit-wolf, obedient as a witch's familiar, it had been a unique combination of the two, and so more dangerous than either. Durant had come across the living creature in a forest in his northern sojourn. And I had been right – it was a fragment of the white wolf's spirit, not his own, which Durant had captured with his photograph. He had grown it and artificially enlarged it, like an exotic culture in a hothouse, in the synthetic white night of the glass room, with its concentrated energy. And that concentration of energy was precisely why he'd had Gabriel put in the glass room – there the *antirentum's* effects, magnified and perverted, would have worked over time to cut the young man's spirit loose of all memory for ever, thus rendering Gabriel utterly malleable, even more so than Felix had been.

Once the spell was complete, the spirit-wolf could be taken wherever its master went, an innocent photograph simply slipped into his pocketbook, till the time was right to unleash it. And unleash it he did, many times, in different places, against any person who stood in his way. Luel thought there were at least a dozen victims, starting from Byelfin the shaman. Without knowing it, I'd even seen a mention of one of those crimes: for the *Kolorgrod Messenger* report had got it wrong. The nameless man in that story hadn't been killed by a shaman's spirit-wolf at all, but by Durant's creature of light.

That was the terrible secret Gabriel had found out, three years before, when he had stumbled across a secret panel hidden behind the bookshelves in Durant's study. He had found a notebook detailing his godfather's experiments with magic. Till then, he had not had the faintest idea of his godfather's double life. 'I hardly knew him,' Gabriel said. 'He was hardly ever home, but he was the last person you'd suspect of sorcery. Not only did he claim to despise magic, he was also a man of action, whose exploits in remote places were the stuff of legend, and he had friends in high places, including the Presidential palace. The rare times he was home, he spent his time locked in the glass room, tinkering with the photographs he'd taken abroad. That was hardly a secret; his photographs were published in magazines and shown in exhibitions. I'd helped him with the work when I was younger. If he seemed even more distant when he came back from those long months in the north five years ago, I did not really pay attention. So I had no inkling – no inkling at all – of this thing that had become an evil obsession, a cancer that gradually ate away everything that had ever been good in him. I suspected that Felix had used some kind of magic to enhance his painting and secure his win, but I had absolutely no idea Edmond was involved.'

'As for me, I'd felt for a while there was something different about that man,' Luel chimed in, 'but never anything I could be sure of, and I was distracted by the painting. Like Gabriel, I suspected something, and when I saw it at Lilac Gardens I was sure it had been magically enhanced. But I didn't suspect Durant. I just wanted to punish Felix for his cheating, so I made the painting vanish from the gallery. I had no idea that would precipitate what it did . . .'

'That was just before I discovered the notebook,' Gabriel explained. 'I had no idea Luel was behind the disappearance of the painting. The day it happened Felix turned up at the house, ranting that I'd done it, that I was eaten up with jealousy because he was a genius and I wasn't. Edmond was there and sent him packing, and the way he did it made me think he too suspected that Felix had cheated, so I told him my hunch about the involvement of magic. He had looked grim and had said he'd investigate, that in the meantime I was to keep quiet.

It was that very night I found the notebook. I could hardly believe it at first. I was in utter turmoil, repulsed by what I'd read. But I could not just betray Edmond to the authorities, not without giving him a chance to explain. He was my godfather, after all – the man who had taken me in when my parents had died, who had paid for my education. He might never have shown me affection, but also never enmity. From honour, from loyalty, I could not forget those things.'

Luel shook her head. 'Ah, but a sorcerer has no honour. No loyalty. Not even family. Nothing left in his heart but the will to power. If you'd come to me first, I'd have told you. But then you didn't know that, and so I couldn't stop him casting the *abartyen* spell. I wasn't even there.'

'And the only bit of good fortune,' said Gabriel quietly, 'was that before the spell had time to work completely, you were able to free me from the room where he had locked me, and spirit me away to a place you thought he could never get me.'

'Why there?' I asked.

It was Old Bony who answered, not Luel. 'Luel knew that in the places under my protection, no sorcerer can set foot. Though to be sure, she did not ask my permission. I knew a fellow *feya* when I saw one, and I sensed no threat from her or the poor creature she was protecting.'

'I knew that man wouldn't stop looking for us though,' said Luel, 'because my intervention had halted the workings of the spell so that its power was incomplete. Until he could be sure the spell had destroyed Gabriel, he could never feel safe. I knew Durant would be scouting the world for us. I knew I could keep the spell in suspension, albeit temporarily. I know how standard *abartyen* spells work and what might be done to break them, but this one wasn't standard or even traditional – it was a hybrid thing, and wickedly subtle. As you know, good magic should fit you and bad magic makes you fit it. But that man's magic was uniquely dangerous because it used small strands of good amongst the bad so as to burrow deeper inside its victim, turning your own impulses against you, destroying everything most precious. A *feya* alone could never break a spell like that. It took me a long time before I had any notion of what might be done. And even then it was only a small notion, as everything really depends on finding the right person to break the spell.'

'And wasn't she ever the right one,' said Gabriel, looking at me in a way that sent tingles of pleasure up my spine.

I leaned against him. 'I'm sure I'm pleased you think that because I think the same of you.'

'That's just as well then,' Gabriel said, smiling. Into my head came my mother's words. *One day, you'll understand what I mean.* A pang went through me.

'What's that sigh for?' he said gently.

'I was only wishing that my mother and sisters could be here to meet you. Then my happiness would be complete.'

'Well, then your wish is granted,' he said, 'for they should arrive by this evening. Isn't that so, Luel?'

'I do believe that is so,' said the *feya*, smiling in calm pleasure at my yelp of joy.

Epilogue

Old Bony did not stay for my family's arrival. 'No need for them to see me,' she said. 'And I have more important things to do.' There was to be a big gathering in the north, to which all Ruvenyan *feyas* had been called to discuss new laws in connection to dealings with human sorcerers, so that a sorcerer like Durant could never exist again.

Luel did not go, believing firmly that her place was with us. And she still says that now, more than a year later. She and Gabriel took a summer house right next to our place in the country, but they also kept the old Fontenoy house in Champaine, where we join them to escape the Ruvenyan winter, so Gabriel and I are rarely parted. He speaks more than passable Ruvenyan now and I get by quite happily in Champainian, so when we are married, our children will have both languages as their birthright.

Luel has become a member of my family now as much as Gabriel's. My mother and sisters took to her at once, and even Sveta sniffily agrees she's all right, for a foreigner and a *feya*. She won't hear of Luel using magic to help the household, though. But she has a sneaking fondness for the pretty things Luel creates – the silk flowers and hat ribbons she is making now not only for Madame Ange in Palume, but the best milliners in Byeloka, too. It is Luel's primary use for magic these days, and she thoroughly enjoys it, though she will occasionally do a couple of other small things.

She also advises Andel on his prototype of the 'armchair traveller'. Though the story of Dr ter Zhaber's legacy wasn't strictly speaking true, the patent most certainly did exist. Upon my suggestion, Gabriel purchased it and bequeathed it to Andel and Olga, who had been so kind to me. It has been an inspired decision for it also means Andel and Olga often come to visit.

I have become fast friends with Olga. Occasionally, she and I speak of Old Bony, because apart from Gabriel, the young werewolf is the only one who really understands how I feel about the forest *feya*. I know my family would not have taken her to their hearts like they have Luel, even knowing of how she helped us. Even when she is helpful, there is something about Old Bony that does not encourage you to be too friendly. She'd hate it, anyway. She likes being respected, even feared. But that does not stop me from remembering her with gratitude and respect. I have not seen her since that time in the Fontenoy house, and I do not wish to go anywhere near the house of bones in the forest again. But I feel that one day our paths may cross once more. And that I'll be pleased to see her.

But if Luel is held in great affection by my family, Gabriel is loved. First it was for my sake, now it is for his own. Liza said to me the other day, 'It's like Anya and I have a brother now, and do you know what? I didn't know that all along we'd missed having one.' As for my mother, she says that the old proverb is right and that she hasn't lost a daughter but gained a son. And they're not just words; she and Gabriel get on so naturally it's as if they have always known one another. Of course, they're both artists, and that makes it even easier.

Things are good in our family. Over winter in Champaine Gabriel introduced Liza and Anya to his circle of friends and one of them, Sebastien d'Roch, has taken quite a shine to Anya, and she to him. He is nice-looking and kind and also he's heir to a large estate, so he fulfils just about every wish Anya had for a match. Funnily enough, it is sharp-tongued Liza who has turned out to be more flighty. She has a great circle of admirers in Byeloka and in Palume, and she goes to just about every ball and party. It was from just such a ball in Palume that she came back with the news that a newly engaged couple had been there: Celeste Durant and Felix Vivian. Felix is by now fully restored to health. He is working for Messir d'Louvat, managing a new art gallery, but has given up painting altogether. 'He's a rather wishy-washy specimen,' Liza said cheerfully, 'but harmless, you know, and he thinks Celeste is the queen of the world, which is just how she likes it.'

Celeste has surprised everyone. After news of her father's death was brought to her – the story was put about that he'd drowned in a deep remote lake, which explained why no body was ever found – she developed a decisiveness that previously had lain quite dormant. As Edmond Durant's sole heir, she had sold the Durant residence, bought a luxurious apartment in the centre of the city and invested some of her money in a little jewellery shop, which she keeps stocked with unusual items. They aren't created with Luel's magical gifts, for the power of those ended when they were no longer needed, but are sourced from the far-flung places her father had once travelled to: Green River pearls from Pandong, delicate gold ornaments from the Prettanic Islands, crystal from the deep mines of Krainos, and even amber from the frozen north. Yes, Celeste has come a long way. Our paths rarely cross; and though I cannot ever really feel warmth towards her, I also cannot think altogether unkindly of her. And to her credit, she did offer Gabriel a small portion of the estate, though he refused it out of principle.

I only have to look down at the ring Gabriel gave me for our engagement, shining with the glow of the ruby and pearl in its setting, and think that we two are the luckiest, most blessed people alive. We found each other in the most unlikely way and in the most unlikely place, and the love between us has bloomed and flourished as we have grown to know each other in the quiet happiness of ordinary days as much as in the thrilling joy of passion. As our love has grown and deepened and strengthened, so too have the gifts we were each born with.

Though I had had a budding literary talent before, it has now opened up and become deeper, richer. And that has changed everything. Eight months ago, the story

I wrote at the mansion, *The White Rose*, was published in *The Golden Pen*, has received very good notices and has been reprinted twice. Since then I've sold nearly a dozen more, new and old, including *The Three Sisters*. Most exciting of all, Gabriel and I are working on a book together. It is a book of tales of love and magic, written by me and illustrated by him. Luel and my family say it will take the world by storm.

Six months ago, Gabriel had a joint exhibition with my mother. It was a beautiful collection of her most striking portraits and his miniature paintings of Ruvenyan landscapes, clustered around *Scarlet in the Snow* – the only painting not for sale. The exhibition was held in Kolorgrod's modest art gallery and was launched quietly. But it did not stay quiet for long. The word spread about how good it was, and soon people were flocking to it from far and wide, including from Byeloka. Even a member of the royal family turned up one day! Everything was sold, and there were even notices about the 'wildly successful and unusual' show in foreign newspapers. Mama has more commissions now than she could ever have dreamed of, including one for a portrait of that same prince who saw the show. As for Gabriel, he has been inundated with offers of shows from just about everywhere. But he's put them all off, for the time being. 'There'll be time for that,' he says, 'later.'

I write this at the desk in my room at home, with the windows open on a bright summer's day. It's nearly midday, and Gabriel and Luel will be along very soon, and we'll all have lunch together at the long table under the big old chestnut tree. Then Gabriel and I will go for a long walk together, till we reach the perfect place to lie in each other's arms in the tall blond grass, as the heady fragrance of roses wafts on the warm air. And that is where I'll end.

Moonlight & Ashes

Sophie Masson

The story of Cinderella as you've never heard it before . . .

A girl whose fortunes have plummeted from wealthy
aristocrat to servant-girl.
A magic hazel twig. A prince.
A desperate escape from danger.

This is not the story of a girl whose fairy godmother
arranges her future for her. This is the story of Selena,
who will take charge of her own destiny, and learn that her
magic is not to be feared but celebrated.

Available at all good retailers

Read on for the first chapter

One

Once upon a time, I would have walked in through the beautiful carved doors of the Angel Patisserie and Tea Salon. Once, and not so long ago either, my feet would have glided across the soft carpet in smart shoes, my long skirts swishing behind my mother's as we headed to our favourite table looking out across St Hilda's Square at the bustling morning crowds. Once, we would have sat on the plush velvet chairs while the waiter brought us plates of cream puffs, chocolate hazelnut tart or cream-layered honey sponge served on delicate china plates edged with gilt. We'd have eaten our cakes and sipped fragrant tea from fine cups as the owner of the Angel, Monsieur Thomas, resplendent in a blue silk waistcoat and white tail coat, would have made sure to stop by our table and wish us good day. He'd have told Mama how fine she was looking, and me how much of a young lady I was becoming. Mama and I would giggle about it afterwards because, although Monsieur Thomas always said the same thing, it was always in such a hushed tone as if he was telling us a secret instead of a rather tedious politeness.

That was then. If I tried to go in through the front door of the Angel now, Monsieur Thomas would have me thrown out. And no wonder for my feet, now clad in old shoes that let in the rain, are not fit to tread on the soft carpets. My skirts, patched and old, no longer swish but flop limply around me. And the taste of those cakes is nothing more than a sweet, distant memory. These days I have to go around the back of the Angel and wait in the dingy little courtyard no proper customer ever sees. I am handed the box of cakes my stepmother and stepsisters have ordered, and am warned that if I so much as think of opening it I will have the police set on me. I am told to 'Begone!' by people who once would have bowed to me as the daughter of Sir Claus dez Mestmor, a rich and important nobleman from one of the oldest families in Ashberg. They all know I have become a servant in my own father's house and that has made all the difference. I used to think people were nice to me because they liked me. Now I know better.

But not everyone is like that. Even at the Angel, where faces are hard as overcooked pastry and tongues bitter as wormwood. There's Maria, the scullery maid, who has never stopped being nice to me even though it would cost her her job if anyone were to find out. When she can, Maria slips me bits and pieces she's kept from the kitchens, and always with a kind word or two which is almost as comforting. This day, she had a surprise for me. As I stood in the courtyard waiting for a box of cakes, trying to avoid the drips from the clearing rain, she crept out and handed me a little parcel done up in brown paper and string. 'Happy birthday, Selena,' she whispered, giving me a quick smile before scuttling back in just as Rudi, a waiter who never misses an opportunity to laugh at me, came out. He's got his eye on my stepsister Babette, and thinks that will get in her good books, though if he thinks Babette will even look once, let alone twice, at a waiter, no matter how fine his waistcoat, he's in for a great disappointment. To her and Odette, waiters may as well not exist, or at least no more than as some kind of useful machine.

That morning, as usual, I put up with his heavy attempts at wit at my expense to avoid a quarrel I could not afford to have. Not if I am to keep the promise I made to my dear mother two years ago on her deathbed, whose loss I still feel like an arrow to the heart. I promised her that I would not abandon my father, no matter what was to happen. Papa is not a man who can cope with illness, and my poor mother had been sick for a year or more. She had lost the good looks that had made him forget her humble origins and fall in love with her. I think she knew he could not stay alone for long, and so it proved – for within a few months he had married Grizelda, a rich widow from the imperial capital, Faustina. She had brought her daughters, Babette and Odette, home to Ashberg and had set about removing all reminders of my mother, throwing out her pictures and books, of which I could save but a few. And so my ordeal began.

Of course, there are moments when rage and sorrow boil within me like scalding pitch. When I think of my weak and indifferent father who seems to have almost forgotten my existence altogether. When I remember the day my stepmother summoned me to triumphantly announce the annulment of my parents' marriage and, in turn, my social demotion in the eyes of the law to a mere 'natural daughter' of my father, dependent entirely on his goodwill. When my mother's portrait was burned and her books thrown out, except for the few I managed to hide. When my stepsisters taunt me with a cruel nickname, Ashes, and delight in tormenting me with tales of the parties they've been to, the young men who shower them with compliments, the fine dresses they've ordered from the best seamstresses in the city, and the exciting trips they'll go on while I have to stay in my kitchen.

In those moments the promise I made to Mama seems like a cross that's much too hard to bear. But, always, I master myself; I cannot break my promise to her for fear of losing my honour. They have taken everything else – I will not let them take my word as well. Alone in my room at night I take out one of Mama's books and, though I've read each many times over the years, cover to cover, I take comfort in it. I remember Mama's voice as she read to me, her smile as she read to herself, and it brings her close to me once again. I whisper to the empty room as though she were there. I whisper how I feel – how I really feel – deep inside. It helps me to be patient, to try and hold fast to the hope that my mother would never have bound me to such a promise if she did not think that one day things would get better for me.

Maria's kindness touched me. Sixteen. I turned sixteen today. I didn't expect anyone to remember. My father's away, like he is nearly all the time these days, and his new family would rather think I had sprung from an amoeba. Anyway, who ever heard of a servant having a birthday? Squelching home through the wet streets, carefully holding the box of cakes, I thought of the pleasure I'd have in opening her little parcel later that night. It would mark the day that someone other than myself had remembered. Sixteen – the coming of age, when you are no longer a girl but a woman. I remember Mama saying how this important birthday was marked in her own forest village, far away. How on your sixteenth birthday you'd be given a dish of honey and cream, a crown of roses and a hazel twig. It seemed a strange combination to me and I always asked why, *why*. But she would only smile and say that on my sixteenth birthday, she would tell me.

I was so absorbed in my thoughts and bittersweet memories that I didn't notice the carriage heading down the street behind me. It was only as it was almost upon me that I suddenly heard the rumbling of wheels and the coachman's shout, and tried to jump aside. Instead, I tripped and fell sprawling in the gutter, the cakes flying out of my hands as the carriage squeezed past me with just inches to spare. As I looked after it, breathless from the fright, I saw it was completely closed with black blinds drawn down across the windows. And my heart skipped a beat as I recognised the crest on the side of the door to be the sinister snake and two wands of the Mancers.

Three Wishes

Isabelle Merlin

Careful what you wish for . . .

When Rose creates a blog for an English assignment, she doesn't realise it will change her life. An elegant stranger arrives to announce that Rose has an aristocratic French grandfather who would like to meet her.

Rose arrives in France to find that her grandfather lives in a magnificent castle. Utterly enchanted, she grows to love her new life – and Charlie, a charming boy who is equally besotted with Rose.

But as Rose begins to delve deeper into her family's past, her fairytale turns into a nightmare. Who is friend? Who is foe? Someone wants her dead. And she must find out who before their wish comes true!

Available at all good retailers

Pop Princess

Isabelle Merlin

A ticket to a millionaire lifestyle . . .
or a one-way trip to the underworld?

It's a simple twist of fate that catapults Australian teenager
Lucie Rees from her ordinary life in an ordinary town to a
strange, exciting job in Paris as friend to ultra-famous but
troubled young pop star Arizona Kingdom. But it is more
than a simple twist of fate that will see Lucie entangled
in mysterious happenings that soon put her in terrible
danger.

Who can she trust? Will the holiday of a lifetime in
Paris turn into her last days on earth?

Available at all good retailers

Cupid's Arrow

Isabelle Merlin

Love at first sight has never been so terrifying.

It's been a while since 16-year-old Fleur Griffon has had one of the weird and scary dreams that used to plague her childhood. So she's really creeped out when she starts dreaming of being hunted through a dark forest by an unseen, sinister archer.

But when her bookseller mother unexpectedly inherits the magnificent library of a famous French author, Fleur forgets all about her fears. Excitedly, mother and daughter travel to Bellerive Manor, near the ancient French town of Avallon, reputedly the last resting place of the 'real' King Arthur. And it is there, in the magical green forest near Bellerive, that Fleur meets a handsome, mysterious boy called Remy Gomert. It seems to be love at first sight, beautiful as a dream.

But Fleur's nightmare is just about to begin . . .

Available at all good retailers

Bright Angel

Isabelle Merlin

Sylvie is in the wrong place at the wrong time . . .

When Sylvie and her older sister Claire survive a horrific encounter with a gunman, they're sent to stay with their aunt in the south of France for a change of scene. There, Sylvie meets a charming, enigmatic little boy called Gabriel, who tells her he can see an angel sitting on her shoulder. Not so charming is Gabriel's fiercely protective older brother, Daniel, who's just plain rude. But it's love at second sight when Sylvie gets to know Daniel better – until Gabriel disappears and Sylvie starts to wonder if Daniel is telling the whole truth about his family. And then there's Mick, the geeky guy who has a major crush on Sylvie . . .

Why does life have to be so complicated? And how can such a beautiful village hide such dark and dangerous secrets? Sylvie will need all her courage, the skills of the mysterious Houdini – and the blessing of the angels – to see her friends and family again.

Available at all good retailers

Loved the book?

There's so much more stuff to check out online

AUSTRALIAN READERS:

randomhouse.com.au/teens

NEW ZEALAND READERS:

randomhouse.co.nz/teens